BUT NOT FORGIVEN

A CLINT WOLF NOVEL
(BOOK 2)

BY

BJ BOURG

WWW.BJBOURG.COM

D1713808

TITLES BY BJ BOURG

LONDON CARTER MYSTERY SERIES

CLINT WOLF MYSTERY SERIES

BUT NOT FORGIVEN
A Clint Wolf Novel by BJ Bourg

This book is a work of fiction.
All names, characters, locations, and incidents are products of the
author's imagination, or have been used fictitiously.
Any resemblance to actual persons living or dead, locales, or events
is entirely coincidental.

Cover design by Christine Savoie of Bayou Cover Designs

PUBLISHED IN THE UNITED STATES OF AMERICA

CHAPTER 1

Sunday, July 6
Main Street, Mechant Loup, LA

Susan Wilson stopped at the corner of Bayou Tail Lane and Jezebel Drive and sat there, her left turn signal clicking impatiently. She gripped the steering wheel of her marked cruiser and stared straight ahead, wondering if what she was about to do was inappropriate. It wasn't illegal, but was it morally okay?

"You're just an officer bringing her chief a birthday cake," she said out loud. "Nothing more, nothing less."

With renewed determination, she jerked the wheel to the left and drove south along Jezebel until she came to Clint Wolf's house. Clint had been hired as the new police chief less than a month ago, but it seemed like a year. A lot had happened in that short period of time and she felt like she knew Clint better than some of the locals she'd known for years—better than her own family, even. She would never admit it out loud, but he was the first man who truly excited her. Sure, his chiseled cheeks, dark features, and muscular build didn't hurt, but there was much more to her new boss. Something deeper drew her to him. *Is it the dead look in his eyes and the fact that he's suffered so much grief?* she wondered. *Is my fascination with him some deep-seeded desire to fix him? Is it a motherly thing?* She grunted and shook her head, laughing at the idea. "I'd rather break someone. Nope, I think I'm—"

Susan suddenly stopped speaking when she saw the vehicle in the yard. She knew it wasn't Chloe Rushing's car, but she didn't recognize it and that bothered her. She knew every car in town. She glanced toward the front of the house and could see through the screen door enough to tell that the main door was open, but she couldn't see inside from that angle. She chewed on her lower lip, wondering if she should get down. What if it was someone from the city—some old friend visiting after everything that had happened? What if it was his mom?

"To hell with it. Everyone likes cake." She slipped from the driver's seat and paused long enough to tug at the bottom of her red dress. It had been years since she'd worn one and she felt ridiculous in it. "Why'd I put this damn thing on again?" she asked herself, snatching the cake from the seat and pushing the door shut.

Susan strode across the yard—the muscles in her tanned legs rippling as she walked—and had just reached the steps when she heard a loud voice booming from inside the house.

"You took away the last thing that mattered to me, Clint Wolf. For that, you have to die."

Susan's heart began pounding in her chest. She kicked off her shoes and tiptoed up to the porch, craning her neck to see inside the house.

"All this time you pretended to be grieving with me, but you were plotting against me," came a heated response. It was Clint and he sounded equally as angry as the other man. "You shady bastard."

Susan inched across the porch and reached for the screen door, pulling it open.

She heard Clint saying, "You don't have the balls to pull—"

Just as Susan stepped through the doorway, a gunshot exploded directly in front of her. It only took a split second for her to take in the scene; some man—a large man—had just shot Chief Clint Wolf point-blank in the stomach. A scream of anger ripped from Susan's throat as she dropped the cake and struggled to rip her gun from the thigh holster. Everything in the room seemed to slow down and Susan found herself thinking very clearly. She was astutely aware that Clint's knees had hit the floor at the same time the cake did and that the man was stepping forward to finish him off. Using her left hand to grip the holster, she jerked upward as hard as she could, ripping the gun free. The metallic click of the man's revolver being cocked was deafening. Susan tried to bring her hand up as fast as she could, but it, too, was moving in slow motion.

Clint knelt before the man, staring up at the revolver that was pressed to his forehead. "Do it," Clint said, straightening his shoulders proudly.

The explosion that followed was deafening and Susan jumped in her skin. Relief quickly surged through her body when she realized she'd gotten her shot off just in time. The man hollered in pain, but Susan didn't waste any time or take any chances. She stepped forward and fired the next shot right into the back of the man's head, shutting him up forever.

The man collapsed and Clint sank to the ground beside him, struggling for air. Susan pulled her phone from a pocket in her dress and called 9-1-1, barking orders at the call taker. When she'd given her location and requested emergency medical assistance, she rushed forward and dropped to the floor beside Clint, cradling his head in her lap. Blood oozed from his belly and matched the color of her dress. He tried to talk but couldn't. She knew it wasn't good and panic started to settle in the pit of her stomach.

"Clint, can you hear me?" she called, trying to project an air of confidence. "It's Susan. Hang on! Keep breathing. An ambulance is en route. Come on—keep breathing!" Tears welled up in Susan's eyes as she suddenly realized what had drawn her to him...he reminded her of her father. "Please don't die, Clint. Please, not you, too!"

CHAPTER 2

Fifteen months later...

Thursday, October 8
Chateau Parish Courthouse

I cleared my throat and glanced around the large courtroom. The hearing was closed to the public, leaving the two dozen wooden pews empty. The only chairs occupied were those in the jury box and at the prosecutor's table. Adjusting the ballistic vest under my tan uniform shirt, I leaned close to the microphone. "I'm Clint Wolf, chief of the Mechant Loup Police Department."

First Assistant District Attorney Isabel Compton nodded, and then asked me to recount the events of July sixth. Although it had been over a year ago, I remembered every detail like it was yesterday. I turned to face the grand jury. There were twelve of them—seven men and five women. The youngest was a female who looked to be about nineteen and the oldest was a man who had to be knocking on seventy.

I'd testified in court dozens of times as a patrol cop and even more as a homicide detective for the City of La Mort, but this was different. A lot was riding on my testimony. What I said would mean the difference between Susan Wilson being indicted for first degree murder or going free. In Louisiana, being convicted of first degree murder meant one of two things—the death penalty or life in prison without parole. I took a sip from the glass of water that the court reporter had offered me. When I returned it to the counter, my hand shook and I almost spilled it. I cleared my throat again and took a deep breath.

"I'd just returned home from the hospital," I began. "My house was a wreck, so I started to clean things up when I heard a knock on the door."

Isabel stepped forward and pushed a length of blonde hair behind her ear, shifted her dark brown eyes—which were even darker than mine—down to her notes. "Before you go any further, can you explain to the jury what happened that caused your house to be in such disarray?"

I nodded and turned back to the jury. Starting from the beginning, I described everything that had happened, down to the very end. When I went over the bad parts, I noticed some jurors shaking their heads and one even gasped out loud. After I was done, I turned to Isabel and nodded. She straightened her red suit jacket and removed several photographs from her file. She then walked to the witness chair and asked me if the photographs accurately depicted what my house looked like after the shooting.

"Yes, ma'am," I said.

"Is there any doubt in your mind that Susan Wilson's actions saved your life that day?"

"No doubt at all." I turned and made eye contact with each of the jurors, one at a time. "Had it not been for Sergeant Susan Wilson's actions, I wouldn't be sitting in this chair talking to y'all today. Instead, I'd be rotting in a coffin and a murderer would be walking free."

Isabel looked out over the jury, pursed her lips, and nodded. "Thank you, Chief. That'll be—"

"Isabel, I have a few questions for Chief Wolf."

I turned to the large man sitting at the prosecutor's table. He wore a dark pinstriped suit with a purple tie. I guessed him to be in his mid fifties. Although we'd never formally met, I'd seen District Attorney Bill Hedd's picture on billboards up and down the parish. The Elvis Presley haircut and large flapping jowls were hard to miss. He'd remained mostly quiet throughout the hearing, but it was clear something was on his mind now.

Isabel looked a little surprised by the interruption, but smiled and took her place at the table as he stood and sauntered over to the witness chair. For those who didn't know better, he was an intimidating figure. He had to be at least seven inches taller than my five-foot nine-inch frame and, at four hundred pounds, was more than two hundred pounds heavier than me. But his hands were soft, and his life marred with tragedy.

"Miss Compton just showed you a series of photographs."

I nodded and waited for a question.

"How many times was the victim shot?"

I scowled. "I'd hardly call him a victim, sir. He came over to my house to kill me."

"Right." DA Hedd stared at me for a long moment. "But he didn't kill you, did he?"

"Not for lack of trying. He shot me pretty good. I was in the hospital for a long time."

"You lived, but he died."

I nodded.

"Please answer out loud, so the court reporter can record your answer."

"Yes, sir. He died."

"Tell me, Chief, what did the victim do after Sergeant Wilson fired the first shot?"

"The would-be murderer who came to my house with the specific intent to kill me screamed when Sergeant Wilson shot him. His eyes grew wide. He was obviously surprised that someone was there to save me."

"Was it necessary for Sergeant Wilson to shoot the victim twice?"

I stared DA Hedd in the eyes for a long moment, anger rising to the surface. When I first rolled into town two years ago, I'd heard whispers about his wife being brutally murdered twenty years earlier by some local bar owner. They said she'd been cheating on Hedd with the man and he wanted her to leave Hedd. When she refused, the man killed her. It was bad enough to learn your wife had been murdered, but to learn she was murdered by her lover? That was just cruel and unusual punishment. Although I didn't know him, I felt a strong connection to him back then. I always said I'd shake his hand and tell him how sorry I was if our paths ever crossed. But now that our paths were crossing for the first time, I only wanted to punch him in the face.

In a controlled voice, I said, "Yes, it was absolutely necessary for her to shoot him a second time."

"In the back of his head?"

"After she shot him the first time, he was still a threat and he aimed to kill me. Had she not taken swift and decisive action, I wouldn't be here today."

"I see." He seemed to be staring at something on the wall behind me. After thirty seconds or so, he looked down at me. "Why did

Sergeant Wilson show up at your house that day?"

I hesitated, not knowing the answer to the question. I remembered the cake falling to the ground and Susan running up wearing a dress—something I'd never seen her wear—but, beyond that, I had no clue why she'd decided to visit my house. I'd thought about it many times in the months following the shooting, but I'd never resolved it within myself. My girlfriend had her own ideas, and she even voiced them once during an argument. According to Chloe, Susan had a thing for me and was trying to get to my heart through my stomach. I had dismissed the notion as foolishness, but Chloe would not be deterred.

"Why else would she bake you a cake and show up at your house in a red dress that revealed more skin than a bikini?" Chloe had argued.

That got me looking at Susan in a different light. Not bad, just different. Before then, I'd looked at her the same as I'd looked at my other officers—only she was much tougher than them. To me, she was just another tough cop who'd have my back in a pinch and who'd sacrifice her own life to save the life of another. Nothing more, nothing less. After Chloe's comments, I still saw her as a tough cop, but I also recognized she was a woman with needs and desires that could only be satisfied by a man. Just the thought of her having those feelings for me made me uncomfortable, considering I was her boss and Chloe was my girlfriend. We'd been alone many times over the course of the past year and I'd thought about asking if Chloe was right, just to clear the air between us, but then I'd talk myself out of it. Some things, I knew, were better left unasked.

When it seemed I had waited too long to answer Bill's question, I shrugged and said, "I don't really know why she came to my house that day, but I'm glad she did. Every breath I take is because of Sergeant Wilson and I will forever be grateful to her."

The district attorney waved his hand toward the door. "You're free to leave now."

As I stood to leave, I saw Isabel sitting at the table frowning. She mouthed an apology as I walked by the table and out the door. My head was spinning as I took a seat in the hallway. Susan was not going down for saving my life—for doing her job. What would I do if the grand jury returned an indictment for murder? When I'd worked as a homicide detective in the city, I'd learned firsthand that the district attorney could indict a tomato can if he wanted to, and that scared the shit out of me. Based on his questions, he seemed to be gunning for Susan. Sure, the man she killed had been an officer of the court, but he was a bad man—a murderer.

Footsteps echoed at the end of the long corridor and I looked up to see Reginald Hoffman approaching at a brisk pace, his fingers dancing across the screen of his phone as he walked. DA Hedd's chief investigator was tall and lanky and looked much younger than his forty-seven years. His dark hair was slicked back with some type of gel, making it seem even darker, and it was parted to the left. It had to be the gel that made him look younger, because his face was a bit weathered—like a man who spent his spare time in the sun.

Reginald didn't seem to notice me sitting there, so I was surprised when he stopped in front of me and nodded. After he finished texting, he shoved his phone in his pocket and pursed his lips.

"Isabel texted me and told me what's happening," he said. "Don't worry about a thing. My investigation was complete and my testimony will be convincing. Sergeant Susan Wilson used only the force that was absolutely necessary—and completely authorized by law—to save your life. When I'm done testifying, that grand jury will put her up for an award. They'll want to name a street after her."

I nodded my thanks, but didn't share his optimism. I'd seen too many good cops get indicted for murder by overzealous prosecutors who took a "Monday morning quarterback" approach to evaluating life-threatening situations that required split-second decision-making. Based on DA Hedd's line of questioning, I feared he fell into that category.

I glanced at the large clock on the wall. Nearly ten-thirty. I had been inside for an hour telling my part, and I could only imagine how long it would take Reginald to lay out the entire case. I figured I had time to kill, so I stood to go outside.

CHAPTER 3

I was pacing along the sidewalk two hours later when the front door of the courthouse burst open and some of the jurors began filing out into the warm afternoon air. None of them looked my way as they congregated at the foot of the large concrete steps. After chatting for about a minute, they separated into two groups, with some of them walking toward the parking lot while others crossed the street and disappeared into one of the many restaurants in the area. I watched the group that disappeared into the restaurant, wondering what they'd decided.

The ancient hinges to the courthouse door squeaked loudly behind me and I turned back in time to see Isabel walking outside with Reginald and DA Hedd. Isabel saw me and nodded. After saying something to Reginald and Hedd, she walked to where I stood.

"What'd they decide?" I asked.

"They didn't. We're on a lunch break."

"How's it looking?"

She frowned, glanced over her shoulder to make sure Hedd had continued in the opposite direction. "I'm not going to lie, he's gunning for Susan."

I clenched my fists. "Why? It was a righteous shooting and he knows it."

"We all know it. I don't know what's going on. We were on the same page when we walked through the door. He told me to handle it, to present the case, and I did. When he stepped up and started asking question…" Isabel shook her head. "I don't know what's going on, Clint, I really don't."

I hesitated, afraid to ask the next question. Finally, I did. "They can't possibly indict Susan, right?"

"Had you asked me that question five years ago, I would've said there's no way in hell she gets indicted." She indicated toward me with a nod. "But you know firsthand how bad things have gotten. You were in the city during the riots."

I ran a hand through my hair, thinking. What could I do to make sure Susan didn't get indicted? Would talking to the DA help? I posed the question to Isabel, but she shook her head. "He doesn't do well with advice," she said. "And once he makes up his mind, there's no changing it. Our only hope is that the grand jury will agree with you and Randall and find a *no true bill*."

A *no true bill* was when a grand jury decided there was no probable cause to believe a crime had been committed. "Will you let me know?" I asked.

Isabel nodded. "I'll call as soon as the decision is rendered."

I thanked her and walked to my Tahoe. I stole one last glance toward the restaurant door and—resisting the urge to walk inside and speak to the jurors—drove away. As I made the long drive back to Mechant Loup, I wondered what I'd tell Susan. I didn't want to worry her needlessly, but I didn't want her to be caught off guard should the worst case scenario become a reality.

There were no cars in the sally port when I arrived at the police department. I parked inside and made my way through the processing center and entered the patrol area where the dispatcher's desk was located. Lindsey was leaning back in her chair with her feet on the desk, reading a paperback novel. She was the daytime dispatcher and was never without a book. Her favorites were mysteries and crime fiction. I guess it made sense that she worked at the police department.

She didn't look up when I entered, so I announced my presence by asking, "What're you reading?"

Lindsey screamed and threw her hands back in surprise. I quickly ducked as the book flew into the air and hit the ceiling. At the same time, her chair flipped backward and she dumped in a heap on her shoulders. I rushed forward to help, but the mess of flailing arms and legs was enough to confuse anyone. She finally kicked the chair off of her and scrambled to her hands and knees. I tried not to laugh as I reached down and helped her to her feet.

"Damn it!" she said, dusting off her jeans and straightening her shirt. "You scared the shit out of me...*again*. We need to put a cowbell on the door or something."

I righted her chair and mumbled an apology, chuckling in the process. "Sorry, Lindsey, I can't help it." As the image of her surprised face being flung violently backward and her legs flying into the air played over and over in my mind, I doubled over and laughed until I almost cried. She wasn't amused.

"Here..." As though she thought she was punishing me, she snatched a message off her desk and shoved it into my stomach. "I need someone to handle this complaint. Melvin's on the water looking for an overdue boater and Susan's on a suspicious subject complaint. I didn't call you earlier because I thought you'd be in court all day."

When my laughing fit subsided, I read Lindsey's scribbling. For a girl, she had a horrible handwriting, but I made out an address and a name and could tell that the man was reporting a minor car crash. I waved to Lindsey and hurried out the door, heading for Orange Way, which was only a few blocks from the police department.

Within a few minutes, I turned my Tahoe down the street and drove toward the back. The sun was beating relentlessly through the windshield and I shoved the visor down and squinted against the glare, trying to read the house numbers on the mailboxes. I had driven halfway down the street when I saw a man standing in the middle of the street about a hundred yards ahead of me. He was waving frantically in the air and jumping up and down. I sped to where he was and pulled my Tahoe to the edge of the street.

"Officer, officer, you have to go after them! The garbage men...they crashed my car!" The man's eyes were wild, matching his thick and unkempt beard and hair. While most of his beard was brown, there were patches of deep red on either side of his face. I could smell him before I stepped fully out of my Tahoe. It was a mixture of stale sweat and armpit juice. Based on the tattered clothes and stains on his skin and face, I figured it had been at least a week since he'd had a shower.

"Did you call this in?" I asked. "Are you Ty Richardson?"

"Yeah, I'm the one who called. They crashed my car with their big truck." The man nodded and tried to get closer to me, but I put a hand out to stop him.

"I can hear you fine from there, sir," I said. Garbage pickup was definitely on Thursdays in Mechant Loup, but when I looked up and down the street I didn't see a garbage truck. "How long ago did this happen?"

Ty began pacing back and forth. "About forty minutes ago. What took you so long to get here? They already escaped. Now we'll never catch them."

"Why don't you tell me what happened, so we can sort everything out?"

The man stopped pacing and took a deep breath. His eyes darted from left to right and he licked his lips several times before telling his story. "I was just sitting there, minding my business, when this garbage truck pulls up to get the garbage. After getting the garbage, it backed into my driveway to turn around like it always does. I'm the last house on the street and they do this every Thursday and Saturday. But this time it rolls right over my car and crushes it. I yelled at them to stop, but they just drove away like nothing happened."

I turned toward his driveway and stared. It was empty. "But...where's your car?" I asked.

"Are you blind?" He looked at me like I was crazy. Marching to the middle of his driveway, he pointed to a spot in the shells near his feet. "It's right there!"

I approached him slowly and turned my attention to where he pointed. There were pieces of what was once a toy car in the shells. "Is this your car?" I asked. "The one the garbage truck smashed?"

"Of course it is. What'd you expect—a mini-van?" Ty scoffed. "I drive nothing but muscle cars."

CHAPTER 4

Once I'd taken pictures of the toy car with my cell phone, I promised Ty Richardson I would file a report and have his car replaced. I then spoke with his mother, who lived in the gray house next to his camper trailer, and she assured me she would take him to his doctor. She apologized profusely and explained how she'd been in the hospital on and off for three weeks with Ty's grandmother and wasn't able to give him the attention he needed. As she talked, I absently wondered what would happen to poor Ty if she died before him.

I drove back to the office and found Sergeant Susan Wilson sitting at the corner of Lindsey's desk looking through a stack of reports. Her brown hair was braided into cornrows and she ran her fingers back and forth through them as she read—a movement that caused the muscles in her arm to stretch the fabric on her tan uniform shirt. A casual observer might think she pumped iron in the gym, but those familiar with her knew better. Her muscles were built from long hours of kicking and punching people and objects. A terror to watch, she was undefeated as a cage fighter and a cop. Of course, the fight you lose in law enforcement is usually your last fight, so the fact that she was still north of six feet was evidence enough that she'd won every fight as a cop.

I didn't know what to say to her about the hearing and thought about turning and sneaking out, but she looked up and caught me standing there. Her dark eyes studied mine for a moment, searching for any hint of what might have happened this morning. I met her gaze and tried not to waver. Finally, she turned her attention back to the reports. In a casual voice, she said, "I hear you met Ty

Richardson."

I nodded and glanced at Lindsey, whose face was flushed.

"Sorry, Chief," Lindsey mumbled. "I seriously didn't know he was mentally ill."

"Ty's been quiet for about four years now," Susan said, "so there's no way she could've known."

Lindsey nodded her head. "She's right. I had no idea."

I grinned. "It's not a big deal."

"I…I just figured you might think I did that on purpose since you laughed at me earlier, and I didn't want you to be mad at me."

"You should know me better than that by now." I turned to Susan. "What do you have here?"

"I'm looking for the report from last year when that suspicious guy showed up at the gas station asking about you. Remember what month it happened?"

"Asked about me?" I could feel my brows furrow. "I thought they asked about Beaver?"

"They asked who the chief of police was and the clerk told them it was Beaver, but she was wrong."

"What makes you want to find it now?"

"Some strange guy walks into Cig's Gas Station this morning and asks if Clint Wolf is the chief of police. I think the two complaints might be connected."

"Connected?" I laughed. "Why are the clerks filing complaints in the first place? It's not a crime to ask about the chief of police."

Susan was thoughtful, then shrugged. "I guess you're right, but I still want to know who the hell is coming here looking for you. If the clerk thought it was suspicious enough to call the cops, I think it's suspicious enough for me to look into."

"Suit yourself." I turned away and called over my shoulder to Lindsey, "I'm heading back to court."

"Wait," Susan said. She dropped the reports on Lindsey's desk and rushed to my side, grabbing my arm and ushering me into the sally port. Once there, she pushed the door shut. In a hushed voice she said, "I know you can't talk about your testimony, but what happened? Did they clear me?"

I lowered my head.

"What is it?" Susan asked. "What's wrong?"

"It's the DA. He's gunning for you."

"That bastard." Susan pursed her lips. "He never did like me."

"Why not?"

She shrugged. "No clue. I never did anything to him."

We were both quiet for a long moment and she finally asked what would happen if they indicted her.

"I don't even want to go there in my head." I squeezed her shoulder and got into my Tahoe.

Before going to the courthouse, I stopped at a department store in central Chateau Parish and walked to the toy section. I pulled out my phone and studied the picture of Ty Richardon's car. It was in pieces, but looked like it might've been a Chevy Camaro. After sifting through the wide selection of Hot Wheels for about five minutes, I found the closest match. I paid for it and drove the rest of the way to the courthouse.

The door to the courtroom was closed when I got there, so I took a seat in the hall to wait—and wait is what I did. I dozed off several times, paced the halls, and even took short walks around the block to try and make the time move faster. It was during one of these walks that my phone rang.

I answered without looking. "This is Clint."

"Hey, Love, how's your day?"

All of my troubles disappeared in an instant when I heard my girlfriend's voice. "Chloe! What's up?"

"Missing you."

I knew she couldn't see me, but I smiled anyway. It had been hard for me to start over after Michele and Abigail were murdered, but Chloe was making it easier. "Will I see you tonight?"

"I have to work." I could almost hear Chloe's bottom lip pouting. "My editor wants me to meet a source for a story. I'm really sorry."

"You know you don't have to apologize. It happens to both of us."

"I know, but I still feel bad."

"Don't. I'll let you make it up to me." We spoke for a few more minutes and then I returned to the hallway.

It was late in the afternoon when Chief Investigator Reginald Hoffman and First Assistant Isabel Compton walked out of the courtroom talking quietly to each other. Reginald waved and walked off and Isabel approached with a look of concern on her face.

"Is it over for us?" I asked.

"I won't lie, it doesn't look good."

I cursed under my breath. "What if I talk to him?"

"I wouldn't," Isabel said. "It'll only make things worse. Besides, Reginald presented a good case for justifiable homicide, so there's still a good chance the jury will return a *no true bill*."

"When will we know?"

"We're bringing them back tomorrow so they can hear from more witnesses."

"What witnesses?"

Isabel's head jerked around when the courtroom door opened. It was one of the jurors. She turned back around and whispered, "I've already said too much."

I nodded my understanding and watched her hurry down the hallway after Reginald.

CHAPTER 5

On the way home, I stopped at Cig's Gas Station, which was the only gas station/convenience store combination in town. When I pushed through the glass door and sauntered to the counter, I pointed past the clerk to the liquor shelf. "Six bottles of the cheap vodka, please."

The clerk was a middle-aged woman with rotting teeth and cigarette stains on her fingers, but she was pleasant. "Rough day, am I right?" she asked, smiling and nodding. "I've got nothing to do later, so if you're partying alone..."

I didn't feel like talking, so I just shrugged. I usually got my alcohol from Mechant Groceries on the south side of town, but the gas station was closer to my house and I was ready to call it a day. An elderly lady from the library once told me Mechant Loup meant Bad Wolf, and I often wondered why someone would name their store Bad Groceries. I didn't care enough to ask about it, but I did check the expiration dates on everything I bought at Mechant Groceries.

When the clerk had finished ringing up the sale, I paid her and gathered up the three large plastic bags. I started to turn away, but remembered the complaint Susan handled earlier. "Ma'am, what can you tell me about the guy who came into the store earlier asking about me?"

The clerk gave me a blank stare, muttered, "I wasn't working earlier."

I nodded my thanks and walked outside. Before the door closed behind me, I heard her yell, "I get off at three!"

I continued on my way home and had just turned onto Jezebel

Drive when I saw Chloe's red car in my driveway. Surprised, I snatched the bottles of vodka off the front floorboard and reached behind me to shove them under the back seat. I parked beside her car and checked to make sure the bottles were concealed before stepping out of the Tahoe.

Achilles must've heard me, because his commanding bark sounded from inside and I could hear him scratching at the door. I groaned. It had taken me several months and two living room sets to break him of his chewing habit, but I couldn't stop him from scratching the door when he detected someone in the front yard.

Before I made it to the porch, the door flung open and Chloe and Achilles came barreling out to greet me. I didn't know who was happier to see me, my solid black German shepherd, or my blonde girlfriend. Achilles beat Chloe to me and dropped to a sitting position and squirmed, begging me to rub his head. I did and it only excited him more. It had taken nearly a year to teach him to stop jumping on me and my guests with his hundred-pound frame. While I had succeeded with him, Chloe was another story. Her blue eyes sparkled as she flung herself into me and wrapped her arms around my neck. She smashed her lips against mine and kissed me like it was the first time. She did that every time.

Achilles had broken from his seated position and was running circles around us, vying for attention. I was only vaguely aware of his actions as Chloe's soft lips and tongue explored mine and we pulled at each other with our hands, trying to get closer than we were. I didn't have any immediate neighbors, so we weren't worried about onlookers—not that I would've noticed anyway. I wanted to rip her clothes off right there in the front yard, but I restrained myself.

Once our lips parted, I stared into her eyes for a long moment and then scanned down her pink blouse to her blue jean shorts. They were cuffed, making her long and sleek legs seem even longer. They disappeared into a pair of leather cowboy boots and I smiled my approval.

"You like them?" Chloe asked.

"Best set of legs this side of the Mississippi."

She blushed. "I mean the boots."

"What boots?"

She laughed and we headed toward the front door. Achilles nearly knocked me over as he bolted between us and crashed into the back of my left knee on his way up the porch and into the house. He skidded to a stop near the table and looked back at me, his tail wagging in furious fashion, as though he felt good about giving away Chloe's surprise.

She had fried some split-back jumbo shrimp and made white beans and jasmine rice to go with it. My stomach growled and it was only then that I realized how hungry I'd been. With the hearing and work and shopping for the perfect toy car, I'd forgotten to eat lunch.

"What's the occasion?" I asked. Normally, I was the one who cooked our food on the back porch grill.

"I wanted to talk to you about something, and I wanted to set the mood with your favorite dish."

All of a sudden, I wasn't quite as hungry, as I wondered what she wanted to talk about. Did she want to break up? Had she seen me hide the vodka bottles? I dismissed the thought immediately. She might've seen me reaching toward the back seat, but there was no way she could've seen what was in the bag. Besides, who cooks someone a meal to announce a breakup?

I held her chair so she could sit and then took my seat across from her. "I thought you had to work late today?"

"My source proved unreliable and the whole story fell through." She shrugged her shoulders. "You know how it goes."

I nodded, shifting my feet under the table. "So, what's on your mind?"

She chewed at the corner of her lower lip and stared deep into my eyes. She hesitated and sat quiet for a long moment, studying me. Just when I thought she would lose her nerve—and I was starting to feel relieved—she lowered her eyes and took a deep breath. "We've been dating for over a year now..."

I nodded, feeling a tinge of panic as I began wondering where she was going with this. What if she wanted to get married? I loved her company and the way she made me feel, but I didn't think I was ready for that type of commitment. I definitely had feelings for her, but I wasn't over Michele yet—and doubted I ever would get over her. It had been more than three years, but I still felt as strongly for Michele today as I did back then. So strongly, that I often felt guilty after Chloe would leave, and I'd later be lying alone in bed staring up at the ceiling. Chloe was making it easier to move on, but I often wondered what Michele would think if she knew about us. What if she *did* know? I shuddered at the thought.

I fidgeted with my fork, not knowing what to say. I kept quiet and the silence grew loud. Finally, Chloe continued.

"So, we've been together for a while now and I really have strong feelings for you, Clint." Her eyes were glassy when she looked at me again. "I was thinking maybe it was time to take it to the next level."

And what level is that? I wanted to ask. Instead, I just sat there looking at her, trying to offer no hint of what I was thinking. I didn't want her to know I was panicking inside, because that would crush her spirits and probably send her fleeing. I wasn't ready for a real relationship, but I didn't want to be alone either. She gave me purpose.

"I was thinking we should…um, what if we moved in together?"

I gasped out loud, a little relieved, and quickly winced. I gave myself an inward kick in the ass for my insensitive reaction.

Her eyes clouded over. "What is it? Why'd you react that way?"

"No reason." I reached across the table and took her hand in mine. "It's not what I expected you to say, is all."

"What did you expect?"

I stammered, finally said, "I'm not really sure what I expected—it just wasn't that."

"Clint, there's something more you need to know."

I felt like vomiting. I just knew she was going to say she was pregnant. I was lightheaded, needed some air. I wasn't sure if I was ready for marriage, but I knew for a fact I wasn't ready to be a father again. Losing Abigail just about knocked the life out of me. I'd spent the next two years in a fog until being offered the job as police chief for Mechant Loup. Hiding out in a sleepy swamp town waiting to die seemed like the right move at the time, but that wasn't exactly how things had worked out. A lot had happened and a lot had changed, especially when Achilles and Chloe came into my life.

While I no longer wanted to kill myself—thanks to a preacher who told me I'd never see my daughter again if I did that—I didn't jump at the sound of gunfire and didn't fear death. I thought it'd be easy to find a way to "check out" accidentally enough to fool God into thinking I didn't have anything to do with it, but it happened to be harder than I'd first imagined. Turns out I'd developed a survival instinct from all my years of refusing to lose—refusing to die—during my work as a homicide detective in the city. It wasn't a conscious desire to live, just a dogged refusal to die. But eventually, under the right circumstances, I would give up the ghost and fade silently into that good night.

I turned my attention back to Chloe. I'd never admitted to her that I was secretly marking time until I could join Abigail and Michele in the afterlife. If Chloe was pregnant, that would really throw a wrench into my plans. I'd have to start giving a shit—had to make a conscious effort to survive, because what kid deserved to grow up without a dad? What woman deserved to be left alone to raise their child?

I could tell Chloe was speaking, but couldn't make out what she was saying. Her lips seemed to move in slow motion and her words were dragging. After she finished talking, she sat there for a moment and then her lower lip started to quiver.

I shook my head to clear it, asked, "Wait...what is it? What's going on?"

"What's wrong with you today?" Tears welled in her eyes and she wiped them with the palms of her hands. "Didn't you hear what I said?"

"I'm not feeling well," I said. "What'd you say?"

She shook her head, frowned. "Never mind. It doesn't matter anyway."

I started to object, but her phone rang and she glanced down, said it was work. "I have to go," she said. "I'll see you tomorrow, okay?"

"But what did you say?"

"We'll talk tomorrow." Chloe gathered her things and hurried out of my house, leaving her food on the table half eaten.

CHAPTER 6

Friday, October 9
East Coconut Lane, Mechant Loup, LA

Betty Ledet wasn't wearing a bra under her dirty white T-shirt, and it didn't take Peter long to realize it. It was a little after midnight and he'd just dragged his lazy ass out of bed. While the rest of southeastern Louisiana was winding down for the night, he was only now getting ready to party. He wiped his pale face and padded across the kitchen floor in his socks and sagging boxers. Betty recognized that look in his eyes and turned away, hoping he would lose interest. She didn't want to be molested while she was on the phone.

Knowing Peter's routine well, Betty had dialed J-Rock on her cell phone as soon as she heard him stirring from the bedroom. She knew the sooner he got his drugs the happier he would be, but she began to worry when the phone continued to ring with no answer. She yelped and almost dropped the phone when Peter stole up behind her and reached under the front of her shirt to place his rough hands on her breasts. She started to protest, but J-Rock finally answered and she turned her attention to the call.

"I need some crumbs," Betty said, pushing the phone closer to her ear so she could hear J-Rock above Peter's heavy breathing. It was difficult to ignore the squeezing and pulling of her nipples, but she somehow managed to block it out.

"How much?"

"I've only got forty. Can you spot me sixty?"

J-Rock's raspy voice broke out in laughter. "Bitch, you still owe me twenty from last week."

"Come on, J.R., I need enough to last the night. You know I'm good for it."

Peter leaned close to Betty's ear and whispered, "Tell him you'll give him a blowjob for it."

Betty gagged at the idea, and the stench of stale beer and rotten cigarette smoke on Peter's breath. She shrugged him off and moved away. "Please…just this one time. I'll pay you when I get my check."

"This is the last time, Betty Jo. You don't pay me by next month, I'm gonna have to hurt you. I like you, girl, but business is business. If I don't handle up on them that don't pay, I'm gonna look weak. You know how it is."

J-Rock hung up the phone and Betty turned to look at Peter. He was thirty-nine, but looked fifty. She knew the last few years had been rough on her, too, but even though she was a year older, she was sure she could do so much better than him now. His beard was more gray than black and his hair was falling out in weird patches. The wrinkles on his pale face looked like elephant skin. She frowned. He hadn't looked like that in high school. There'd been no hint of what was to come. Back in those days, he was the backup quarterback and the hottest thing on the field. His dark hair flowed like a horse's mane down his white neck and his brown eyes were mysterious and piercing. She had been surprised when he took an interest in her, considering she wasn't a cheerleader, and even more surprised when he asked her to marry him right out of high school.

"What you looking at?" Peter wanted to know.

Betty made an effort not to focus on the sores on his forehead. They'd been there for months now and wouldn't heal. He was self-conscious about it. "Nothing. I'm looking at nothing."

"Is he bringing a hundred?"

Betty nodded, turned her head to hide the tears that threatened to flow from her eyes. She wanted to tell Peter how cheap he made her feel when he tried to make her exchange sexual favors for his drugs, but she was afraid he would hit her again. The last time she complained about something he did it got bad—really bad. She ended up in the hospital with a broken jaw, fractured orbital socket, and cuts and bruises all over her face and head. While that was scary, it was nothing compared to what she thought he might make her do when the money ran out. At the moment, her waitressing job paid their bills and provided enough money to feed the crack habit. But tips were slow a week ago and they fell behind. If she couldn't get caught up, they'd have to choose between paying the rent and paying

J-Rock back. Somehow, she figured being evicted would be easy compared to whatever J-Rock had in mind.

Betty spent the next thirty minutes cleaning up the trailer. She had just finished shoving some dirty plates into the dishwasher when a car pulled into the front yard. She pushed back the towel that hung over the small window in the kitchen and recognized J-Rock's car.

"He's here," Betty called over her shoulder.

"Make it quick." Peter scrambled from the sofa and darted toward the back of the trailer like he always did when J-Rock came over. Betty had once asked him what would happen if J-Rock got out of hand with her, and he'd only smiled and said she was being paranoid.

Betty walked to the door and opened it. She peered out into the darkness. The wind was blowing, but it was warm. The weatherman had mentioned a cold front coming through the area later in the evening, but it either hadn't arrived yet or that was as cool as it was going to get.

"Hey, girl," J-Rock called from somewhere in front of her, his voice startling her.

His dark features were hard to discern in the limited light, so she reached for the switch just inside the door and flipped it up. The porch light came on and cloaked the area in a pale yellow hue.

J-Rock was smiling, but not in a nice way. He was looking at her like a hungry vulture. She forced a smile, but shifted her eyes to the ground. He made her feel uncomfortable—terrified, even. She reached out and handed him two twenty dollar bills. "It's all I've got at the moment," she said. "I promise to get the rest by the end of next week. It's hunting season, so we'll get more customers in the restaurant and I'll earn more tips."

"I don't care how you get my money—just get it." J-Rock snatched the bills from her hand and held them up to the light. "These better not be fake."

Betty tried to quiet the pounding in her ears and mask the quiver in her voice. "Come on, J-Rock, you know me better than that."

He grunted and pulled a small baggie from the front pocket of his jeans. He dangled it in front of her like candy. The top of the baggie was twisted into a knot and she could see the crack rocks through the clear plastic. They looked small. She took it and held it closer so she could inspect them. Peter would be pissed if she got shortchanged again. She turned to look inside the trailer. *Why didn't he handle his own business like a man?*

"Bitch, what you looking at?" J-Rock asked, suspicion evident in his voice.

As Betty turned back toward him, there was a whisper of wind and something struck her in the chest. It was sudden and shocking. At first she thought she'd been punched, but it was much worse than any punch she'd ever felt. She gasped at the severity of the pain. It was deep and penetrating, like nothing she'd ever experienced. She stood frozen, unable to speak, unable to move. Everything around her seemed to slow to a crawl. J-Rock said something, but his voice sounded muffled. He looked over his shoulder toward his car, then snatched the baggie from Betty's hand and ran off.

Betty tried to cry out, but only managed a moan. She was dizzy. Weak. She reached for her chest and felt a hard object protruding from a spot between her breasts. Her head fell forward as she tried to see what it was. Too dark.

The engine roared as J-Rock backed out of the yard and tires screeched as he sped off down the road. Although everything was happening right in front of her, it sounded like it was across town.

Peter would be mad that she didn't get the drugs. She turned to go inside and explain, to get help, but her knees buckled. She fought hard to stay on her feet. It was a gallant effort. But in the end, she couldn't do it. She dropped straight downward, her kneecaps making a sickening sound as they connected with the top step. She then lurched forward onto her face and stomach, crashing into the concrete surface and sliding roughly down the remainder of the steps. When she reached the bottom, she crumbled in a heap on the ground. The object in her chest had been pushed deeper into her body and felt as though it had punched a hole in her back. Unable to scream, she cried in silence. She knew it was the end. She was dying—could feel the life leaking out of her with every drop of blood that poured from the hole in her chest. She'd felt it once before when she'd hemorrhaged after giving birth to Landon, but she'd been in a hospital surrounded by doctors. Here, she was on the dirty ground surrounded by mosquitoes and gnats...and no one knew she was hurt. Well, except for J-Rock. J-Rock knew she was hurt, but he had done this to her. He was probably halfway to Mexico by now.

Landon...

Betty smiled through the pain. She would finally get to see Landon again.

CHAPTER 7

Getting up early the next morning, I headed straight to the courthouse and had to wait fifteen minutes for the bailiff to open the front doors.

"Back so soon?" asked the old timer.

I nodded and hurried to the courtroom we'd been in yesterday, hoping to catch Isabel or Reginald before they walked inside the closed-door hearing. I was too late. The grand jury filed in later and I tried to make eye contact with some of them, hoping to get a sense of where they stood, but it was no use. They all turned their heads when they noticed me sitting in the metal chair across from the courtroom. The judge's secretary let them in through the side door and they all disappeared inside.

Grunting, I settled in for a long morning. To my surprise, the door to the courtroom opened a few minutes later and Bill Hedd himself walked out. He didn't turn his head. Instead, he looked directly at me as he walked by and didn't take his eyes off of me until it would've been awkward to keep looking at me. He disappeared down the stairwell. When he returned, I nearly choked on my tongue. Walking beside him was William Tucker, one of my officers who worked the night shift.

I jumped to my feet. "What the hell are you doing here?"

William's tanned complexion turned to ash when he saw me. He put both hands up and shook his head, mouthing the words, "I have no idea!"

"Chief Wolf, this is a closed hearing and you're out of line," DA Hedd said, his voice thunderous. "You shouldn't even be out in this hallway. If you don't vacate the premises, I'll have the sheriff send his men here to remove you."

A look of worry on his face, William turned and walked into the courtroom. Hedd stood in the doorway and glared at me. "I mean it, Clint. If you don't leave, I'll have you removed in handcuffs."

I wanted to tell him where to go, but Susan's freedom was worth more than my pride. "I'm sorry, sir. You're right. I was out of line. Just surprised, was all." I nodded and headed for the exit. "I'll see myself out."

Anger turned my knuckles white as I gripped the steering wheel on my drive back to the police department. *Why in the hell is William testifying for Hedd?* He hadn't even been at the shooting, so he could offer nothing substantive. I was still mulling it over when my radio screeched to life and Lindsey asked me to call her at the office.

"What is it?" I asked when she answered.

"A postal carrier was delivering mail on East Coconut Lane earlier and discovered what looks like a body lying near the steps to a trailer," she explained. "She was too scared to get close, so she drove up the street and called 9-1-1. It's probably nothing, though. Remember that time we got the call about the dead body hanging on the porch, but it was a Halloween decoration?"

I remembered. "Can Melvin check it out? I'm just leaving the courthouse and it'll be a little while before I can get there."

"Melvin took the boat out to look for an overdue fisherman," Lindsey explained.

"What about Susan?"

"She's in the booking room wrapping up a DWI arrest."

I glanced at the clock on my dashboard.

"I could call out William," Lindsey offered.

"He's busy," I said.

"What about Amy?"

Amy Cooke worked nights with William Tucker. I'd hired her a few months earlier to fill a vacancy on the night shift. She was working for the Chateau Parish Sheriff's Office and had recently graduated from the police academy when I first met her at Cig's early one morning. I was heading to the office and she was just getting off the night shift at the detention center. She expressed an interest in working patrol and I needed a hand, so we sealed the deal on the spot with a cup of coffee. Two weeks later she was roaming the streets of Mechant Loup with William and making one hell of a name for herself in the ticket department.

"No, I'll handle it," I said. "Have Susan meet me at the scene when she's done."

I started to hang up, but Lindsey called my name. I put the phone back to my ear and asked her if there was more.

She hesitated for a moment, and then asked, "Will Susan be okay?"

"I sure hope so."

"Is it true she could go to prison for murder?"

I sighed as I stared blankly at the highway in front of me. I wanted to tell her there was no way in hell that could happen, wanted to reassure her everything would be fine and Susan would be completely exonerated, but even I didn't believe it. "I don't know, Lindsey. I really don't. I guess anything can happen in this day and age."

As I continued heading south, I tried calling Chloe, but she didn't answer. I frowned, tossed my phone on the console just as I drove over the bridge that separated Mechant Loup from the rest of the world. When I'd first landed the job here, I didn't know how I felt about living in a town located at the southernmost tip of a rural parish with only one road in or out. I also didn't like having to cross a single bridge to get there. While I started to grow used to the idea, I often wondered what would happen if the bridge broke.

CHAPTER 8

The mail carrier was not very happy when I pulled onto the shoulder of the road near East Coconut Lane and approached her Jeep. "Well, it's about time you get here," she said. "Thanks to you, I'm an hour behind schedule."

"I'm sorry, ma'am." I stuck out my hand and she shook it. She was tall and on the heavy side, but she carried her weight well and her grip was strong. Her dirty blonde hair was wavy and fell across her shoulders, nearly long enough to cover the postal service emblem on her light blue uniform shirt. She wasn't wearing a name badge, so I asked her name.

"Sandra Voison." She crushed out the cigarette she'd been smoking on the bumper of her Jeep and tossed it to the ground. I thought about warning her not to litter, but decided against it when I saw the hard lines on her face. It looked like she'd been through enough already.

"So, you've been here about an hour?" I asked.

Nodding her head, she turned away from me and walked to the back of her Jeep. I followed and watched as she opened the back door and grabbed a large box filled with mail. It looked heavy, but she lifted it with ease. I hurried forward and reached for it. "I'll get that for you."

She stopped in midair and turned slowly to face me, her eyes squinting. She was only inches away and I could smell spearmint-covered cigarette smoke on her breath when she asked, "*Get this for me?* Why? You don't think I can handle it?"

I stared at her. "No, I just thought it'd be nice to offer. I mean, I realize you probably do this all day, every day, and I know you're capable, but I figured it might be nice to have a break."

She studied my face with her green eyes. A smile tugged at the corners of her mouth and it caused her face to light up a bit. "And here I was thinking chivalry had died a slow, painful death many years ago."

"I guess it's still here," I mumbled, not real sure what to say or do next. She finally stepped back and allowed me to grab the box. "Where do you want it?" I asked.

She led me to the passenger's side of the Jeep and opened the door. After removing an empty mail box, she pointed to the wooden platform. "Put it right there."

I did as she instructed and then followed her back to the rear of the Jeep, where she tossed the empty box and slammed the door shut.

"Thank you," she said. "No one's ever offered to do that for me."

I shrugged it off and asked her what she witnessed.

"I didn't witness anything. I just saw what looked like a body on the ground by some steps down the street."

I looked in the direction she pointed. The left side of the street was lined with trailers and on the right side there was nothing but trees. "Are you sure it was a body?"

"No—and I wasn't getting close to find out."

I smiled my understanding. "Which house was it?"

"417. The last trailer on the left."

"Do you know who lives there?"

She grunted. "I know where everyone lives. That trailer belongs to Betty and Peter Ledet. They've lived there a long time."

"You know where everyone lives, do you?" I asked.

"I sure do."

"Where do I live?" I challenged.

"326 Jezebel Drive. You have a black German shepherd and you need to cut your grass."

I whistled, thoroughly impressed. "Damn, you're good."

"I know." She turned back to her Jeep and slid into the driver's seat. "Is there anything else? I mean, I'd love to sit and chat all day, but someone's got to deliver this mail."

"Just give me your number in case I need anything further." Once I had Sandra Voison's information, I drove to the last trailer on the left and stopped in the middle of the street. Even from that distance I could see what looked like a body on the ground in front of the trailer, but I couldn't be positive it was a real human. I called Lindsey on my police radio to let her know I was there and pushed my door open.

After grabbing a set of gloves from the console, I picked my way along the driveway. I was still fifteen feet from the trailer when I realized this wasn't a drill—it was the real deal. I moved closer and stopped when I was standing over the body. It was a white female and she was lying face down at the foot of the steps. It looked like she had been standing on the steps and just crumbled to the ground in a lifeless heap. There was a lot of blood in the dirt around her body, so I wasn't expecting much when I felt for her pulse. As I figured, there was none.

What used to be a white T-shirt was now reddish brown in most places. Something protruded from her back under the shirt. It pushed the fabric of her shirt up like a short tent pole. The tip of a knife, perhaps? It was right over the back of her heart. I bent over and reached for her shirt when I heard a creaking sound coming from the interior of the trailer. Pausing where I was, I listened with my mouth open to better hear movements from inside.

After several long seconds, there was no other sound. What if it was just one of those natural Louisiana marsh sounds, like the creaking of two giant tree limbs rubbing against one another in the wind, or an alligator rustling in the bushes behind the trailer? Maybe it was the wind pushing against the trailer. It did seem rather old, and a little wind could be enough to make it shift on its foundation.

When I didn't hear the sound again, I shrugged and turned back to the body. Just as I reached for the woman's shirt again, I heard a loud and distinct bumping sound.

I whirled around to face the trailer and jerked my Glock from its holster. Dropping to my knees beside the concrete steps, I pointed the muzzle of my pistol at the front door. The bumping sound came again and I wondered if this was a murder scene and if the killer was still inside. Knowing I was exposed to the windows above me, I scurried under the trailer and held my breath, listening for the slightest sound above me.

CHAPTER 9

Except for a couple of spots, I had a good view of all sides of the trailer from where I huddled. Tall grass lined the entire back of the trailer, but if someone tried to escape through the back door I'd be able to see them. Trying not to make any sounds that would give away my position, I eased my radio from my belt and spoke softly into it, asking Lindsey if Susan was finished with the prisoner. Before she could answer, Susan's voice came over the speaker.

"Headed your way. About two minutes out."

I studied the front yard. A gray four-door truck was parked in the driveway and Susan could use it to cover her approach. I whispered as much into the radio and settled back to wait for her.

I didn't have to wait long. It took Susan a little more than two minutes to get there, but not by much. She parked her Charger behind the truck and rolled out of the driver's door. I lost sight of her as she moved around the back of the car. When she reappeared near the front of the truck, I scooted out from under the trailer and pointed to the windows on the left side of the door to let her know I would watch that side. She nodded and sprinted toward my location, staying low and keeping her pistol aimed at the windows to the right.

When she reached the trailer, we each moved to opposite sides of the concrete steps, and I leaned closer and mouthed, "I heard something from inside. It could be the killer."

Susan nodded to let me know she understood, but I wasn't so sure. While she was only several feet from me, she seemed miles away. The muscles in her left arm rippled as she adjusted the twin pigtails that dangled behind her neck. She then returned to a two-handed grip on her pistol and bit her lower lip, as though lost in thought. There were worry lines on her forehead and I realized just then she had to be thinking about the hearing. I frowned. We were about to enter what might be a hostile environment and I couldn't have her mind on anything but the task at hand.

"You with me?" I asked.

As though I'd interrupted some inner monologue, she turned to me with a blank expression on her face. "What?"

"Are you focused?"

She shook her head to clear it, and then nodded. "I'm ready."

I reached up and tested the doorknob. It was locked. She pointed to her thigh and then to the door. I nodded and she crept up the steps. When she reached the second to last step, she lifted her right leg. The snug-fitting uniform pants stretched over her muscular figure. I'd seen firsthand how powerful her kicks could be, and I knew the door was no match for her. In a flash, her boot shot toward the area of the door just inside the knob and it crashed inward, disturbing the stillness of the late morning air.

Susan rushed into the trailer and I scrambled up the steps and darted through the door behind her. We found ourselves in a kitchen and living room combination, and quickly hunkered down beside a small bar. We waited, listening. Other than the trickling of splintered wood onto the linoleum floor, all was quiet. I was starting to doubt what I'd heard when footsteps suddenly pounded down the hallway to our left. We sprang to our feet, but not before we heard what sounded like a door being smashed open toward the back of the trailer. Light spilled into the hall and we heard someone grunt as they thudded to the soft ground.

"The back door!" I bolted from my position and raced down the hallway and toward the bright light. Susan had turned to jump out the front door, and she reappeared around the outside corner of the trailer just as I leapt through the back door. There were no steps and I fell for about four feet before landing hard on my heels. I cast a quick glance around. Susan was pointing toward a stretch of trees that lined the back yard.

"He ran that way," she said, giving chase.

I followed her and we plunged into the trees. Branches whipped at us and stung with each strike. The leaves had been falling for a week, or so, and made it easier to track the half-naked figure that zigzagged ahead of us, trying to dodge trees and picker bushes.

"Police," I called, unsure if he could even hear me. "Stop or we'll shoot!"

Susan also began yelling commands as we started to catch up to him. The trees parted suddenly and we found ourselves racing across a small clearing beside a dry canal. The man was now in full view and only several dozen feet ahead of us. I hollered at him again and he skidded to a stop, spun around to face us. There was a large kitchen knife in his hand and I slid on one knee, extending my arms to point my pistol at him. While I was focused on the knife, I couldn't help but notice he wore nothing but sagging boxers. They could've had a print pattern or been a solid color at one time, but now looked like an old door mat that had been rubbed free of any discernible tint. His pale skin appeared chalky and thin and was littered with sores.

"Drop the knife or I'll shoot," I ordered.

Susan had fanned out to my right and was approaching him with bad intentions. She'd already holstered her pistol and her hands were extended above her waist as she measured the man in front of her. He looked rough. His face was darker than the rest of his exposed body, but the same types of sores were present. His dark hair was falling out in weird patches and his beard didn't know if it wanted to be gray or black. He held the knife in his right hand and his left hand was palm out, facing us. Both hands were dry and cracked. Looked painful. His eyes were wild as they shifted rapidly from me to Susan.

"Y'all not J-Rock," he said.

"No, we're not." I motioned toward the ground. "Now put that knife down before she hurts you."

"Y'all really cops?"

I pointed to the badge pinned on my tan uniform shirt. "As real as it gets."

He was thoughtful. Finally, after about a minute, his trembling hand opened and the knife dropped to the ground. He crumbled to his knees and fell forward, crying. "Thank God! I thought y'all were here to kill me."

Susan hurried forward and kicked the knife away. She grabbed him under the arm and jerked him to his bare feet. "Put your hands on your head," she ordered.

The man did as he was ordered and Susan grimaced as she frisked the lining of his boxers for other weapons. When she was satisfied he was unarmed, she waved for him to put his hands down. I walked to where she had kicked the knife, but had to search in the dry leaves for several moments before finding it. I used two leaves to retrieve it from the ground and turned to Susan. She was questioning the man, who identified himself as Peter Ledet.

"Why'd you run?" she asked.

"I thought y'all were with J-Rock and that y'all came back to finish me off."

"Who's J-Rock?"

Peter hesitated and stared down at his cracked and bloody toes.

"It's okay," she said. "We're here now. This J-Rock can't hurt you."

"It's just that…well, J-Rock was Betty's dealer."

"Betty's dealer?" Susan raised an eyebrow. "What about you?"

He shook his head, picking at the sores on his face. "I…I don't do nothing."

"That's bullshit." Susan stepped closer to him, checking his fingers and pushing up his lip. "You've got burn marks on your fingers and lips. Care to tell me how those got there?" Peter just stood there fidgeting, so Susan continued. "I'm betting you don't have a job and all you do is stay home and get high. But where do you get the money? You can't keep a job in your condition. Shit, you can't even dress yourself. I bet you send poor Betty to work to support your habit. Do you make her turn tricks?"

"What do you know about Betty?" Peter stared wide-eyed from me to Susan. "Is she okay? I thought she was dead. Did you talk to her?"

"No, she's gone."

"Then how'd you know all that?" he asked.

"I know a lot of things." Susan folded her arms across her chest. "Now, tell me about this J-Rock."

Peter slumped forward, which pushed his bony shoulder blades out like twin shark fins. "I'm on probation and I already got three felonies on my record. The judge said if I caught another one he was gonna put me away for a long time."

When Susan told him we weren't interested in his petty drug use, Peter seemed to relax a little—as much as any crack-addict could in his situation—and started talking.

"Betty called J-Rock up and asked him to bring some crack over to the house. She owed him money and I guess it made him mad when she couldn't pay it."

"Are you saying J-Rock killed her?" Susan asked.

Peter nodded. "I heard his voice. He was the only one at the door."

As we walked back to the trailer, Susan continued to question Peter, but he couldn't tell her more than he had already. When she asked why he hadn't called 9-1-1, he said he didn't have a phone. She pointed out that Betty was able to call J-Rock, so one of them had a phone. He started to answer, but winced and doubled over in pain when he stepped on a small cypress knee that jutted out of the ground. He held onto a tree while he rubbed the bottom of his foot, explaining Betty had a cell phone, but he hadn't been able to find it after the murder. Fearing J-Rock was lurking in the darkness and waiting to kill him next, Peter had armed himself with a kitchen knife and hid under a pile of clothes in a closet. Somewhere in the middle of the night he drifted off to sleep and didn't wake up until he heard our voices outside the house. When the front door crashed open from Susan's kick, he thought it was the end of the line.

We finally reached the trailer and he limped toward the back door.

"You can't go inside," I said.

"Why not?"

"It's a crime scene now." I nodded to Susan and she led him to her car.

Once Peter was secured in the back seat and the car was running to keep him comfortable, Susan returned with her crime scene kit and set it on the ground away from the body. As she bent to open it, I stepped closer and squatted beside her. "What happened back there?" I asked.

"What do you mean?"

"When we were about to go into the trailer. You seemed lost."

She sighed. "I got this sick feeling in my stomach as I wondered..."

I waited for her to continue. When she didn't, I asked, "What did you wonder?"

"Before, when I'd face a dangerous situation, I'd wonder if I was going to come out alive. Now, I wonder if I'm going to go to jail for doing my job."

I picked at the dirt in front of me, debating whether or not to tell her about William. She must've sensed that something was up, because she said, "Just spit it out already, Clint."

"I saw William at the hearing this morning."

She gasped. "William? What the hell was he doing there?"

I shook my head. "That's what I'd like to know."

"But he wasn't even at the shooting."

"I know. When I asked what he was doing there, he said he didn't know."

Susan was thoughtful, and then shook her head to clear it. "I guess this case won't investigate itself, so..."

We spent the next hour and a half documenting the scene and

searching the house. There was drug paraphernalia in the house and some baggies with possible cocaine residue in them, but nothing related to the murder. The phone was nowhere to be found. Susan had checked on Peter during one of our breaks to change gloves, and found him stretched out on the back seat sleeping.

After everything had been documented, we set out to move Betty's body. I positioned myself on one side and Susan on the other. I took hold of her right shoulder and Susan grabbed her right leg and we gently pulled her onto her back. My mouth dropped open when I saw it. I glanced over at Susan and her eyes were wide.

"What the hell?" she blurted.

CHAPTER 10

Susan and I stared in disbelief at the large arrow protruding from Betty Ledet's chest. It had been hidden under her body and we hadn't noticed it until we'd turned her over. I now knew what was sticking out of her back. A cold chill ran up the back of my spine. During my years working as a homicide detective in the city, I'd seen people murdered with every type of weapon imaginable. Firearms, knives, hatchets, hammers, pencils, cars—even a blow dryer. But never an arrow. There was something primal and creepy about it.

I glanced at Susan, who was more familiar with working in swamp country. "Ever seen such a thing?" I asked.

Susan eased Betty's stiff leg onto the ground and straightened. She shook her head. "We've got a lot of hunters around here who use bows on wild boars and deer, but I've never seen one used on a human before. Not saying it can't happen—just saying this is a first for me."

"When's bow season start around here?"

"It started the beginning of the month." Susan cocked her head sideways and stared at me. "You're not thinking this was a hunting accident, are you?"

"We have to consider every possibility—hunters, J-Rock, and anyone else we come up with." I scanned the clearing on which the trailer squatted. Directly behind the trailer and to the right of it was a patch of thick forestland. To the left, a line of azalea bushes separated their yard from the neighbor's yard. But this arrow didn't come from any of those directions. I turned and looked toward East Coconut Lane. A few bushes stood guard on either side of the driveway and that was the only foliage on this side of the street. But on the other side—thick swampy woodlands that disappeared into forever. I pointed in that direction. "You don't believe it's possible an errant arrow flew in from the woods and got her?" I asked. "Someone could've been hunting across the street and missed their target. It's about a hundred yards, or so. You think that's possible?"

"The trees are too thick for it to have been fired from deep in the woods." Susan smirked. "Besides, this arrow looks like it was meant for her."

The shaft of the arrow was solid red, which seemed appropriate given it was plunged through Betty's heart. Two of the plastic vanes were white and one was blue. It actually appeared patriotic. I lifted her crimson-stained shirt and glanced under it. There was a gaping hole—had to be at least an inch in diameter—in her chest. "Damn, Susan, it looks like she was shot with a twelve-gauge slug."

We gingerly turned Betty onto her side so we could inspect the tip of the arrow. As I held the body in position, Susan lifted her shirt. I whistled when I saw the tip of the arrow. There were three razorblades protruding from the sides of the arrowhead and the tip looked strong and pointed. I could visualize it spinning like a top, drilling a hole into Betty's chest and straight through to her back. I shuddered. It was a horrible way to go. "It looks vicious," I said, studying the arrowhead.

"This is a three-blade mechanical broad-head. They're designed to create a large wound channel and spill lots of blood so hunters can track their prey." Susan tapped the tip of it with a gloved finger. "It would give a DeWalt drill a run for its money."

It had certainly spilled a lot of Betty's blood. "What do you think?" I asked.

Susan shrugged. "Whoever did it can shoot a bow, that's for sure. It could be a hunter, a hobbyist, someone who took archery in high school—or a drug dealer named J-Rock. Whoever it was, I think this was definitely murder—and I don't think it happened from that tree line."

"You don't?" I asked.

"I don't think the arrow would have enough energy to punch a hole clean through her after traveling a hundred yards."

I was thoughtful, turning my attention to Betty's open eyes. They looked hazel, but death had clouded her corneas, so it was hard to be sure. There was an expression of surprise on her face, as though she wasn't expecting what had happened. I'd seen that look many times before. It seemed most murder victims were surprised to learn they would only have a handful of seconds left on earth.

I moved on to the rest of Betty's features. Despite being dead, I could tell she had been pretty at one time—probably many years ago—but it appeared life hadn't been good to her. I said as much to Susan and she nodded.

"She's clearly made some poor life choices." Susan moved to the base of the steps and looked up toward the door. "If it *was* J-Rock, do you think he shot her from here?"

I studied the angle of the arrow in Betty's chest. It was about as close to ninety-degrees as possible without going over. The top of the concrete steps was about four feet off the ground, so if J-Rock shot her from the base of the steps, there would've been a severe upward angle. I shook my head. "I don't think so."

Susan chewed on her bottom lip and scanned the front yard and the street. It had to be forty yards to the closest edge of East Coconut Lane. She pointed. "It could've come from the highway."

I considered that, and couldn't argue. Betty and Peter's trailer was one of only a half dozen other trailers and, since arrows didn't make a sound, there was little hope of locating a witness who might tell us when the shot happened or where the shooter was standing when the arrow was fired. At the moment, our only suspect was a drug dealer named J-Rock, and we didn't know anything about him.

I dropped to my knees and began rifling through Betty's pockets and even checked her hands. Nothing. No money, no drugs, no phone. If Peter was telling the truth—

"Where're the drugs?" Susan asked.

"That's the million dollar question." I stood and flicked at the inside of my ring finger with my left thumb, frowned when I remembered the wedding ring was no longer there. It had been years since I'd worn it, but I found myself reaching for it often. I missed wearing it, and I missed Michele and Abigail even more. I'd been told repeatedly it would get easier over time, but those were all lies. Every day felt like the day I lost them and I had finally realized it would never get easier and I'd have to live forever with the pain in my chest.

I blinked back to the present, pointed down at Betty. "If she was killed before the transaction, she should still have money and a phone. If she got killed afterward, she should still have the drugs."

"Unless he robbed her."

I nodded. "That could be it. Peter did say she owed him money."

We made a search of the yard and then concentrated our efforts in the area of the driveway and across the street, but found nothing worth noting. I glanced up at the sun. It had to be getting close to three o'clock. The coroner's office had called twenty minutes earlier to say they would be here within the hour to retrieve the body, and Peter had been getting restless.

"Can you take Peter down to the office and try to get a statement from him?" I asked. "Find out Betty's phone number from him and contact the phone company to see if they can ping it. When we find the phone, we'll probably find J-Rock."

"Will do."

I let her know I'd wait for the coroner's investigator to retrieve Betty's body, and asked her to see to it that Peter got something to eat.

Susan turned to walk away, but then stopped and stared down at her boots. "Um, did you hear anything from anyone at the hearing? It should be over by now, right?"

I frowned and glanced at my phone. No missed calls. I'd forgotten about the hearing and suddenly wondered why I hadn't heard anything. "It should be."

She shuffled her feet for a few seconds, then asked, "If you were a betting man, would you bet on me getting indicted or not?"

My heart ached as I stared into Susan's dark brown eyes. "I...I think the hearing went okay, as far as I could tell. Reginald did say there's nothing to worry about."

Susan grunted. "Then why do you look worried?"

I sighed. "You know I can't talk about my testimony, but I didn't like the direction Hedd was going with his questions."

"Why do you think William was there?"

I didn't know, but I could only imagine it was from some previous event, so I said as much.

"What previous event? You mean, like a use of force situation?"

I nodded, thinking back to last year. "He did see you heel stomp—"

"That had nothing to do with this case! Besides, I was cleared of any wrong doing. I already explained to Reginald that a heel stomp to the throat is no different than a bullet to the chest when your life is in danger."

"I agree with you one hundred percent—about all of it. You were justified in using deadly force and the shooting at my house had nothing to do with what happened the week before, but I'm trying to look at it from Hedd's point of view. I guess he's trying to use that situation to show a propensity for violence on your part."

"Why doesn't he just present videos from my cage fights while he's at it? It doesn't get more violent than that."

"Don't think he hasn't presented that to the grand jury. I think he'll throw everything he can at you."

"And why'd he wait so long to come after me? I mean, this was over a year ago."

"I guess whatever you did to him happened over the last fifteen months." A thought occurred to me. "And he might be looking at current events around the country and he thinks this is the right time to go after you. You know yourself it's not a good time to be a cop."

Susan stood silent for quite some time, lost in thought. Finally, she spoke in a soft voice. "When I first took this job, I'd worry about being involved in a shooting and hitting some innocent bystander, or get in trouble for injuring someone while driving too fast to an emergency call. I never dreamed I'd face prison time for killing someone who was actively trying to murder another person—someone who deserved it. That's just plain ludicrous. How'd we even get to this point?"

I didn't have an answer for her and I already felt guilty that she might lose her freedom for saving my life, so I kept my mouth shut. After a long and awkward silence, she mumbled a goodbye. I grabbed my phone and dialed Reginald's number as I watched her walk away. The least I could do was try to find out what was going on. It rang seven times and then went to voicemail. I left a message and shoved the phone in my pocket and walked back to Betty's body. Blowflies were starting to gather and I waved them off as best I could.

Ten minutes later tires squealed on the street behind me and I turned to see Melvin Saltzman turning into the driveway. He worked the day shift with Susan and was as hard a worker as they came. He was also the most loyal person I'd had the pleasure of meeting.

Melvin stepped out of the department pickup truck and made his way toward me. His bald head and thick face were blazing red from recent exposure to the sun. At twenty-nine, he was only two years younger than me, but we didn't look even close to the same age. Most people took me for late thirties and him for a first-year college student.

"That poor lady," Melvin said when he was standing beside me. "When Susan told me who it was I had to come out and see for myself."

"You knew her?" I looked down at Betty's bloodless face and tried to age her. It didn't seem possible they attended school together.

"She graduated high school with my sister, who's ten years older than me. She would come by the house and they'd hang out. I had a crush on her when I was little, but I wouldn't admit that out loud now."

"You just did," I pointed out, but he pretended not to hear me.

"I hadn't seen her again after they graduated—until about five years ago, that is. I got called out here for an accident." Melvin frowned. "Poor girl ain't never been the same since."

"What kind of accident?"

"Her little boy was killed."

My head snapped around and old memories came flooding to the surface. Although my eyes were wide open, I could still see the masked man pushing his tongue through the gap where his front left tooth used to be. He had been the ringleader of the group. I could hear Abigail cry out loud as he shoved the muzzle of his pistol against her temple. Could see the look of utter horror on her little face. Could feel my lips move as I begged Ringleader not to hurt my little girl, pleading with him to spare her life.

CHAPTER 11

"Chief, are you okay?"

Melvin's voice broke through the fog. I had to blink away the blank expression that fell over Abigail's face when the bullet ripped through her brain and took her precious life with it. Melvin's mug slowly came into view in front of me. "What's that?" I asked.

"You were mumbling something." Melvin's face was twisted in concern. "Are you okay, Chief?"

"Yeah, yeah. I'm fine." When I'd become the police chief of Mechant Loup, I'd spent the first six months tenure trying to convince Melvin it was okay to simply call me "Clint". Susan once told me it had taken her a month to break him of the habit of calling her "ma'am" and "Ms. Susan", but I had no such luck and had finally given up. I smiled to reassure him. "I'm fine. I was just wondering what happened. How was her little boy killed?"

He hesitated, as though he was unsure that I was okay, and then told me the story. Betty was working at the hospital north of Mechant Loup and was late for her night shift. She had rushed out to the car and started the engine, not realizing the house door hadn't shut behind her. She checked her mirrors, but Landon was too short and she backed right over him.

"That's horrible," I said.

Melvin nodded. "Poor lady didn't even realize she'd hit him. Peter was freaking out and screaming from the steps and she couldn't make sense out of what he was saying. She jumped out the car and that's when she saw him lying there."

I knew the pain and guilt she felt—or used to feel. I stared back at her body and no longer felt pity for her. She would never have to live another day with the sharp pain in her chest, or the lack of sleep, or the hole in her heart. No, I didn't pity her…I envied her.

"I guess that's the day her life turned to utter shit," I said.

"Yeah, that day totally screwed up her life." Melvin sighed. "It changed my life, too, a little."

That got me curious and I asked what he meant.

"I saw how much it destroyed her when she lost her son, so it made me not want to have kids. I figured if losing a kid hurt that bad, I'd be better off not even having any."

I started to tell him he was wrong, that the memory of Abigail and the time I got to spend with her was the only thing that kept me from shoving the muzzle of my Glock down my throat and pulling the trigger, but he said, "And then Bethany was born and I realized the love you feel for your child is worth the risk of possibly losing her."

I smiled at the mention of his firstborn child. She had just made a year and was as funny as any kid I'd ever seen. I liked it when his wife dropped by the station with her. She brightened up the place— reminded me of Abigail.

It was right then that the coroner's investigator arrived to retrieve Betty's body. I left Melvin to wrap things up at the scene and attend the autopsy, and then I headed to the station. When I walked through the door I saw Susan on the phone in her office, so I continued to my office. I nearly bumped into William as I walked through the door.

He started in place. "Sorry, Chief. I was just putting the reports from last night on your desk."

He couldn't make eye contact with me as I stood staring at him. I wanted to ask him what he'd said in the hearing, but I knew we'd both be violating the sequestration order. Instead, I simply walked by him and around my desk. I cursed when I slammed my shin against the bottom drawer, kicked it shut with my boot. I rubbed my shin as I sat and looked at the stack of reports. William was still standing in the doorway, apparently unsure of what to do. I scowled, pointed to the chair across from me. "Why don't you have a seat? You don't go on shift for another hour."

He nodded and dropped into the chair, his shoulders slumped forward.

I couldn't help but feel bad for him. "So, anything interesting happened last night?"

William shrugged. "Nothing much. A few speeders, a gas drive-off, and a prowler complaint that turned out to be bullshit."

Curious, I asked about the prowler complaint.

"Some guy on Orange Way saw a bush walking through the neighbor's yard. I wrote it up as unfounded, because he clearly had some problems."

"Ty Richardson?" I asked.

"That's him."

"I met him yesterday." Remembering, I reached in my pocket and pulled out the Hot Wheel I'd bought for Ty. "I need to bring this to him as soon as I get the chance."

"Why?" William asked.

"Just 'cause." I shoved it back in my pocket. "So, what'd you do with him?"

"I talked to his mom and she said she would make sure he takes his—"

"What the hell are you doing in here?" Susan demanded from the doorway. "I heard you testified in the hearing today. You don't know shit about what happened out at Clint's house, so why in the hell were you testifying?"

William stood and held up his hands. "Susan, I'm sorry. It's not what you think."

"That's what they all say right before they screw you over."

I watched Susan closely; worried she might take a swing at William. If she hit him, he'd end up in the hospital. I'd seen her destroy professional fighters in the cage, and William wasn't a trained fighter.

"I didn't ask to be there," William explained. "A sheriff's deputy showed up at my house this morning with a subpoena from the judge saying I had to show up today. The DA asked me what—"

"William, don't," I warned. "You can't talk about your testimony. You took an oath."

"Sorry, Chief, but I'm more afraid of Susan than any old DA."

Susan stood poised for a few tense moments, then exhaled forcefully. "Clint's right. I'm sorry for getting in your grill. I shouldn't have asked you about the hearing and I shouldn't be mad at you."

"Look, I'd be mad, too, if I didn't know what was going on." William lowered his head. "I feel like shit, you know? Like a sellout. I didn't want to be there, but they threatened to arrest me if I disobeyed the order to appear."

Susan walked over to him and slapped his shoulder. "It's okay, Will. We're good."

"Look, they asked about the heel stomp and I told them it was totally justified."

I cringed when he began talking about his testimony. "William, don't…"

"Okay, that's all I'll say," William said, looking right into Susan's eyes. "But I want you to know I had your back."

Susan nodded. "Thanks. I owe you."

"Go ahead and hit the streets," I said. "Susan and I have some things to sort out on this case and then we're heading in to get some rest. I want you and Amy pairing up tonight. There's a killer on the loose and until we know who it is, we need to be careful."

William nodded and walked by Susan, who smiled to reassure him everything was okay. When he was gone, she walked around my desk and leaned over me, typing on my keyboard. "The phone company called back," she said. "They were able to ping Betty's phone." She pulled up a map on my computer and tapped the monitor. "It's hitting on the tower in this area."

I studied the map, not exactly familiar with the area. "Is that in the central part of Chateau Parish?"

She nodded and drew a circle with her finger. "It could be anywhere in this vicinity."

"Was Peter able to give you any more info on J-Rock? A real name, or anything?"

"No, but I put in a call to a narcotic detective I know in Chateau. She said she'll run the nickname through her database and let me know what she finds."

I looked toward my door. "Speaking of Peter, where is he?"

"He's on the floor in the interview room. He's been snoring since we got here." She hefted her digital recorder. "Everything I could get out of him is on here."

I nodded my approval, asked her to have William and Amy put him up at a relative's house, and we walked out of my office together.

"Where're you going?" she asked.

"I'll try to call Reginald again and then I'm heading home. Let me know if your friend finds something on J-Rock."

Reginald didn't answer, so I left another message. The lack of response was starting to worry me. When there was good news, people fought to spread it, but when it was bad, no one wanted to answer the phone. I called the main line at the DA's office, but the girl who answered said Isabel and Reginald were both in court. I asked her to leave a message for Isabel to call me as soon as she got back in. I thought about driving to the courthouse, but that would seem desperate and would probably piss off DA Hedd even more. I glanced at the time on the wall clock. They would be closed before I arrived anyway, so I walked out into the sally port and then made the short drive home.

As always, Achilles was excited to see me. I headed toward the back door, but he wasn't about to wait for me. He dove headlong through the flap in the doggie door that I'd cut into the rear wall of the house long ago. With my job the way it was, I never knew when I'd be able to come home to let him out, so Mrs. DuPont—the lady who'd given Achilles to me—suggested the doggie door. She said it would allow him to become acclimated to the outdoors while still living like a king indoors. For security reasons, I didn't like having to cut such a large hole in the house—he topped the scales at a little over a hundred pounds—but I realized no one was coming near the house with him on duty.

Achilles was off the back porch before I opened the door. I watched him bound about the yard. I grunted. Sandra Voison was right—I needed to cut the grass. As I sat on the wooden steps wondering who killed Betty Ledet, Achilles snatched up a chew toy and ran toward me, stopping several feet away. With his hind side high in the air, he lowered his face to the ground and slowly opened his mouth, daring me to reach for the toy. I pretended not to look at him, and then made a jump for it. He jerked like he'd been shot and bolted across the yard, the toy clamped securely in his teeth. He seemed to smile as he took his victory lap. I chased him around for thirty minutes, or so, trying my best to take that toy away from him when a voice called from the back porch.

"Aren't you two just a couple bundles of joy?"

I turned to see Chloe standing there wearing blue jean shorts that had been cut so short the pockets were hanging out the bottoms and a shirt with a giant flower on it. When she lifted her hand to wave, her shirt rose with it and exposed her perfect bellybutton. I hurried to meet her and she met me half way, nearly taking me off my feet. After a long kiss, I leaned back, asked, "Do you want to finish where we left off last night?"

She smiled. "I'd like that very much."

I held her hand as we walked inside and we worked together in the kitchen until dinner was on the table. We made small talk as we ate and it was late into the night when we finally settled on the sofa, me sitting up and her lying in my lap. She had been unusually quiet and I knew it had to do with the way our conversation had ended the night before. I was scared to ask what she'd said, but I knew she was waiting for it, so I just came out with it. "So, what did you want to tell me last night?"

"I told you."

I rubbed the side of her face. "I know and I'm sorry I wasn't paying attention. I've just had a lot on my mind lately."

"I understand." She stared off across the room. "It was nothing, really."

"If you cared enough to say it, it was something. I want to know what's on your mind." I turned her head until she was looking up at me, bent close, and kissed her soft lips. "Please...can you say it again?"

She hesitated for a long moment, searching my eyes. I wasn't sure what she was looking for—or if she'd found it—but she finally sighed. "I said I love you...I love you, Clint Wolf."

CHAPTER 12

An hour later…

I moved up beside Susan, who was propped against a giant oak tree, and peered through the darkness at the small brick house. Everything was dark except for a rectangle of light coming from a window on the right side of the front door. I could make out a set of brown cabinets across the room from the window, so I suspected we were staring at the kitchen. A sheriff's deputy I'd never met approached at a crouching run and dropped to a knee next to Susan. He was short—I doubted he even touched the five-foot mark on a measuring tape—and stocky. He wore dark blue BDUs and carried a submachine gun. I felt naked with only my Glock, but four SWAT officers were slinking through the muggy night air and were about to kick down the front door, so I didn't want to miss the fireworks to get a shotgun from my Tahoe.

As it turned out, Susan's friend from narcotics, Trinity Bledsoe, knew J-Rock well—she'd arrested him four times in the past two years. His real name was Jerome Carter and he lived two blocks from the cell tower that was communicating with Betty's phone. When Trinity had run his name through the system, she found an active warrant for him from out of Magnolia Parish. It was for distribution and the bond was $70,000. Although his rap sheet was respectable by street standards, there was nothing violent on his record. It didn't mean he wasn't a violent person—it just meant he hadn't been caught yet. Every killer had to start somewhere, and his first kill could be a young woman with no life and a broken heart who owed him a few dollars. I'd known people who killed for less.

Stocky's muffled radio scratched to life and Trinity's voice came across the speaker. She called the entry team to attention and counted down from three. When she reached one, a flash-bang exploded somewhere behind the house and the entry team smashed open the front door and piled through the opening, disappearing from our view. To the untrained eye, what followed might've appeared to be mass confusion, but to someone who'd been in deep more than a few times, I saw it for what it was—a well-timed and superbly executed high-risk entry.

The SWAT officers announced their presence before the splintered door was fully open and they flooded the house just as quick. I heard at least two people scream when the flash-bang went off, but their screams were quickly drowned out by the authoritative voices of the officers commanding them to show their hands and get to the floor. Within seconds, everything was quiet again.

Moments later, Stocky spoke into his radio and stood. He gave us a nod. "All's clear. Trinity said y'all can go inside."

I thanked him and we walked across the damp grass. Once we reached the front door, Susan and I picked our way through the rubble and walked to where Trinity stood over two men wearing designer jeans that were baggy and T-shirts that were skintight. One of the men wore a pink shirt and the other wore a blue one; both were handcuffed and lying on their faces. Trinity turned to us, nodded. Her silky brown hair was pulled back into a tight bun and there was perspiration high on her forehead. She appeared to be of Asian descent and her almond-shaped brown eyes were beautiful and inviting, but I knew she could be deadly—could see it in the way her jaw was set. She pointed to the man on the ground who wore the blue shirt. "That's Jerome Carter."

J-Rock twisted around on the ground to look up at us and grimaced when the cuffs bit into his wrists. "Bitch, these cuffs are on too tight."

Unbothered by J-Rock's remark, Trinity instructed one of the SWAT deputies to take both of the men to the sheriff's office. Her voice was quiet, but confident. She was a little taller than Susan and, while not as toned, the muscles in her slender arms rippled as she reached down and pulled J-Rock to his feet.

J-Rock's head had been recently shaved and looked to have a day or two's growth on it. He tried to maintain a hard look, but there was worry in his eyes. "Who're these pigs? I ain't never seen them before. They feds or something?"

Susan and I were also dressed in jeans—and our uniform shirts—

but there was nothing designer about what we wore. "We're from Mechant Loup," I said, noting the slight widening of his eyes at the mention of our small town. "We've got some questions for you."

J-Rock looked around like he was weighing his options. He glanced down at his companion, then back at us. He swallowed hard and shook his head. "Look, we don't know nothing about that girl. We just—"

"Shut your mouth, J," said the man on the ground.

Trinity nodded for the deputy to take J-Rock away. She pulled the other man to his feet and I noticed the initials "NB" tattooed on the left side of his neck. "This handsome devil," Trinity said, "is Neal Barlow." The hair on his head was a little shorter than J-Rock's, but he had a thin moustache and a thick puff of hair under his chin. His thin-rimmed glasses were crooked on his face, and I didn't know if it was from being face-planted on the ground or if it had always been that way. "J-Rock's an angel compared to this good citizen. What're you doing here, Neal? You and J-Rock aren't best buds."

"This is a free country, Hoe. I can go where I want."

"Well, right now you're going to jail." Trinity led Neal outside and sat him in the back of a patrol car and instructed the deputy to put him in a separate holding area from J-Rock once they got to the sheriff's office. She then turned to Susan and me. "Y'all can follow my deputy to the office and start questioning them about the murder. I'll need to stay here and finish tossing the house. We found a few illegal guns and some drugs, but, so far, no bow or arrows and no cell phone matching your victim's."

Susan and I walked to my Tahoe. Before driving away, I grabbed my phone from the console and glanced at it. It was after midnight. I sighed when I saw two missed calls from Chloe and a text message wanting to know when I'd be getting back home. There had been panic in her eyes after professing her love for me earlier in the night. I guess the awkward silence that followed didn't help. I wanted to be honest with her—to tell her I needed more time—but I was afraid she'd leave me if her feelings weren't reciprocated, so I had just stared at her. When I felt like I'd been silent for too long and that I'd have to say something, one way or the other, the phone rang and rescued me.

It had been Susan calling to tell me her friend had a lead on J-Rock and we needed to meet her pronto. The fact that Susan was calling certainly didn't help, but Chloe tried to sound supportive as she told me she understood how it was when duty called. I'd promised to continue the conversation when we got home and that seemed to reassure her. I still wasn't sure what I'd say to her, so I tossed my phone back on the console and drove away, following the deputy to the sheriff's office.

CHAPTER 13

1:37 a.m., Saturday, October 10
Chateau Parish Sheriff's Office

"You mentioned a girl back there at your house," I began when Susan and I were seated across from J-Rock in an interview room. We'd already read him his rights and he'd agreed to speak with us. "What were you talking about?"

J-Rock shook his head. "Man, I don't know nothing about no girl."

"Why don't you tell us what you did on Thursday," I said. "Beginning earlier in the day, say, the afternoon, and going into the night."

J-Rock shrugged. "I don't remember."

"Why don't you try to remember?" I pressed.

"Nah, I'm good." J-Rock put his head down on the table and closed his eyes.

I looked at Susan. "Let's go talk to Neal and see what he thinks about what J-Rock said."

That brought his head up from the table. "What're you talking about? I didn't say nothing."

Susan and I stood and started to walk toward the door, but J-Rock jumped to his feet. He reached out with his cuffed hands, pleading with us. "You can't do that to me. I didn't say nothing. If you tell him I talked to y'all, he's...he's gonna kill me. He don't play. Neal's mean. I've seen him...um, he's just mean."

"I'm not playing either," I said. "I don't have time to be jerked around. Are you going to tell me what you know about Betty Ledet or not?"

"I...I don't know nothing about that."

"Suit yourself." I opened the door, but J-Rock grabbed my wrist in his hands. When I turned toward him he quickly let go and mumbled an apology.

"Wait," he said. "Where're you going?"

"I'm going talk to Neal," I said. "One of you kicked down Betty Ledet's door and raped her on her living room floor before plunging an arrow through her heart, and I'm going to find out which—"

"Whoa!" J-Rock's mouth dropped open and he fell to his knees on the floor. "Please, you have to listen to me. I didn't rape or kill nobody. I didn't even go in the trailer."

I eased the door shut and then helped J-Rock from the floor and back into his chair. Susan and I reclaimed our seats and I leaned across the table. "So, you didn't go in the trailer?"

J-Rock's eyes were wide. He shook his head.

"Let's start from the beginning," I said. "What brought you to Betty Ledet's trailer?"

J-Rock licked his lips, hesitated.

Susan shot an inquisitive look my way and I nodded. She turned to J-Rock and said, "Look, we're not interested in your petty crimes. We need to know the reason you were there, but we don't care about it—we care about finding the person who murdered Betty Ledet. So far, you're number one on our short list of suspects."

"I didn't kill Betty. We were friends." His voice was pleading. "But if I catch another drug charge, I'm going up the road for a long time."

"Like Sergeant Wilson mentioned, we don't care about your petty crimes," I said. "We know you were there selling drugs, but our main focus is on who killed Betty Ledet. At this point, you're the only one with opportunity and motive."

"I got motive? Why would I want to kill Betty? I make money off of her. If I'd go around killing all my customers, I wouldn't have a job." He snickered and settled back in his chair. "What kind of businessman you think I am?"

I raised an eyebrow and stared at him, watching as the realization of what he'd said slowly dawned on him. He shook his head, said, "You told me you weren't worried about petty crimes. That was a trick!"

I waved him off. "It wasn't a trick. We know Betty owed you money. Did that piss you off?"

"Nah, that didn't piss me off. I knew she was good for it, and I knew it wasn't all for her, anyway. It was mostly for that lazy piece of shit, Pete."

"Tell us what happened when you went out to Betty's house," I said.

J-Rock once again licked his lips and sat up in his chair. "Betty called me like she usually did, saying she needed enough to last the night. I drove over there with my boy, Neal, and I went knock on the door. Betty came out and gave me the money and I gave her the"—J-Rock glanced around, as though searching for a hidden camera—"stuff. And then, next thing I know, there's an arrow sticking out of her chest." He snapped his fingers for emphasis. "It happened just like that. One minute we were talking and the next minute she was shot and looking at me all weird."

"What'd you do next?" I asked.

"I looked behind me to see who shot her, but I didn't see nothing. At first, I thought it was Neal, but I knew he didn't have no bow and arrow. After that, I just ran to the car and told Neal to get the hell out of there before we got killed, too."

I turned his story over in my head. Due to the slight upward angle of the arrow, it was more likely it was fired from a distance. Had he fired it from the base of the steps, the angle would've been sharply upward. "Do you know anyone who has a bow?"

He shook his head.

"We didn't find this 'stuff' you mentioned in Betty's possession," I said. "And her cell phone was missing. Know anything about that?"

"Yeah, I took it back. She looked dead on her feet, so I knew she wasn't going to use it. I thought I could sell it to somebody else and make double the money."

"And the phone?"

"It fell on the ground next to my feet. I knew the cops would see my number on it and use it to track me down, so I took it and threw it in a dumpster behind my house."

Susan pulled her phone from the left breast pocket of her uniform shirt and started texting, and I knew she was letting Trinity know where to find the phone. After talking with J-Rock for another hour, it was clear he didn't know more than he was saying, so Susan and I left him with a deputy and met with Neal in the next room.

I read Neal his rights and then asked him if he would be willing to talk to us about what happened out at Betty Ledet's house. Neal was thoughtful, then pursed his lips. "Can I write something down before I answer that question?"

"Sure." I slid my notebook across the table and handed him an ink pen. In my peripheral vision, I saw Susan shift in her chair, and I knew she was thinking what I was—this might be a ploy to get a weapon in his hands. Although his hands were cuffed in front of him, he could still be dangerous, and I sat poised to take action should he try something. Unaware he was sitting across from two tigers that would pounce on him in a split second, he scribbled some words on my notebook and slid it back with the ink pen. His face was twisted into a smug grin, which made the patch of hair on his chin push forward like a third foot.

I glanced down at my notes and smiled when I read what he wrote. I turned it so Susan could see. "Go to hell," she read out loud. We both started laughing, and it seemed to confuse Neal.

"I mean it," he said. "Go to hell! I ain't saying shit. I want my lawyer and I want y'all to leave me the hell alone."

I'd been doing police work too long to get angry over a suspect exercising his right to remain silent. "That's fine," I said. "Just give us a call if you change your mind."

Susan and I walked out, leaving Neal Barlow with a befuddled expression on his face. When we walked into the Detective Bureau, Trinity was there. She handed us a clear plastic evidence envelope that contained a cell phone. "You were right," she said to Susan. "It was in the dumpster."

Trinity showed us the long list of evidence recovered from J-Rock's house and we examined it carefully, but none of it seemed to be connected to the murder. It was mostly drugs and drug paraphernalia. After thanking her for the assistance, we drove to the police department, where we pulled on latex gloves and examined the cell phone for clues. We searched through every contact, text message, phone call, photograph, video, voice note, and social media site, but found nothing that brought us any closer to finding out who wanted her dead.

It was almost four in the morning when we decided to call it a night. Before parting ways, Susan and I studied the photographs, evidence sheet, and notes Melvin had left on my desk from the autopsy. There were no surprises—Betty Ledet had been shot through the heart with an arrow and the manner of death was homicide. The big question was, *"Now what?"*

Susan had learned from Peter that Betty worked at M & P Grill. Since her family was out of the picture, her job was our next best lead. Maybe the other waitresses knew something about her habits. Her supervisor could probably tell us about any problems with other employees or customers. Hell, even some of her regular customers might know a thing or two that could prove helpful.

"Let's meet at M & P Grill first thing in the morning," I said. "We need to learn all we can about Betty, and her co-workers probably know the most about her at this point."

Susan nodded in agreement and I waved goodbye. As I watched her walk to her Charger, I couldn't help but wonder what she might be thinking. We'd been busy and that kept our minds occupied, but I knew she would now be alone with her thoughts and I was sure they would turn to the hearings and what would become of her career…or even her freedom.

I had a lot on my own mind as I turned into my driveway and walked toward my house. In addition to being worried sick about Susan, I couldn't stop wondering what kind of person would put an arrow through another human's heart. Whoever it was, they definitely wanted Betty Ledet dead. If not J-Rock, then who could it be? Had she ripped off some other drug dealer? According to Peter, J-Rock was their only supplier, but what if Peter was lying to protect someone he feared more than J-Rock? From everything we'd gathered Betty had been eking out a meager existence since losing Landon. Her family had disowned her when they learned she'd turned to alcohol and drugs to cope with her depression. According to Peter, she didn't have any friends. But what about enemies? Was it possible for her to make enemies when she didn't even have friends? What if she was messing around with a married man? They say hell hath no fury like a woman scorned, and it would take a hell of a lot of scorn to send an arrow through a person, so a jealous wife was certainly a possibility. I had to figure this thing out and do it soon before—

"It's about time you get home."

I nearly jumped out of my skin when the voice came from out of the darkness to my right. I squinted to improve my night vision and saw Chloe crouched on the porch, her arms wrapped around her knees.

"What are you doing?" I asked, confused. "Have you been out here all night? I thought you went home when I left."

She looked up, the dim glow from the distant streetlight catching on her face, and I gasped when I saw streaks of tears running down her cheeks.

CHAPTER 14

I dropped beside Chloe and took her in my arms. "Baby, what's wrong?"

"I'm terrified, Clint."

Had something happened? Had someone threatened her? I knew she had been busy trying to develop a story she was working on, but things weren't working out like she'd hoped. Was her job in jeopardy? What if someone associated with the story came after her?

"What happened? Did someone do something to you?" I looked toward my house. Achilles had the tendency to play rough. "Is it Achilles? Did he bite you?"

"No, no...none of that." Chloe shook her head from side to side, and took a deep breath to calm herself. "It's you."

My heart fell and my chest ached. It was in that moment I realized I had strong feelings for Chloe Rushing. Michele used to ask me how I knew I loved her and I could never answer the question to her liking—that is, until Abigail was born. Every time Abigail used to laugh, my heart would swell with joy, and every time she'd cry, my heart would break.

I took Chloe's face in my hands and eased her lips to mine. I tasted the salt from her tears as we kissed. When I pulled away from her, I looked into the shadows that were her eyes and said, "I love you, too, Chloe."

I saw her expression change. "I don't want you to say it just because I said it."

"I'm not."

"Then why'd you hesitate earlier? You just stared at me, not saying anything." She shuddered. "That was the scariest moment of my life. I thought I'd pushed you away. And then you left and were gone forever. You didn't answer my calls, didn't call back, didn't respond to my text. I thought it was over between us."

"I'm sorry. I was busy."

Chloe seemed to be thinking. After a long moment, she said, "If you really love me, you would've said it right away. There wouldn't have been any doubt."

"Look, I'm not good at these kinds of things, but I know I love you."

Chloe's face looked ghostly in the dim glow from the streetlight as she peered up at me. "How do you know you love me?"

"Because I'm happy when you're happy and I hurt when you hurt."

She seemed to be considering this. "Don't you feel bad for strangers when bad things happen to them?"

"Sure, I feel bad for them, but I don't hurt inside. I don't lose sleep over it." I ran a finger down the side of her neck to her chest. "When you're upset, it ruins my day."

This seemed to satisfy her. She threw her arms around my neck and squeezed harder than I thought she could. "It feels so good to get that out of the way." Her voice was somewhat muffled by my shoulder.

"What do you mean?"

"I've wanted to tell you for a couple of months now, but couldn't bring myself to do it."

Curious, I asked, "When did you know?"

"Last year…when I thought you were dead." She reached up and scrubbed at the tears spilling from her face. "I felt like my life was over. I didn't think I could survive the day. That's when I knew."

We stayed in that position until I couldn't feel my legs anymore. All of a sudden, I was aware of mosquitoes buzzing around my ear. They'd found us. Although the town had an aggressive mosquito abatement program, it was no match for the Louisiana state bird. I helped Chloe to her feet and we walked inside. Achilles bounded across the living room floor and shoved his cool snout against my hand, his tail wagging a greeting.

"I fed him and let him out about an hour ago," Chloe said, as she walked to the bedroom.

I let him out again and watched him patrol the back yard, my thoughts turning back to the murder investigation. First on my to-do list was the restaurant. I was hoping it would lead in other directions and eventually lead to the murderer—if it *was* a murder. What if this was nothing but a tragic hunting accident?

When Achilles was done marking his territory, we went back inside and I gasped when I saw Chloe standing in the kitchen wearing nothing but one of my white muscle shirts. It was too big for her and the neckline hung low on her breasts.

"I take it you're sleeping over?" I asked.

"Is that okay?"

I smiled and took in all of her beauty. I was tired, but never too tired to be with her. My smile faded when I saw her frown and adjust my shirt. "What is it?" I asked.

"For tonight...um, I just want to be held."

I nodded my understanding. It had been an emotional night for her. I took her hand and led her to my room, where we both got ready for bed in the master bathroom—the *only* bathroom. Afterwards, we slipped under the sheets and she placed her head on my chest. Soon, her breathing changed and I knew she was asleep. My eyes dragged shut and I started to doze off, my thoughts on the future of us and contemplating if it was possible to love two women. Had Michele still been alive, I wouldn't be here. I would've never met Chloe or been interested in her—or any other woman. Michele was everything to me until Abigail came along—

I jerked awake as images of Abigail's face popped into my mind's eye. Chloe stirred beside me, but turned over and continued sleeping. I tried to sleep, but every time I dozed off, those horrific images from three years ago kept flooding back. Finally, and taking great care not to disturb Chloe, I eased out of bed and tiptoed to the kitchen. I knelt and opened the cabinet under the sink, wincing when the hinges squeaked. I paused, but didn't hear any movement from my room. When I knew it was safe, I reached behind the garbage can and pulled out the bottle of vodka that was hidden there. I twisted off the cap and put it to my lips, scowled when only a drop came out.

Remembering the bottles I'd purchased the day before, I grabbed my Tahoe keys and headed out the front door. With Achilles at my heels, I picked my way through the damp grass and retrieved one of the vodka bottles from the back of my Tahoe. I then settled on the front porch to consume it. I sighed as the liquid slid down my throat and wrapped its warm arms around my insides. I wondered if I'd ever be able to sleep without it.

Right after Michele and Abigail were murdered, I started drinking a few shots before bed and that would help, but, eventually, it wasn't enough. Before long, I upgraded to a glass. When that didn't help anymore, I started downing a bottle a night. I often wondered what I'd do if it ever wore off.

I'd once confided in Chloe that I needed vodka to sleep, but never admitted to how much. She started pressing me to get help—to see a psychologist and talk about my feelings—but I was having none of it. When it started to feel like she was nagging, I told her I was better and I didn't need it to sleep anymore. It was easier to live with the guilt of hiding my problem than to be constantly reminded that something was wrong with me and I needed fixing.

I stared down at the empty bottle. My lips were numb, my chest warm. It had done its job. I'd now be able to get a good night's sleep and I'd be better in the morning. No need to talk about my feelings and hear how messed up I was and be offered some multi-step program that would help me get better. Nope, this was a miracle in a bottle, and it was all I needed to get through my nights. As I tossed the bottle under my house, I wondered what Chloe would do if she found out I was still drinking.

CHAPTER 15

Isaac Edwards dropped his tired legs to the floor beside his bed and rubbed the sleep from his eyes. The red digits on the clock were blurry, but he could tell it was six-thirty. *Too damn early to be up on a Saturday*, he thought.

Wearing nothing but his plaid boxer shorts and his white night shirt, Isaac walked to the bathroom to relieve himself—cursing the slow stream that flowed from his member—and then stopped in front of the mirror to wash his hands. He splashed some of the cold water on his face. It shocked him at first, but it felt good. He rubbed the water into his salt-and-pepper hair in a futile attempt to flatten the unruly tuft sticking out like a unicorn's horn on the left side. He finally gave up, started to turn away from the mirror when something caught his attention. He leaned closer, but had to back off so the blemish could come into focus. It was another pesky skin tag and it hung under his right eye like a third ear.

"You're like an old beat up truck with rust spots and fading headlights," he said to his reflection in the mirror, taking note of his grayish eyes—eyes that had once been bright blue and sparkling. His mom had often said his eyes were too pretty to be on a boy. He grunted. "Nowadays, that'd be no problem. There's a surgery for everything."

Isaac padded to the front door in his bare feet and stepped onto the porch to retrieve his newspaper. Some kid—a sandy-haired boy with mischief written all over his dirty face—whisked by on a skateboard and jerked his head around when he saw Isaac standing there in his boxers.

"Put some clothes on, you old goat!" the boy shouted, shaking his head and lurching forward as though he were vomiting.

Isaac only smiled and returned to the kitchen to make coffee and enjoy what was left of the printed paper. It had been getting thinner and thinner over the years, as people like him slowly died off to make room for a younger generation who preferred their news on rectangular-shaped intelligent phones that did all but scratch their asses. He only hoped he would die before the newspaper did, because he would certainly miss it more than it'd miss him.

After drinking a tall cup of coffee and reading about some drug dealer who'd been killed in the northern part of the parish—"Good riddance," he thought—he made his way back to the master bathroom to change into his running shorts and shoes. His back hurt a little more than it used to as he bent to lace up his shoes, and he had to keep reminding himself why he was doing it. He stood and tested his legs. The shoes he'd just bought were lighter than the last pair and seemed easier on his old legs. He was approaching seventy at breakneck speed and after running nineteen marathons over the years, he didn't think there was anything left to learn. But when he'd started experiencing new pains in his ankles and knees and his doctor's only advice was to stop running, he'd gone to the Chateau Parish Library and researched some alternative methods—something to take the pressure off of the joints just long enough to run this last marathon for Stella. In this one book about running, the author claimed if he ran on the balls of his feet it would relieve the pressure in his ankles and knees. He was doubtful, but had tried it anyway. Three miles later, he had been pain-free and running strong, while cursing himself for wasting money on the doctor visit.

Isaac walked outside to begin the last run of his fifth week of training. He and Stella—his wife of forty years—had signed up for the event six months ahead of time, as they had every alternating year for the past forty years, and were set to accomplish Stella's goal of completing twenty marathons before reaching seventy. But when Stella was hit by a car two weeks earlier during a late night run and hospitalized in critical condition, she'd made him promise to complete the race without her—to do it for her. She insisted he wear one of those camera helmet gadgets that everyone was wearing these days so she could experience the training and the event with him.

Isaac sighed. Running was Stella's passion, not his, but he loved her more than life itself, so he wore the goofy helmet and gutted through the lonely morning runs while she recovered in the hospital. He wanted to spend every minute beside her bed, but she'd insisted he keep up the house and his training. So he did.

It was an unusually warm October in Louisiana and it made his runs tougher. He thought about skipping that morning, but Stella would find out when she downloaded the video to her laptop that afternoon. *Damn the kids for buying her a laptop and the grandkids for teaching her to use it,* he thought.

It suddenly dawned on him—the videos were to keep tabs on him, to make sure he was still training! He smiled. That Stella was a sharp knife for sure.

Isaac pressed the button on the recorder and strapped the helmet in place. Taking a deep breath, he set out on the concrete road. He fell into a comfortable pace, landing on the ball of one foot and then the other, moving ever forward. He knew not to get in a hurry, especially in that heat. The air was so humid it felt as though he was breathing through a wet towel, but he pressed on. Somehow, he managed to reach the end of the five-mile run in under an hour.

He'd sprinted the last hundred yards and was gasping by the time he reached the finish line, which was his driveway. He slowed to a walk in front of his house and wiped sweat from his face and neck, took several deep breaths to calm his beating heart. "Not bad for an old man," he shouted to no one in particular. He walked back and forth in front of his house for a few laps, traveling about twenty yards each way, slowly cooling down. He scanned the neighborhood as he walked. Other than the swamp rat of a kid on the oversized skateboard, there wasn't a soul in sight.

He smiled to himself. While his other neighbors were either still in bed or shuffling around in their pajamas, he was outside living life. He hated to run, but always felt a sense of accomplishment when he finished a training session. Tears welled up in his eyes as he thought of Stella lying in a hospital bed waiting for him to visit. She'd want to hear all about the run. He remembered the video and reached over his head to turn it off. "I love you so much, Boo-Boo," he said, walking toward his mailbox.

He'd seen the mail truck in the neighborhood during one of his laps and hoped Stella's present had arrived. His daughter had helped him order a new watch for Stella on the Internet and it was set to arrive any day. He reached for the flap to the mailbox and groaned when he caught a whiff of his armpits. He kept forgetting to put deodorant on before the runs. That never happened when Stella was home. She always made sure to remind him. As he sifted through the mail—campaign ads, bills, and other junk—he wondered what he'd do if Stella were taken from him for good. He immediately dismissed the thought, as he couldn't bear to imagine life without—

"What the hell is this?" The last envelope in the stack was from the Chateau Parish Clerk of Court and it had "Jury Duty" stamped on the outside. It was addressed to him. Scowling, he ripped it open and read the enclosed letter. The part that grabbed his attention most was the part that read, "You are hereby summoned to appear for Jury service on February 22 at 9:00 AM through March 3 at 4:30 PM and there remain until duly discharged."

"No!" Isaac slammed the flap to the mailbox shut. He had served on a jury once before—twenty years earlier—and they'd been forced to work all day, every day of the week, with barely any breaks. They got out late at night and even had to work Saturday and Sunday. He looked at the date again. The marathon was on February 28th, and that was right in the middle of the trial. "Damn it to hell! This is going to kill Stella." His mind racing, he thought he remembered the presiding judge of the other trial excusing one of the ladies for being too old. He was about to be seventy, and surely that was plenty old enough to be excused. Excitement surging through him, he walked toward his door while scanning the letter for the telephone number. He would have to wait until Monday, but he would call first thing to get this—

A sudden and penetrating pain smashed into his back and shot through to his chest, stopping him in midstride. He glanced down. "What the *hell?*"

A pointed object had pushed the front of his running shirt out like a tent pole. The pain was so severe his legs buckled and he fell to his knees. The mail slid from his hands as he reached for the bottom of his shirt. Confused and disoriented, he pulled the shirt upward until it was high enough to reveal the object—*a razor-bladed arrowhead attached to a red arrow!* Blood oozed from the hole in his chest. He suddenly realized he was in trouble—bad trouble. He was dying. Someone had just killed him! Had it been an accident? Was it intentional? Who would want to do such a thing to him? Fear clutched at his heart, constricted his throat. "Help! Help me!"

Isaac pawed at the arrow as he screamed for help. Blood leaked down his belly and stained his shorts. He fell to his hands and knees and turned to begin crawling toward the road. There were no neighbors across the street from his house—only an open field—but he needed to get out from behind his hedges and to a place where someone could see him. He thought he saw that punk kid ride by again on his skateboard, but his vision was getting fuzzy and he couldn't be sure. Blood dripped freely to the ground beneath him and he could feel himself fading. He began to cry as he thought of Stella and how she would be waiting for him to visit her later in the day. What would she think of him? Would she be mad that he didn't show up? He didn't want her mad at him. And who would take care of her? She was set to be released from the hospital in a week, but she would need assistance getting around. Who would help her? The kids had lives and children of their own to care for. He cried out in sorrow. "Stella! Oh, Stella, please forgive me for not being there!"

Isaac made it to the street and collapsed onto his side. The sun was hot as it beat down on him, but the pavement was even hotter. It burned his face. He wanted to move, but couldn't. He was too weak. He called out for Stella, but he could no longer hear his own voice. Was he actually talking, or was he only imagining it? His eyelids started to slide shut. He heard what sounded like a skateboard whisk by and then heard it come to a stop. Through the mirage of pain he saw the sandy-haired swamp rat from earlier. He called out to him for help, but the boy only stared. His jaw was hanging and his eyes were wide. After standing frozen for a long moment, the boy spun around and headed back in the direction from which he'd come. "Mom!" he yelled as he sped off. "Mom! There's a dead man in the road!"

CHAPTER 16

I met Susan in the parking lot at M & P Grill a little before eight o'clock. The first thing she asked was if I'd heard from Reginald Hoffman. I ripped my phone from my pocket and checked it, feeling guilty for not knowing. Chloe had forced me awake this morning at six and I'd awakened in a fog. I'd been disoriented and the splitting headache I often got from drinking was even worse than usual, causing her to ask a million questions. I chalked it up to lack of regular sleep, and that seemed to calm her suspicions. I'd rushed through a light breakfast and a shower and then left before she could interrogate me more.

I shook my head when I didn't have any missed calls, looked up into Susan's troubled eyes. "Nothing at all."

She frowned and turned toward the entrance to the restaurant.

M & P Grill was a small restaurant on the corner of Kate and Main that served mostly seafood and hamburgers, but they also cooked a killer breakfast. The smell of greasy bacon and scrambled eggs greeted us as we stepped through the front door. Malory, who was the restaurant manager, smiled when we entered.

I'd first met Malory last year while working a murder investigation—she'd been the head waitress at the time—and I'd come to know her better over the months that followed by stopping in every now and then for lunch. Her hair was long and wavy at the moment—dark brown nearest the crown of her head and fading to a lighter brown at the shoulders—but that could change in an instant. There was this one time when her hair color and style had changed three times within the same month. She'd blamed it on boy problems and told me all about it, but I tuned most of it out. She was a little heavier than Chloe and appeared softer, but she was attractive nonetheless, and I hadn't wanted anyone getting the wrong idea. I was a one-woman man, and that woman was Chloe.

Malory pointed to the corner of the room. "Your spot's open," she said, knowing I preferred the corner table, where I could face the door while keeping my back to the wall.

I frowned. "I wish I hadn't eaten breakfast yet, because that stuff"—I shot a thumb toward the kitchen—"smells good."

Malory looked puzzled. "If you're not here to eat, then..."

"We're here on business," I said. "Betty Ledet's been killed and we need your help to try and figure out who'd want her dead."

I was surprised when Malory only nodded and waved us toward her office.

"I can't believe she's dead," Malory said when we were seated around her desk. "We heard someone had been murdered in her neighborhood and when she didn't show up for work Friday night, I put two and two together. I don't know that I can help with anything, though. Nothing ever happens here at the diner."

Susan shifted in the chair, her leather gun belt creaking as she moved, and asked, "Did Betty have any enemies that you know of? Either here at the restaurant or someone from her personal life?"

Malory didn't hesitate. "No way. Everyone loved Betty. I mean, she was quiet and not very outgoing, but I think that's why everyone loved her. She didn't get involved in restaurant gossip and was always willing to work an extra shift if one of the girls needed someone to cover for them."

"What about men?" I asked. "Did she have any admirers?"

"Sure, she had lots of admirers. Guys would flirt with her all the time. She was a pretty girl."

"How'd she respond?" I wanted to know.

Malory shrugged. "She'd flirt back, like the rest of the girls, but it was all innocent, really."

"She was a married woman," Susan interjected. "There's nothing innocent about married women flirting. It usually means there're problems back home."

"Well, Peter wasn't the greatest husband," Malory acknowledged. "But I don't believe Betty would ever step outside of her marriage. Of course, Peter thought differently."

When asked to explain, Malory told us Peter had come into the restaurant one day while Betty was chatting with a customer and he had caused quite a scene. "It was an old man. I hadn't seen him in here before, but Betty seemed to know him. They were talking and laughing and carrying on like old friends when Peter walked in. He went straight to the table and started bitching at Betty. Called her a whore and accused her of cheating." Malory shook her head. "It was quite ridiculous. The old man could've been her great grandpa, but Peter didn't care."

"Who was the old man?" Susan wanted to know.

Malory just shrugged and said, "I'd never seen him before. He came in a few times since then—once a month, I guess—but he always asked for Betty, so I never did get his name."

"Has Peter come in here often?" I asked.

"He's come in the restaurant a few times over the years. Mostly, he pulls Betty outside and talks to her in the parking lot and then leaves—except for that outburst. The poor old man didn't know where to put himself. He kept apologizing and saying he was just an old friend and that he didn't mean any harm."

"What else do you know about Peter?" I asked.

"Only what Betty told me. He was a bum. Never wanted to work and he expected her to hand over everything she made. But the worst of it was when…" Malory hesitated, chewed on her lower lip. "I feel like I'm violating her trust or something. I know she's gone, but she made me promise never to tell."

Susan and I exchanged looks. Susan leaned across the table and, in a soft voice, said, "When Betty made you promise not to tell her secret, she had no idea someone would've shot her through the heart with an arrow."

Malory threw a hand to her throat, gasping. "*What?* Shot with an arrow? That's the most horrific thing I've ever heard!"

Susan nodded. "Had Betty known this was about to happen, she would've given you the green light to tell us. Anything you know—no matter how insignificant it seems—might be the tiny puzzle piece that brings the whole picture into view. Trust me…she'd definitely want you sharing that with us now. So, please, tell us everything you know."

Malory nodded slowly. "I know you're right, but I just feel bad saying it out loud." She glanced around the tidy office, brought her eyes back to us. "Well, about three months ago she was closing up and I came in to check on her. I found her crying in the kitchen. I asked her what was wrong and she said Peter's drug problem was worse than ever. We all knew he was an addict and we suspected he beat her, but we didn't know the extent of his addiction." Malory paused and I thought she was going to shut down, but she continued after a long moment. "She kept saying she should've let Peter go to jail and I asked what she was talking about. It took some time, but I finally got it out of her." She paused again.

"Got what out of her?" Susan asked when Malory had been silent too long.

"The truth about her baby."

CHAPTER 17

We sat with Malory for about ten minutes and she went over the story exactly as Betty had relayed it to her. We were about to leave when the radio on my belt scratched to life and Lindsey notified us that a dead body had been found in a posh neighborhood at the southwest corner of town. Susan and I exchanged looks and rushed out the door, leaving Malory sitting alone at her desk with a befuddled look on her face.

"Leave your car and jump in with me," I called to Susan, hitting the unlock button on my keyless remote.

The southern sky was clear and blue, and the air warm as we sped across town. A recent cold front had reduced the temperature from ninety-five degrees to ninety. Sweat caused my tan polyester uniform shirt to cling to my back, but I wasn't complaining. Not one to relish cold weather, I welcomed the unseasonal temperatures and embraced it like an old friend. Most of the townspeople made their living hunting, trapping, and trawling, and the weather was taking a huge bite out of their economic pie. While I felt bad for them, I was happy for myself. I was feeling like I landed in a tropical paradise. I'd always told Michele I wanted to live so far south that all four seasons were summer, and she'd agreed. My disdain for winter had come from spending too many wet and freezing mornings huddled over dead bodies on the mean streets of La Mort, which was the third largest city in Louisiana. As for Michele, she just hated being cold.

I frowned at the thought of my wife. She and Abigail would've loved living in Mechant Loup. Michele's parents had moved here after she graduated and left the nest. She had tried to visit as often as she could, but the trips were always brief, so she never got to appreciate the area. Back then, I would've never considered leaving the city to move to some backwoods town with one road in and one road out, but a lot can change in a few years.

Susan pointed to a street sign that was approaching at breakneck speed. "That's it!"

I smashed the brake, turned right onto Lacy Court, and cruised toward the back of the street.

"It's after Second Street, the third house from the end, and it's on the right." She nodded. "Can't miss it—it's the only house with a dead guy in the driveway."

The first thing I noticed when we drove up to the scene was the red arrow sticking out of the man's back. Although we were twenty yards from the body, it was hard to miss. My blood slowed in my veins—whoever killed Betty Ledet had struck again. We had a hunter on our hands, and he was preying on humans. I snatched my phone from the console and dialed the office. I didn't need every nosy townsperson with a scanner knowing what was going on. Hell, *I* didn't know what was going on. Lindsey answered on the first ring. "Run this address through every system and program you have," I said. "I want to know everything about the people who live here...what they drive, where they work, who their family and friends are—everything. I even want to know if they do it with the lights on."

There was a long pause on the other end of the line.

"I'm joking about the last part," I said.

Lindsey laughed. "Okay, I was wondering how I'd find that out." She cleared her throat. "I already ran the address through the complaints computer. The owners are Isaac and Stella Edwards and I found two calls for service in the last eight years that are associated with them."

"What're they about?"

"The first one was because someone broke into their shed. That was eight years ago. The other complaint was...oh, wow." Lindsey paused and I could hear her fingers dancing across the keyboard. "Stella Edwards was hit by a car two weeks ago."

That caught my attention. "Here? In town?"

"No. She was hit a couple miles north of town." Lindsey paused again, mumbling to herself as she read the report. "Okay, it seems she was jogging with her husband along the highway and a car swerved toward them. She saw the car and pushed Isaac out of the way and it ran smack over her."

"Why do we have a complaint on it?" I asked.

"The sheriff's office got into a high speed chase with the car and it was heading back toward town, so they asked us to set up a roadblock by the bridge. They blew out the tires with spike strips before the suspect got to the bridge, though, so we didn't get involved. William was working the night shift at the time."

I mulled over the information for a minute, asked, "Do we know who the suspect was?"

"No, but I can find out."

"Thanks." I shoved my phone in my shirt pocket. There might be a connection between the crash and the murder. But what was the connection between Isaac Edwards and Betty Ledet? I stepped out and followed Susan to the body.

The second thing I noticed as we got closer was the camera attached to Isaac Edwards' head. "Is that a GoPro?" I asked.

Melvin, who had arrived before us and already roped off the scene, wiped sweat from his forehead with the tan sleeve of his uniform shirt. "It sure is, Chief. I think we just got a major break in this case."

I resisted the urge to immediately rip the headgear off his head. Instead, I directed Melvin and Susan through the process of documenting the scene and searching for evidence. It was a simple scene—a man in extremely short shorts shot through the back with an arrow after checking his mail. Based on the blood around the body, he had been shot with the same type of three-blade mechanical broad-head as Betty. I lifted his shirt and the large wound canal through his body confirmed my suspicions.

When we'd finished searching and photographing the scene and surrounding area, Melvin recovered the mail while Susan and I took measurements.

"Hey, Chief," Melvin called from his knees in the driveway, "Isaac's going to be late for jury duty in February."

I looked up from the body of the elderly man and watched as Melvin carefully placed a jury duty subpoena in an evidence envelope.

"You think he killed himself to get out of jury duty?" Susan asked.

I stifled a grin, not wanting any neighbors to see us laughing at a murder scene. Neighbors. I scanned the street. It was empty. "Who called this in, anyway?" I asked.

"Some kid on a skateboard found him," Melvin said over his shoulder. "The kid's mom called." Melvin had located more mail under the hedges where the wind had blown it. A little thick in the belly, he had to take a deep breath and hold it as he bent to retrieve the envelopes. When he straightened, he exhaled and wiped more sweat from his face. "That boy was scared stupid. Said he had just waved to the man a minute earlier and told him good morning, and when he saw him again he was dead on the ground. I asked him if he saw or heard anything suspicious, but he said everything was quiet."

Melvin went inside to search the house next, while Susan and I finished measuring the position of the victim's body in relation to the surrounding area. Based on our recreation of the scene, it appeared the arrow had been fired from across the street. I walked to the edge of the road and surveyed the area. A ditch separated an empty lot from the street. The lot stretched for about two hundred feet from the ditch and was lined with trees on the backside. One lone tree was situated near the middle of the lot. The leaves were still thick and hung low to the ground. I nodded. That was the spot.

When Melvin came outside and announced there was nothing of evidentiary value inside the house, I said, "Can you call your canine buddy—Seth, right?—and see if he can pick up a track from that tree? It's got to be where the killer fired the arrow."

Melvin, who was always eager to please, nodded his head. "I'm on it!" He turned and walked up the street to make the call.

Susan had finished what she was doing and joined me near the body. I pointed to the GoPro camera. "You ready to see what's on that thing?"

Nodding, she squatted beside the body and eased the camera from the man's head with her gloved hands. We then walked to my Tahoe and she removed the mini SD card from the GoPro. Digging her laptop from one of her bags, she shoved the mini into an adaptor and plugged it into her computer. Within seconds, she'd pulled up the video files from the GoPro.

We watched as Isaac walked up the driveway—the camera bobbing up and down with each step—and to Lacy Court. He faced toward the back of the street and then his pale and wrinkly legs suddenly came into view as he bent to stretch. When he straightened, it appeared he nodded to himself and then broke into a nice jog toward the back of the street. His pace was steady and brisk—not at all what I would've expected from someone his age. He didn't slow down until he reached the end of the concrete road, where he turned around and headed toward the front of the street.

"Rewind it to the end of the street and pause it there," I told Susan. When she did, I studied the picture, which was crisp and detailed. Where the concrete ended, a dirt road began and extended for what looked to be a mile, or so, until it reached a line of trees. On either side of the dirt road were deep ditches separating the road from fields of rich grass that were bordered by thick lines of trees and shrubbery. A barbed-wire fence stretched from a locked gate to the tree lines on either side. They were littered with *No Trespassing* signs and other signs warning that violators would be prosecuted to the fullest. There were a few good hiding spots from which an archer could launch an attack, so I wondered why the killer hadn't shot Isaac when he reached the back of the street. It was possible the killer staged in that area and stalked Isaac from there, so I covered every inch of the screen, searching for the tiniest hint of a human's presence. There was none. I sighed, motioned for Susan to continue the film.

Isaac maintained his impressive pace toward the front of the street. He passed dozens of houses, most of them sprinkled with Halloween decorations. Every yard was manicured, every tree and bush trimmed to perfection. Nearly every driveway had at least one car—most had multiple—but no one was outside except for one man toward the beginning of the street. He could be seen opening the door to a white SUV and stepping out. He was too far from the camera for me to make a proper identification, but the house and four cars in the driveway would make him easy to find.

When Isaac reached Main Street, he turned and made his way back down Lacy Court, turning once more at the end of the street. Not wanting to miss anything, we watched every minute of his hour-long jog and were nearing the end of the video when a sandy-haired kid on an oversized skateboard popped into view. His hair was bushy and he appeared dirty and he was scooting away from Isaac. "Is that the kid, Melvin?" I asked when the boy turned and whisked toward Isaac.

Melvin, who was waiting for his buddy from the sheriff's office to show up with a K-9, walked over and confirmed it was the kid. "That's the little shit. He looks like he's up to no good."

"Yeah," Susan agreed. "If he hasn't been arrested yet, he will be."

"Maybe seeing this dead body will scare him straight," I said, shooting my thumb toward Isaac Edwards.

"Maybe he's the killer," Susan countered.

I glanced down at the indicator bar at the bottom of the video player. We were nearing the end of the footage. "If someone doesn't pop up soon and shoot this man with an arrow, I'm going to start thinking it *was* the kid."

Susan and I leaned closer to the computer screen—our mouths open with anticipation—as we watched Isaac draw to within a hundred yards of his house. He suddenly broke out into a sprint, as though he were trying to finish strong, and didn't slow down until he reached his driveway. He walked back and forth in front of his house a few times and then his arm came into the camera's view, appearing to wipe sweat from his head. He shouted, "Not bad for an old man," and then—

"What the hell?" Susan blurted.

CHAPTER 18

"You've got to be shitting me!" Susan said.

"We should've known it was too good to be true." I sighed, staring at the blank computer screen. Isaac Edwards had turned the camera off moments before his murder. Had he known what was about to happen, would he have left it running? A car approached behind us and we turned to see a sheriff's office cruiser with a large "K-9" emblem on both front doors approaching the scene. It stopped a few feet behind my Tahoe, and Seth stepped out.

Seth was a young fellow with a shaved head and he was dressed in dark blue BDUs. I remembered him from a year earlier when he and his runt of a German shepherd named Coco had helped us recover a dead body from Bayou Tail. He'd told us that Coco was strictly a cadaver dog, so I wasn't surprised when he opened the back door and a large black and tan German shepherd bounded out.

Seth put him on a long leash and made his way to where we had moved to the side of the road. He shook each of our hands and greeted us like it had only been a few weeks since we'd last spoken. He nodded to his canine companion. "This monster's name is Buddy, and he's as mean as he looks."

Melvin nodded his head up and down. "I can vouch for that! I wore the bite suit a few times when Seth was first training him and he nearly ripped my arm off."

I didn't argue and I didn't want to find out how mean he was. I pointed to the tree. "We're thinking the killer fired from that vantage point," I said. "No one has gone near the tree, so everything's still fresh."

Seth nodded his approval and turned to Melvin. "You gonna

cover us?"

Melvin looked at me and I gave him a "thumbs up". He grinned and followed at a safe distance behind Seth as Buddy began working side to side, his nose buried in the grass. When they reached the tree, Buddy sniffed around, but didn't alert on anything. Seth began directing him in linear sweeps across the property and Buddy finally alerted on a spot in the grass directly across from the victim's body. They then set off toward the tree line, hot on the trail.

Susan and I waited at the scene until a coroner's investigator arrived to transport Isaac Edwards' body to the morgue. While Susan got the information from the investigator, I stepped away and, although it was Saturday, made a call to the district attorney's office. The answering machine picked up telling me they were closed for the weekend. Next, I called Reginald Hoffman's cell phone. It rang to voicemail and I left yet another message for him. I was becoming increasingly frustrated with him, and I was sure he'd be able to hear it in my tone of voice. I swiped my finger across the screen to shut down my phone and watched Susan jotting information in her notebook. She had saved my life on more than one occasion in our short time working together and I was not going to let her go down for doing her job.

When Susan was done and the coroner's investigator had driven away, we pulled down the crime scene tape and headed toward the front of the street. I stopped when we reached the house with the white SUV, and stepped out. Susan walked around the Tahoe and we strode up the driveway together. "How are you and Chloe getting along?" she wanted to know.

"We're getting along great." I was tempted to ask about the day she showed up at my house, but decided against it.

"You've been with her—what?—a little over a year now?"

I nodded and knocked on the door to the house. Susan stepped to the right and I stepped to the left. Within seconds, the storm door was sucked inward as the main door opened. A man stood there in gray slacks and a light blue dress shirt. He frowned. "Can I help you?"

I explained that we were working a death case involving a jogger in the neighborhood. "Did you notice anything suspicious or out of the ordinary this morning?"

"A jogger?" The man scratched his head, ruffling his thinning white hair. "Are you talking about Isaac? I saw him running this morning. Did something happen to him? I always said that poor bastard would have a heart attack running around like he does. He's too old for that shit. "

"I can't release the identity of the victim at this moment," I explained, "but if you saw anything out of the ordinary—anything at all—it might help us answer some questions."

The man was thoughtful. "I left for the store early this morning. The neighborhood was quiet when I left. Other than Isaac and some hunter, there was no one else in the area."

I felt my ears perk up. "A hunter?"

The man nodded. "His car was parked off of Main Street, just south of Lacy Court."

"How do you know he was a hunter?" Susan asked.

"He was wearing an orange hunting cap."

"Did he have a weapon?" I asked.

"I didn't see one, but that doesn't mean he didn't have one. When I pulled out of the street, he had just stepped out of the driver's door and walked around to the trunk of his car. He was still leaning in the trunk when I drove away."

"Have you ever seen him before?" I asked.

"No. I mean, I don't think so."

I frowned. "Would you recognize him if you saw him again?"

"I didn't get a look at his face, but I did see what kind of car he was driving." The man looked up toward the ceiling of his carport, as though trying to recapture the image. "It was a faded green Thunderbird. Old—at least fifteen years or better—and the paint was chipped in places. It definitely stood out."

"You said you didn't see his face," Susan began. "Are you sure it was a man?"

"Hmm…" The man rubbed his face. "You know, come to think of it, I don't know if it was a man or woman. I guess I just assumed it was a man because he was wearing a hunting cap."

"Did you assume anything else?" Susan wanted to know.

"No, I did not," the man said curtly.

"How tall was this person?" I asked.

He shrugged. "I couldn't tell. He was leaning into the back of the trunk mostly."

"What about the build?" I pressed. "Thin? Heavy? Medium?"

"That was hard to tell, too. He was wearing some bulky clothes, like camouflage, and he probably looked bigger around than he really was." The man nodded his head. "Yeah, I remember thinking it was odd he'd be wearing all that bulky clothes in this heat."

Despite our probing questions, the man was unable to remember more than he'd already provided, so we left our cards and asked him to call if he remembered anything.

Next, we headed to Chateau General Hospital, which was twenty minutes north of town. Well, everything was north of town. To the south, there was nothing but acres and acres of marshland separating the town from the Gulf of Mexico. As for me, I was starting to buy into the hype. I never dreamed of working or living in a dead-end town like Mechant Loup, but it was growing on me faster than weeds in the summer. It was peaceful here...and slow. I'd grown accustomed to the pace of small town Louisiana and didn't think I could ever go back to the rat race of the big city. What killed me most was the idea that Michele and Abigail would've loved this place. *Why didn't we move here when they were alive?* I frowned and tried to change the subject in my mind. "Focus on your work," I thought to myself.

I managed to distract myself by trying to figure out a possible link between Betty Ledet and Isaac Edwards, and before I knew it we were at the hospital. Once I parked, I sat for a moment staring at the front entrance. I didn't relish what we had to do, and I could tell Susan felt the same way.

"I never know what to say," she said, and then was quiet for a long moment, lost in her own thoughts. I could hear her soft breathing and felt her eyes on me. When I turned, our eyes locked. "You don't have to do this, Clint. I can take care of it. After all you've been through..."

I pursed my lips, shook my head. "I appreciate you offering, but I need to do this."

We entered the hospital through automatic sliding doors. It was much cooler inside, but the smell of freshly cut grass and oak trees was replaced by a strong disinfectant that singed my nose hairs. The lady behind the help desk was elderly and dressed in a plain blouse and dark brown polyester pants. She looked too old to be working of her own free will. I figured she needed the money to supplement her social security pay or she had a grown kid living at home.

The woman's eyes grew a little wider when she saw our uniforms. She asked if she could help us. Her voice was soft and sweet—like my grandmother's before she passed away when I was young.

"We need to speak with Stella Edwards," I said.

She scanned a list of extensions, then called someone and spoke briefly. She looked back up at us and smiled, her false teeth extending farther than seemed natural. "She's in room two twenty-two."

We made our way up the elevators and to the hospital room,

where we found Isaac's wife sitting up eating lunch from a plastic tray resting in her lap. Her face and arms were pale and gaunt, and her skin was stretched tight over her collarbones. She didn't look strong enough to even lift a fork full of food. When she turned toward us, her hand paused in midflight and her eyebrows arched upward. "Are y'all here about the accident? I already gave my statement to the other deputies."

"No, ma'am," Susan said. "We're here about a different matter."

This caused Stella to place her fork down. It clattered against the plastic tray as concern lines appeared on her face. She started wringing her hands. "Is it Isaac? Is it? Please tell me he's okay."

Susan moved closer to the bed and placed a hand on Stella's arm. "Ma'am, there's been a terrible accident."

"No." Stella began shaking her head from side to side. "No, don't say it. It's not true. No, I refuse to hear it. He's fine. He'll be here after his run." Even as she tried to sound sure of herself, tears began to flow from her eyes and rain down her cheeks. "Y'all have the wrong person. It's not my Isaac."

"We're so sorry Mrs. Edwards," Susan said in a soft voice. "Your husband was murdered this morning."

Stella's gasp was throaty. What little life she had left seemed to drain from her. "Murdered?" Her head sank against the white pillow behind her and tilted away from us. "Oh, God...no! Not my Isaac!"

She wailed in silence for several long minutes. When she had somewhat regained what composure she had, Susan asked about Isaac's habits.

Stella took a deep and quavering breath. "He has his coffee with the paper every morning. We would then go for a run. Now that I'm hurt, he runs alone. After we run, we piddle around the house. Isaac does yard work or finds something to repair. He's always fixing something—whether it's needed or not." Stella chuckled through the tears. "He can't wait for my car or his truck's engine light to come on so he can figure out what's wrong with it. He has one of those little car computers and he says it gives him some codes and he gets to figure out what they mean. He loves a challenge. Always has. After lunch, we usually watch a little television and then he takes a nap while I knit. That's about all he does." Stella stopped and was thoughtful, as though going over his routine in her head. She lifted a finger. "Oh, there is one other thing. Once a month he goes to M & P Grill for a shrimp po' boy or soft shell crabs, which are his favorite meals. I'm allergic to shell fish—my throat swells up if I even smell it—so a few months ago I suggested he start going out for seafood."

She paused and wiped tears from her face. "I hate that I can't cook his favorite—"

"M & P Grill?" I fished an enlarged copy of Betty Ledet's driver's license photo from my folder and held it so Stella could view it. "Do you recognize this woman? She works at M & P Grill. Does Isaac know her?"

Stella shook her head. "I've never been in the place. I told you already—if I smell seafood it makes my throat swell, and most of what they cook is seafood. I can't even kiss Isaac until he brushes his teeth and washes his face after he eats the stuff."

"Ma'am," I insisted, "are you sure you don't know Betty Ledet? Maybe Isaac mentioned her in conversation?"

"Why are you asking me about this lady?" Stella asked. "I don't care about her! I just want to know who killed my husband."

"We were hoping you could help us with that." Susan put a hand on her shoulder. "I know this is difficult and I can't imagine what you're going through right now, but I need you to be strong for just a moment longer." Susan took the picture from my hand and leaned closer to Stella. "This woman was killed in the same manner as your husband, so there must be a connection between them. Are you sure you don't know her?"

"I already told you no. I've never seen her before and I've never been to that restaurant." Stella then turned her face back toward the wall.

Susan chewed on her lower lip. "What about enemies? Did Isaac have any enemies—anyone who would want him dead?"

Stella was silent for a while longer. Other than the low hum and occasional beeping from the machines in the room, there were no sounds. I began to think Stella had fallen asleep when she spoke softly. "Gene Rudolph."

I barely understood what she said. "What was that, ma'am?" I asked.

"Gene Rudolph...that's who killed Isaac."

Susan glanced over her shoulder at me. I shrugged and she turned back toward Stella. "Who's Gene Rudolph?"

Without looking at us, she pointed to her bandaged legs. "He's the man who did this to me. Isaac saw his face—can identify him. That's why he killed my husband."

CHAPTER 19

Susan and I were walking out the hospital when my phone rang. It was Chloe. "Where are you, Clint?"

"Leaving the hospital," I said. "I'm heading to the sheriff's office to get a lead on a suspect."

"The one who's hunting people with a bow?"

I paused by the open driver's door to my Tahoe. "Where'd you hear that?"

"It's my job, remember?" There was hurt in her voice. "Why didn't you tell me? Why'd I have to hear about it off the street?"

I sighed. "We agreed to keep our jobs separate from our personal lives—you know that. I was just honoring that agreement."

"So, if I get a tip on this murder case you're working, should I keep that to myself in honor of our agreement?"

I sensed a trap, so I merely said, "You know the rules of your job better than I do."

"You couldn't even tell me there had been a murder? I'm dating the chief of police and I didn't even know someone had been killed yesterday. And then someone else gets killed today and there might be a connection to the first murder. The whole town's talking about it, but I still know nothing. Do you know how bad that makes me look to my editor?"

"How'd you find out?" I asked.

"So, it is true, isn't it?"

I didn't like the way this was going and I certainly didn't want to fight with Chloe. "Yes, it is true, but we didn't want to put anything out to the public until we had a handle on what was going on." Chloe was quiet on the other end of the phone, so I asked, "Can you keep a lid on it until I'm ready to make a press release?"

Chloe gave an audible exhale. "Yes, but only because I love you." There was another short pause, and then she asked, "Does this mean you'll be working late tonight?"

I moved the phone away from my head to check the time. It was after one o'clock. I had been wondering why my stomach ached. "Yeah," I said. "I'll probably be late tonight."

"Maybe we can hang out tomorrow night, then?"

"I'd love to." I slipped in my Tahoe and headed back to M & P Grill.

As I drove, Susan got on her phone. "Lindsey, pull up a picture of Isaac Edwards and text it to me as soon as you can. Right. Yeah, a driver's license will do." Within a few minutes of hanging up, Susan's phone beeped and she turned it so I could see. "Let's show this to Malory when we stop to get my car. If Isaac's the man who was talking to Betty when Peter barged in the restaurant, then he's as good a suspect as Gene Rudolph."

"Better, even. So far, there's no obvious connection between Betty Ledet and this Rudolph fellow. If we can't find a reason for Rudolph to kill Betty, Peter's our prime guy."

Susan and I said little until we arrived at the restaurant. We walked inside and took our usual table at the corner. There were only a handful of people in the dining area. Most of them had finished eating and were engaged in idle chatter, and they all looked up when we entered. Several waved. When a young waitress I'd never seen came by to take our order, we told her what we wanted and then I asked for Malory. The waitress—a skinny kid who looked young enough to be in middle school—cast a nervous glance over her shoulder and then back at me. I smiled. "We need her help to solve a case."

The teen, whose unnaturally red hair almost matched her lipstick, sighed. "God, I thought I messed something up already. It's my first day and I've been screwing up all morning. It's just so much to remember, you know?"

I nodded, remembering my first day as Mechant Loup's chief of police. "It could be worse," I said. "Much worse."

The girl disappeared through a swinging door and, moments later, Malory appeared. She hurried to our table, wiping her hands on a blue towel as she walked. "Did y'all find out who killed Betty?"

Susan showed her the picture of Isaac Edwards.

Malory's mouth dropped open. "Oh, my God, that's him! That's the man who Betty waits on. Do you think he killed Betty?"

"No." Susan tucked the picture away. "He was murdered this morning in front of his house—the same way Betty was killed."

Malory wrung the towel in her hands.

"You mentioned earlier that he came in here a few more times," I said. "Is it possible Peter saw him come into the restaurant again?"

"I…um…I guess it's possible." Malory's face was pale. "You think Peter did this?"

"We're not sure at this point." I thanked her and explained we couldn't say much more than we already had. When she'd walked off, Susan and I discussed the case while waiting for our food. We agreed to go after Peter first and save Gene Rudolph for later.

"Can you call Detective Bledsoe and see if she can put a car on him until we finish with Peter?"

Susan nodded and made the call. I only heard Susan's half of the conversation, but I heard enough to know a tail wouldn't be necessary. Gene Rudolph was still in jail.

"He can't make bail," Susan explained. "He's been locked up since the crash."

The waitress brought our food and my thoughts turned to Peter Ledet as I ate. Jealousy was a strong motivator for murder, but what would make him jealous of a man old enough to be his wife's grandfather? Some girls dug older men, but this seemed a bit extreme. It might make more sense if Isaac Edwards was single and a millionaire, but Betty had nothing to gain by cheating with him. Could there be another motive? Perhaps Peter thought Betty shared their secret with Isaac and killed both of them to keep them quiet. She did tell Malory, so it wasn't impossible that she told someone else. *And what's up with the arrow?* I thought. *Why didn't he just shoot them with a gun like a normal person?*

When we were done eating, we walked out and a gust of warm air greeted us. I enjoyed it while I could; knowing winter was right around the corner. We went to our separate vehicles and Susan followed me to the police department, where she parked her car in the sally port and jumped in with me again. Melvin drove up as I was about to pull out, and I stopped beside his car to see what he'd found at the scene.

He wiped his shaved crown while waiting for his driver's window to slide down. There were dark blotches of sweat on the front of his tan uniform shirt and around his armpits. "Hey, Chief, where y'all heading?"

I told him, and then asked about the track.

"The dog tracked south to the woodline and then headed east all the way to Main. It ended on the shoulder of the road."

"Yep," I said. "The killer drove away in an older model Thunderbird—faded green. Get with Lindsey and run a search to find every vehicle ever registered to Peter and Betty Ledet."

Melvin nodded and parked his car while Susan and I drove off to find Peter.

CHAPTER 20

4:15 p.m.
Mechant Loup Police Department's Interrogation Room

The scabs on Peter's forehead had been bandaged. Other than that, he didn't look much different from when we pulled him out of the woods. He sat slouched in a chair on one side of the table and I sat beside him, leaning forward with my elbows on my knees. Susan sat on the opposite side of the table, her eyes squinting as she paid close attention to every word that was spoken between us.

"How are you, Peter?" I asked.

He shrugged and passed a hand across his salt and pepper beard. "How do you think I'm doing? My wife was just killed." As he spoke, an invisible cloud of rancid air floated from his mouth and engulfed me. Trying not to gag, I leaned back subtly and took small breaths through my nose until I reached cleaner air.

"Sir, I know this is hard, but I need you to go over every detail of that night again. You know, just in case we missed something the first time." I paused. "As you might have heard, there's been another murder and we think it might be linked to Betty's case."

The wrinkles on Peter's forehead deepened. "Linked to Betty? How?"

"We're not sure at this time, but we think we're getting closer." I nodded. "Can you go over the details of that night again?"

Peter let out a grunt, but recounted the story exactly as he'd told it the first time. When he was done talking, I leaned forward again. "I understand this isn't the first time you've had to deal with tragedy."

Peter shook his head. "My son died when he was little."

"I'm really sorry about that," I said. "What happened?"

Peter sank deeper into the chair and put his head in his hands. "I don't want to talk about it."

"It might be connected somehow. I need you to tell us."

Without looking up, he said, "Betty ran him over one day. She was late for work and didn't look when she backed out the driveway. She didn't see him, you know? It happened really fast. One minute he was in the house, the next he was under the car. It was an accident. I really believe she probably looked, but he was just so small she couldn't see him." He paused and I thought I detected some tears dripping to the floor. When he spoke again, his voice was so low I barely made out his words. "She really beat herself up over that. It changed everything. Ruined our lives."

"That's a nice story and all," I said, "but I want you to try it again. This time, tell the true version."

Peter's face twisted in feigned confusion. "What are you talking about? I am telling the truth."

"Come on, Peter, you didn't think Betty would keep your secret forever, did you?"

Peter fixed me with dull eyes, trying to decide if I was bluffing. I kept quiet for at least a minute, creating an awkward silence between us. I was hoping to elicit a comment from him—anything I could use against him—but it didn't work. He was content to stare at me. I decided to play loose with the definition of a legal term in order to get him talking. "Do you know what a dying declaration is?"

Peter's scowl indicated he wasn't familiar with the term, so I figured my tactic might work.

"It's when someone makes a statement—a declaration—and then dies shortly afterward. Normally, a statement by a deceased witness can't be used against a perpetrator because of the Hearsay Rule, but the dying declaration is an exception." I paused to let him process the information. I'd conveniently left out a few details, such as Betty had to know she was dying when she made the statement and the information had to relate to her cause of death. When he didn't respond, I continued. "So, Betty goes around telling this fascinating story that could get you a lot of jail time. She says she didn't kill Landon." I shook my head, as I studied Peter's squinting eyes. "No, she says it wasn't her who ran over your son—she says it was *you*." I pushed my finger in Peter's face and he recoiled against the back of his chair. His eyes were wild as he stared around the room, searching for a place to hide.

It was time to move in for the kill with another bit of deception—

this one a little more sensitive. "Betty declares you were pissed off at her and you ran over Landon intentionally just to cause her pain and—"

"That's bullshit!" Peter lunged from his chair. "It was an accident! I would never hurt Landon on purpose!"

I had leaned back and folded my arms across my chest, ready to drive the heel of my boot into Peter's crotch if he decided to make a move. Instead, realization of what he'd said settled like lead in the pit of his stomach. He sank to his knees on the floor and cried. "It was an accident! I didn't mean to do it."

"Then why'd you make her take the fall for you?" I asked.

Peter was bawling now, saliva and mucus leaking down his face and spraying from his mouth as he talked. He shook his head from side to side, his wild and thinning hair flailing about. "I didn't ask her to cover for me—she did it on her own. She decided to do it."

"Why?"

"I was drunk, don't you see? I would've gone to jail and she knew it." Peter leaned forward and pounded his head on the floor. I didn't try to stop him. "She loved me so much," he said. "That's why she covered for me. Maybe if she would've just let me go to jail she'd be alive today."

"No, Peter. She'd still be alive if you wouldn't have shot her in the chest with an arrow. You knew she couldn't keep your secret anymore, so you killed her to shut her up. Problem is, she'd already told Isaac Edwards about Landon, so you had to go out and kill him, too."

"I don't know what you're talking about." Peter's chin was quivering. "I...I didn't kill Betty. I would never. I love her too much to ever kill her."

"You wouldn't kill her, but you'd let her risk going to jail to cover your sorry ass and you'd beat her ass." I shook my head. "That's not love, buddy."

He wiped his nose and face with his dirty hands. "Look, I realize now that I made some mistakes—some bad ones—but I didn't kill my wife, and I don't even know that man you're talking about."

"Oh, you know him." I fished the picture of Isaac from the file and showed it to Peter. "Recognize him now?"

"That's the old guy from the restaurant." Peter's eyebrows furrowed and he cleared his throat. "Is he dead, too?"

"Yeah, he's dead. Killed in the same manner as Betty. Didn't you have a beef with him?"

"I saw them talking one day at the restaurant and got jealous." He sighed. "It was stupid, I know, but I was high and was out of my mind. I didn't realize what I was doing."

"Maybe you were high and out of your mind when you killed Betty and Isaac."

"Chief, I swear I didn't kill anyone."

I studied Peter, trying to see past his rough exterior and through to his soul. I hated to admit it to myself, but I believed him. I glanced over at Susan. She nodded to let me know she thought he was being truthful, too. Peter seemed to be the only common denominator between our two victims, so if he didn't kill Betty and Isaac, then who did?

I told Peter to get back in his chair, and Susan and I stepped out into the hallway. "I believe him," I said.

"I do, too." Susan chewed on her lower lip. "Two murders in two days and no suspects yet—not good, Clint."

I leaned against the wall. When I didn't say anything, she asked, "What about his son's case? Do we reopen it?"

As tempting as it was to arrest Peter for vehicular homicide based upon his confession, we needed evidence of impairment to get a conviction. I thought about calling Isabel, but she probably wouldn't answer anyway. "Let's send him home for now," I said. "We'll forward the report to the district attorney's office and see what they think."

Susan grunted. "They'll never call us back."

As we talked, I heard the phone ring and Lindsey answered it in a pleasant voice. After a few seconds, she turned toward us and mouthed the words, "Are you here?"

I looked down at my boots, and then back up at her. "I'm pretty sure I am."

"Yes, ma'am, he'll be with you in a minute." She pressed the hold button and pushed the receiver in my direction. "It's someone from one of the national news stations. She wants to get a statement about your possible serial killer case."

CHAPTER 21

Sunday, October 11

I turned my gaze from Achilles, who was sniffing the many cardboard boxes littered around my living room, to the clock on the wall. It was an hour before midnight and no one had been killed yet today.

"Are you thinking what I think you are?" Chloe asked. She was curled up beside me on the sofa, her sun dress pushed up over her knees, and her bare feet tucked under the side cushion. The local news had just ended on television and she'd turned her attention to me.

I looked down into her soft eyes. "And what's that?"

"You're wondering if there's going to be a murder before midnight."

"Damn. We've only been living together for four hours and you can already read my mind."

She giggled and I smiled. I loved how her eyes squinted when she laughed and how her face seemed to light up. Seeing her like that sent a wave of guilt flooding through me. Her smile faded and I knew she knew something was wrong. She sat up, cocked her head sideways. "What is it, Clint?"

I pushed myself upright and sat there staring at the television. I wanted to tell her, but I didn't know if I should.

"Clint—what's wrong? Is there something going on?"

I waved her off. "It's nothing, really."

"Is it her?"

I jerked my head around. "Her? Who are you talking about?"

Chloe swallowed hard. "Susan. I saw the way she looked at me when I stopped by the office yesterday. Does she know I'm moving in? She's mad about that, isn't she?"

"God, no. Nothing like that."

"I don't know. She likes you—I'm sure of it."

I squirmed in my seat. "I think you're wrong."

"I'm a woman, Clint. I know things."

I realized if I didn't tell her what was going on, she'd torture herself trying to figure it out, and I certainly didn't want her thinking something that wasn't so. I turned and looked her in the eyes. "I have a problem, Chloe. I've been hiding something from you."

She was quiet for a moment, and then asked, "Will it affect us?"

"I don't know."

The corners of her mouth turned down and I thought I saw her chin quiver. "Please tell me it has nothing to do with Susan and you."

I shook my head. "I'm a Wolf, Chloe—I mate for life. I love only you."

"Then what is it?"

I took a deep breath and slowly exhaled. *Just say it.* "Okay, Chloe, here goes...I'm dependant on alcohol. I need it to sleep."

Her brows furrowed. "I thought you were better? I mean, I've slept here many times and you didn't need a drink to fall asleep."

I admitted what I'd been doing and even offered to show her the empty bottles under my house.

"But...but why would you hide that from me?"

"That's not something you go around telling people, you know?"

"I'm not *people*. I'm your girlfriend." Chloe waved her right hand at the boxes on the floor. Most were already empty. We'd begun merging her things with mine earlier in the day, packaging duplicate items to give to charity. "I'm moving in with you. That takes commitment—trust. I have to be able to trust you, Clint."

"You can trust me."

"I can?" Chloe stood and began pacing back and forth in front of me, wrapping herself in her own arms. "You've been keeping a secret from me. Sneaking out of bed in the middle of the night to drink a bottle of vodka and then hiding the evidence. How can I trust you now?"

"Look, I'd never lie to you and I'd never cheat on you. Now that I know I love—that I can admit I love you—I'm totally committed to you. Had you asked, I would've told you the truth. I never would've lied about—"

"But you did lie. You lied by omission." Chloe stopped in front of me and tapped her foot on the floor. "So, if you were sleeping with Susan and I never asked about it, that would be okay, right? You wouldn't be lying to me, because I never asked about it. Is that your logic?"

I leaned back on the sofa and sighed. "I'm not trying to justify it. I screwed up bad. I know I did. I'm sorry."

"Oh, my God, this is horrible!" Chloe put her hands to her forehead and pushed back her hair, pacing circles in front of me. "How could I've been so blind? First it was Beaver lying to me, and now you. I'm such a terrible judge of character!"

"Don't compare me to that piece of shit. He's a criminal."

"And a liar like you," Chloe retorted.

"I told you the truth. I came clean."

"After hiding it for—what?—a year?" Chloe shook her head and began aggressively gathering up some of her things in the living room and throwing them into the empty boxes. Sensing something was wrong, Achilles slinked to the kitchen and cowered next to his food bowl, his ears perked up and watching Chloe move around the room.

"What are you doing?" I asked.

"I can't do this. I don't even know who you are. I can't be with someone who's living a lie. Been there, done that, and it didn't work out so well for me the first time."

"I'm not that guy, Chloe." I stood and took a step toward her. "I love you. I want you to stay."

"You love me?" Chloe grunted and shook her head. "I don't believe you anymore."

I shoved my hands in my pockets, biting down hard as I watched her slam the lids shut on the box she'd filled up. "How can you say that?" I finally asked. "You know I love you."

"I had my doubts when you hesitated for so long after I shared my feelings with you, but now—after finding out you've been lying for all this time—I know it's not true."

"I only hesitated because I wanted to be sure of my feelings. I needed to know I was ready to move on. Otherwise, it wouldn't have been fair to you."

"Well, I'm sure I love you." Chloe paused over one of the boxes and turned to look at me. Her blonde hair fell across her face and her eyes sparkled. I didn't know if it was from hurt or anger. "I don't need to think about it and I don't need to wonder if I'm ready to have a future with you."

"Jesus, Chloe, I didn't get a divorce—my wife died. There's a big difference. By the time a couple gets divorced there's usually so much shit between them that they both know it's over. Michelle died while I was very much in love with her. I wasn't ready for her to go. It took me a long time to realize it's okay to move on. Can't you respect that?"

She hoisted the box she'd been working on and rested it on her jutting hip. Blowing her hair out of her face, she said, "Yes, I can respect that. What I can't respect is you lying about your alcohol addiction." Holding the box against her with one arm, she snatched her purse off the end table, kicked her feet into her sandals, and headed for the door. "I'll be back later for the rest of my stuff," she called over her shoulder.

CHAPTER 22

Monday, October 12
Mechant Loup Police Department

A white news van was blocking the entrance to the sally port when I arrived at the office Monday morning. I grunted, and the reaction made the pounding in my head worse. I started to step out of my Tahoe to tell the driver to move, but he waved his apologies and pulled forward, nearly bumping the van in front of him. The garage door opened and Susan stood there waiting for me. A sea of reporters moved toward her, but she ordered them back. I drove through them and parked in my spot, catching a glimpse of Chloe in my rearview mirror. She was amongst the other reporters—like when I first met her—but she was staring at the ground. I frowned. She hadn't taken any of my calls and hadn't returned any of my messages. Were we over for good? Was this the end of our relationship? I cursed myself for being such a fool, and shoved the gearshift in park.

"They've been here all night," Susan said. She lowered the automatic door on the sally port and I stood next to her watching the door slowly block our view of the reporters. My eyes were fixated on Chloe until I couldn't see her anymore, but she never looked in my direction. "William threatened to arrest one of them for following him into the sally port at about midnight," Susan explained, "and that kind of put them in check a little."

I was about to respond when my phone rang. My heart raced as I jerked it from my pocket. Could it be Chloe? A quick glance at the screen showed a number I recognized, but couldn't place. When I answered I heard First Assistant DA Isabel Compton's voice on the other end.

"Hey, Chief, the DA wanted me to call and see what's the status of your murder investigation. We've been getting calls all morning from the national news media and we don't know what to tell—"

"Tell him to go to hell," I said.

There was a startled pause on the other end, and then Isabel said, "I don't think it would look good if I told the national media to go to hell."

"Not the media...the DA." I tried to remain calm, but I was seething on the inside. "I've been calling all weekend to try and find out what's going on with this damn hearing, but no one will return my calls. Until you're ready to talk about the hearing, I've got nothing to say about this ongoing investigation." I slid my thumb across the screen and ended the call. I looked up and saw Susan staring at me with her mouth open.

"What have you done?" she asked. "You shouldn't piss off the people who are investigating us. I know you're frustrated—so am I—but Jesus Christ, Clint, don't give them a reason to hang my ass out to dry."

My phone rang again and I glanced down. It was Reginald's cell. I sighed, answered the call.

"Chief, I need you to understand I'm risking my job by talking to you," said Isabel. "I'm putting my ass and Reginald's ass on the line here—do we understand each other?"

"What is it?" I asked. "What's going on?"

"The DA's coming after Susan. I don't know why, but something happened in the past to cause some bad blood between them. Whatever it is, it's bad enough to make him want to bring the full power of his office down on top of her." Isabel paused to let the information sink in, and then continued. "If he has his way, Susan's going to be indicted for murder, later convicted, and then spend the rest of her life in prison. She'll have to die to get out, is what he said."

My stomach churned. I felt bile rise up and burn my throat. I'd brought down some big names in the parish and knew I'd pissed off some people in high places, so I'd always known that case would not go quietly into the night and I figured there'd be hell to pay at some point. But what did Susan have to do with all of this? As far as small town politics go, it didn't get much higher than the district attorney, and what could she have done to piss him off to this point?

I felt dizzy and put a hand against the garage door to steady myself. "What can I do?" I asked.

Isabel sighed. "Let's hope the grand jury doesn't buy what he's selling. Reginald did a good job in his testimony. I can't discuss it, but I can say it was favorable to your side. He's been in law enforcement a long time and he knows how these things work. Even better, he knows how to explain it so a jury can understand."

"What about William Tucker? He wasn't at my house, so why'd Hedd subpoena him for the hearing?"

"Again, I can't discuss his testimony, but I can say Bill had a subpoena issued for Tucker immediately after Reginald finished testifying. I don't know what prompted him to do it or how he knew what Tucker would say, but he thinks Tucker's testimony supports his case that Susan has a history of using excessive force."

"Damn it!" I blurted, which caused real concern to show on Susan's face. I averted my eyes, because I couldn't bear to face her.

"Look, Clint," Isabel said, "for what it's worth, I don't believe Susan did anything wrong. I'm in your corner and I'm doing everything I can on my end to persuade Bill to stop this insanity."

I mumbled my thanks and an apology for earlier. "When will we know for sure?"

"The grand jury's reconvening in two weeks to hear more testimony and they should make a decision soon afterward."

I was scared to ask the next question, but did anyway. "If she *is* indicted, what are the chances she gets convicted?"

I heard Susan gasp and saw her eyes widen in my peripheral view.

"I don't know, Clint," Isabel said. "I really don't know."

I asked Isabel to hold on while I explained what was going on to Susan. She took it all in, scowled. "I don't know what he's talking about," she said. "I've never said ten words to the man. I mean, I've seen him, but we've never been introduced."

"Did you hear that?" I asked Isabel.

"Yeah, I did." She was quiet, then said, "Ask her if she ever arrested someone who threatened to go to the DA, or maybe got into a fight with someone with ties to him."

I asked the question and Susan shook her head.

"That stuff from last year was it," Susan said. "I didn't testify, but Randall said the DA himself presented that one, too, and agreed that I hadn't done anything wrong. Whatever it is, it had to have happened during the year, because he wasn't out to get me back then."

I mulled it over, searching the deepest recesses of my brain, trying to remember if anyone had complained about Susan since I'd been there. Sure, there had been complaints—there always are in this line of work—but nothing major. Nothing to warrant a witch hunt that could result in her spending the rest of her natural life in prison. At a loss and needing to get to work, I turned my attention back to Isabel and gave her the rundown on the case. When I was done, she thanked me and left me her cell number. "Don't call me or Reginald at the office," she said. "The phone lines here are recorded and Bill will throw us out on our asses if he knows we're talking to you about the hearing."

When I disconnected the call, I turned to Susan. "You okay?"

"I'm fine." She grinned and the dimple on her upper left cheek appeared. "Even if I do go to prison, it was worth it to kill that slimy bastard."

"You're not going to prison," I said. "I'll make damn sure of that." I didn't know what I would—or could—do, but I meant what I said.

When Susan and I walked inside the police department, we found Melvin and William in the administrative section of the building. They were sitting around Lindsey's desk talking and joking. They looked up when we entered and their expression changed to a more serious tone. I waved them off. "Carry on."

Melvin swallowed. "Sorry, Chief, we were just visiting with Lindsey."

Although I didn't feel like doing it, I smiled to let him know all was well. "You should know by now that I don't mind y'all taking some down time."

Melvin relaxed, grabbed a chair and slid it in my direction. "Care to join us?"

I dropped into the chair and it was then that I realized how tired my legs and back were. William slid a chair in Susan's direction, eyeing her cautiously as he did so. Susan hesitated, fixing him with a cold stare. Finally, she laughed and took the chair.

William sighed. "Damn, Sue, you scared the shit out of me."

We all laughed and made small talk for a few minutes. Finally, Melvin asked, "What're we supposed to do with the case now, Chief?"

I was thoughtful, glancing from one to the other. All of their eyes were suddenly on me—waiting for something…anything. I was their leader and they were looking to me for guidance. Truth was, I didn't know what to do next, and I was having a hard time focusing on the investigation. The images of Chloe packing her stuff and walking out of my life were still very clear in my mind's eye and the idea of

Susan going to jail was even more disturbing. With time, I knew I could get over losing Chloe—those kinds of things happened all the time—but I couldn't let Susan go to jail for saving my life.

"Is everything okay?" Susan asked.

I nodded, rubbed my face. It was too early to have a drink, but I felt like I needed one. I forced my attention to the case and took a breath. "Well gang, we need a reason to kill Betty and Isaac."

William's face twisted in confusion. "But they're already dead."

"Find the motive, find the killer," Susan said. "How many times has he told us that?"

"And we need to find a connection between the two victims. We know they were friends, but we need to find out how they first met. I'm betting that'll shed some light on why they were killed."

"But how are we supposed to do that?" Susan asked. "Peter doesn't know anything about Isaac, and Stella doesn't know anything about Betty. If their spouses don't even know who their friends are, who else would know?"

"That's a good question." I looked over at Melvin. "Did you bring the evidence to the crime lab?"

He nodded. "I dropped it off first thing this morning. They said they'll process it for prints and DNA and get back to us by the end of the week."

"With luck, they'll get a hit on DNA or prints." I turned to William. "Any sign of the green Thunderbird? Betty's murder happened at night, so he might be driving around after dark, as well as during the day."

William shook his head. "Nothing at all. I've been keeping an eye out and asking around, but it seems to be a ghost of a car. I even asked the clerk at the gas station and stopped at M & P Grill to talk to the customers and waitresses, but no one remembers ever seeing a green Thunderbird in town."

I nodded and glanced at the clock. It was almost nine. I told William he could turn in for the day, considering he had to be back at the office for six that evening. He stood and stretched, his gun belt creaking as he moved. "Yeah, I guess I need to get some sleep. I've got a murderer to catch tonight." Waving goodbye and promising to be back early for his next shift, he disappeared through the door that led into the sally port.

I watched him leave, wondering what in the hell he had said to bolster Hedd's case. Susan's eyes were on him, too, and I knew she was thinking the same thing.

The phone rang for the fifth time since I'd been sitting there, and

Lindsey looked at the display screen. "More calls from the media. What do I tell them?"

"Tell them I don't comment on active investigations." I turned my attention back to the case, mulled over what we knew so far. A thought suddenly occurred to me. "Where's the closest place we can buy arrows? Do we have any in the parish?"

Melvin thoughtfully rubbed his bare dome. "There's a hardware store in northern Chateau that sells archery equipment," he finally said. "I can check it out if you like."

"Do that," I agreed. "Bring a picture of the arrows we removed from the bodies. If they sell the same kind, find out when they sold some last and who purchased them."

As Melvin gathered up his things, the door burst open behind us and William stuck his head inside. "The news vans are gone," he said in a hurried voice. "They're nowhere to be seen."

CHAPTER 23

"Gone? What do you mean?" I asked, rising from my chair.

William shrugged. "When I opened the garage door I expected to have to tell everyone to get back, but they were all gone. No reporters, no vans, no nothing."

Susan and I followed William through the processing area, the sally port, and out onto the sidewalk, where the sun was shining bright. I looked up and down Main Street. Other than a warm breeze rustling the leaves on the trees that lined the street, there was no movement. What had once been a circus of reporters was now a ghost town. "What the hell? Where'd everyone go?" I thought about calling Chloe, but every time she refused my call I cringed a little inside.

"This is some Walking Dead-type shit," William said.

Melvin joined us on the sidewalk. He was carrying a manila folder and his car keys. "This is weird. Why would they just pack up and leave? You think they finally realized you won't give a statement?"

A sinking feeling started to settle in the pit of my stomach. Susan studied my expression, asked, "Are you thinking what I'm thinking?"

I nodded and hurried into the office. "Lindsey, switch to the sheriff's office channel to see if anything's going on."

She did and we listened for a few minutes, but radio traffic was low. The phone rang and Lindsey picked it up without looking. "Mechant Loup Police Department," she began. "How may I help you?"

My fears were confirmed when I heard her voice grow excited. "Sure, he's right here." She turned and pushed the phone in my direction. "It's Sheriff Buck Turner. He needs to talk to you right away—it's an emergency."

Buck Turner was the recently-elected sheriff of Chateau Parish. After working cows his entire life, and with no political experience to his credit, he'd decided to run for the top law enforcement job in the parish. There had been a lot of mudslinging and accusations between him and his opponent during the campaign, but Buck had done what no one else had been able to do in sixteen years—unseat the most popular sheriff in Louisiana.

Buck had been in office for three months and I'd only met him on one occasion, but he seemed nice enough. During our one conversation, he expressed an interest in working closely with me and the other police chiefs who served the incorporated towns in the parish, and he promised to offer whatever assistance we needed. I wasn't positive why he was calling, but I was betting it was to ask for my assistance.

Buck didn't waste time with pleasantries. Instead, he said, "Chief, we've got a major problem...there's been another arrow attack and I'm sure it's related to your case."

Although he couldn't see me, I nodded. "I was afraid of that. The news reporters disappeared from around here like we had Ebola, so I figured something must've happened somewhere outside of town."

"Yeah, the attack took place at The Keeper's Cemetery in the central part of the parish, about fifteen miles from the town limits."

"You got anybody on the scene?"

"Yeah," Buck said. "I'm here, myself, along with my best detective and five of my patrol deputies. I have to say, Clint, it ain't good. If you don't mind, I'd like you to take the lead on the case since two of the attacks happened in your jurisdiction and you know more about it than any of us." Buck paused, then said, "My deputies will be assisting you with whatever you need."

"Okay, thanks. Susan and I will be right there. What's the address?"

He gave me the address, and then said in a slow voice, "This attack...it's not like the others."

"What do you mean?"

"Telling you wouldn't do it justice. I...I think you need to see it to believe it. We're definitely dealing with a crazy son of a bitch."

Susan and I jumped in my Tahoe and hurried to the cemetery. When we arrived, we saw a crowded mess of news reporters standing by the road, their cameras trained toward the tombs. Three deputies clad in dark blue polyester uniforms stood in front of them with arms crossed, keeping them at bay. I parked the Tahoe and Susan led the way through the reporters. When they noticed who we were, the reporters started bombarding us with questions. I recognized Chloe's voice and my heart stopped in its place. I turned and scanned the crowd as I walked, spotted her short frame off to the side.

"Chief," Chloe hollered, "is this case connected to the murders in Mechant Loup?"

Our eyes met, but hers seemed distant. I frowned and turned away. When Susan and I reached the crime scene tape, we nodded to the deputies and ducked under it. I immediately spotted Sheriff Buck Turner a hundred yards away standing in front of a mausoleum. Of course, he was hard to miss. His worn leather boots and large Stetson made his six-foot-three, two-hundred-forty-pound frame seem larger than it was. Combined with the single-action 1875 Outlaw Colt .45 revolver that hung low in a leather holster on his hip, it looked like he'd just stepped out of a Louis L'Amour novel. He was flanked by two of his patrol deputies and they were talking to a detective I'd never seen before.

Susan and I walked up and we shook hands with the sheriff and his deputies. "Thanks for coming out, Clint," Turner said, rubbing a thick hand over his weathered face. "I know I ain't been at this job long, but this has got to be the weirdest thing I've seen in my entire life."

I scanned the face of the undisturbed mausoleum, furrowed my brow. When he saw the puzzled look on my face, Turner waved for us to follow him. "It's back here," he said, "on the northern side."

Susan and I followed him along the clean sidewalk and we both gasped when we rounded the corner.

"You don't see that every day," Susan said, nodding for emphasis.

I had to blink several times to be sure my eyes weren't playing tricks on me. The granite crypt front of one of the coffin slots had been destroyed and the wooden coffin had been dragged from its resting place and left leaning against the mausoleum at an approximate forty-five degree angle. The door of the coffin had been pried open, but I couldn't see inside because the back of the smashed door was propped up on my side, obstructing my view. "Is there a body inside?" I asked.

Turner only stepped back to get out of my way. I slowly walked around him to the foot of the coffin and caught sight of a pair of legs, confirming my suspicions. More of the body came into view as I moved to a better vantage point and I nearly choked on my tongue when I saw what all the fuss was really about...a red arrow was buried deep in the corpse's chest.

CHAPTER 24

"What is it?" Susan asked. My chin must've been hanging on my chest, because she rushed forward to stand beside me. She drew to an abrupt halt when she saw the body. "Oh, shit! What the hell is that about?"

Sheriff Turner removed his hat and wiped sweat from the white hair plastered to his scalp. "I told you it was bad," he said, pushing his hat back in place and adjusting it until it was perfect. "I'll go keep the media busy while y'all figure out what happened here."

I nodded, still shocked by the scene. "Who shoots a body that's already dead?" I hadn't posed the question to anyone in particular, but Susan answered.

"Someone who's really pissed off. Unless these are random attacks, our suspect is mad as hell at this guy, Betty Ledet, and Isaac Edwards." She leaned close to inspect the arrow. "What could three people do to piss off one person this much?"

I turned to Sheriff Turner's detective, who had introduced himself as Doug Cagle, and asked, "Any idea who this poor soul is?"

Cagle shook his head. "Once we realized what we had, the sheriff said to turn everything over to you, so we didn't touch anything."

I stepped back and studied the surrounding area. The expansive cemetery was nestled up against a patch of woodlands and was located along a lonely stretch of highway. "Any neighborhoods around here?" I asked.

Cagle pointed to the north. "There's one about a mile that way, but that's the closest. I'll take them"—he shot his thumb at the two deputies—"with me and we'll canvas the area for you. There're also a few houses along the highway and we'll check them out, too."

I nodded my thanks and Susan and I got to work processing the scene. After we'd documented the scene with photographs and measurements, I studied the broken pieces of granite crypt front that were scattered on the concrete sidewalk, some of which were under the suspended coffin. "We need to figure out this guy's name."

Susan dropped to her knees with me and we carefully moved two large pieces and a dozen smaller ones into place like a giant puzzle, and a name emerged. It was Frank Rushing and he was eighty-seven years old when he died four years ago.

Frank *Rushing!*

"Hey," Susan began, "isn't that—"

"It is!" I snatched my phone from my pocket and dialed Chloe's number. I walked around the side of the mausoleum and looked toward the road, where the reporters were still milling around. I couldn't see Chloe, but she answered the call on the fourth ring. "Hey, we need to talk—it's important."

Chloe sighed. "Clint, we're both at work, so it's not a good time to discuss what happened last night. Maybe later, when we've both had time to process everything, but—"

"Look, if you don't want to be with me, that's fine," I said. "Life goes on. But this is about work—about this case. I'm going to call one of the deputies and have them escort you over here so we can talk. Make yourself easy to find." I hung up and called over my police radio, asking one of the deputies near the media staging area to find Chloe Rushing and escort her to my location. One of them responded and I saw movement near the highway.

"Keep her away from the coffin," Susan said. "If this guy is related to her, she doesn't need to see him like this."

I agreed and walked across the cemetery grounds to meet Chloe and the deputy halfway. I thanked the deputy and he returned to his post. Chloe had a puzzled expression on her face. "What is it? Why'd you have me brought here?"

"Does the name Frank Rushing mean anything to you?"

Chloe's brow furrowed, as she looked past me toward the mausoleum. "He's my grandfather. Did someone desecrate his grave?"

I pursed my lips. "It's worse than that."

She started to step around me, but I took her arm gently in my hand. "I can't let you go up to the mausoleum, but I can tell you it's bad."

"Bad? How bad?"

I hesitated.

"Tell me, Clint. I need to know what's going on."

"Someone removed him from his coffin and put an arrow through his chest."

Chloe threw a hand over her mouth and collapsed to her knees, tears welling up in her eyes. "Oh, God, no!"

I dropped to my knees beside her and held her, allowing her to cry against my chest. "It's okay," I soothed. "I'm going to find out who did this to him."

After about five minutes, Chloe pulled away from me and I helped her to her feet. She wiped her eyes and face with her palms, took several deep breaths. When she was calm enough to speak again, she asked who could do something so horrible.

I shook my head. "I don't know, but I'll need to meet with you and everyone in your family to try and figure out what he has in common with Betty Ledet and Isaac Edwards."

"The other victims?" she asked.

"Yeah, but keep that to yourself. Don't give it to your boss or anyone else in the media."

Chloe stared me right in the eyes. "I won't...I'm *trustworthy*." Without saying another word, she turned on her heel and walked away. "I'll be in touch," she called over her shoulder.

When I returned to where Susan was photographing the crypt front, she asked, "How'd she take the news?"

"Not good."

Susan studied my face. "Is there something going on between you two?"

"What do you mean?" I tried to sound casual, as I approached the coffin and examined the arrow.

"The way she looked at you this morning—it looks like y'all aren't getting along. Like maybe y'all were having a fight or had broken up."

I sighed. It was impossible to keep anything from Susan. "She broke up with me."

"Why? What'd you do?"

"I told her I was dependant on alcohol to get some sleep."

"She broke up with you because of that?" Susan's voice was incredulous.

"No. She broke up with me because I've been lying about it for a year now."

Susan was quiet for a long moment. "So, what you're saying is she didn't know you need alcohol to sleep?"

"No. I mean, I mentioned it to her last year, but I began hiding it from her after a while. I wanted her to think I was better, you know? I didn't want her thinking I was damaged, or something."

"I knew you needed alcohol to sleep."

I nodded.

"But she didn't?"

"No."

"Wow, that's screwed up."

"What is?"

"You trust me more than you trust your girlfriend."

I scowled. "It's different. You don't nag me about it."

Susan raised her hands. "I'm not judging you or anything. It just says something about your relationship with her—if you feel you need to hide things."

It was my turn to be thoughtful, as I stood there studying Susan. She had a point, I knew, but I just didn't feel like hearing it day in and day out. I said as much and Susan smirked.

"If that helps you sleep at night."

"No, the only thing that helps me sleep at night is vodka."

"Did you try sleeping pills?" Susan asked, turning to grab her camera.

"No. Don't you have to see a shrink to get a script?"

Camera held poised in front of her, Susan smiled. "You're cute when you're being stupid."

My jaw dropped. "What'd you say?"

"Clint, go to a family doctor and tell them you're having problems sleeping. They'll write you a script and your days of burying alcohol bottles will be over." She pointed to the corpse. "Now, can you turn the body over, so I can photograph the arrowhead?"

As I processed the information she'd provided, I grabbed a hold of Frank Rushing's left shoulder and pushed him onto his opposite side, standing as far at the head of the coffin as I could to allow Susan some room to work. He was surprisingly light and I held him in place with one hand while leaning back out of the way.

"The arrowhead's the same as the others," Susan said, snapping a few pictures of the arrowhead and the corpse's back while I held it in place. "Want me to unscrew the broad-head so we can remove the arrow?"

I nodded. There was no need for an autopsy, so it was up to us to recover the evidence. My thoughts were on Chloe while Susan put down her camera and changed out her latex gloves. If I did find a doctor to prescribe some sleeping pills, would that change things between us? Would she then give me a second chance? Sure, I'd eventually be fine if she didn't take me back, but things were comfortable between us and I wasn't ready for it to end yet—if ever.

I caught a whiff of a sweet fragrance as Susan moved next to me once again and reached for the arrowhead. She grasped it with the tips of her fingers and began to gently unscrew it, but the whole arrow turned. I reached up with my free hand and held the arrow in place while she removed the arrowhead. Once it was free, she packaged it into a small evidence box and sealed it shut.

I allowed the body to rock back into place and held it there as Susan prepared to remove the arrow from its chest. She gripped the arrow with both hands and planted her knee against the coffin. She gave me a nod and then jerked on the arrow, but it offered little resistance and she was able to easily pull it out. We didn't have evidence boxes for arrows, so she secured it in a box designed for long guns.

We made one last sweep of the area to make sure we hadn't missed anything, and then relinquished the scene to the funeral director.

CHAPTER 25

I didn't see Chloe in the crowd of reporters as we drove away, so I tried calling her to find out if she'd spoken with her family. She didn't answer.

Susan was on the phone with Detective Cagle and she pointed toward the north when we reached the highway. "Go left," she said. "Cagle's got something."

Although it was cloudy, it was still hot and the Tahoe felt like an oven. Sweat gathered on my forehead and I slid my window down to let in some air until the air conditioner could cool us off. I drove for about a mile until I saw an unmarked detective car parked on the shoulder of the road. I pulled beside it, waited for Cagle's window to slide down.

"Does a green Thunderbird mean anything to you?" he asked.

Had I been Achilles, my ears would've perked up. "Yeah, it was seen at the scene of the last murder."

Cagle flipped through his notepad, read over what he'd written. "Two different people drove by the cemetery yesterday at about noon and saw a green car parked beside the road," he said. "One of them described the car as an old green Thunderbird and the other person just said it was a faded green sports car."

"Damn, that's brazen," Susan said. "Breaking into a tomb in the middle of the day and target practicing on human corpses."

"Did either of them see a driver?" I asked, hopeful.

"No, they both said the car was unoccupied when they drove by the cemetery." Cagle looked up from his notes. "One of them—a lady who was making a trip to the grocery store—drove back by an hour later and the car was gone."

We discussed the case a while longer with Cagle and when we'd had everything we needed from him, Susan and I drove back to the office. A gray Ford pickup truck was parked in front of the police department and I recognized it to belong to the new mayor, Dexter Boudreaux. A former alligator trapper, he was so popular no one would run against him when he decided to throw his hat into the political arena and run for mayor. When asked by a local reporter why he'd decided to run for mayor, Dexter had spat a long stream of tobacco onto the street and lifted the nub where his left arm used to be. "The missus won't let me trap alligators no more since this happened," he'd proclaimed, "so I figured I'd do something just as dangerous and unpredictable—get into politics."

I waved at Lindsey when we walked inside and she pointed to the kitchen. "He's getting coffee."

I nodded and joined the mayor in our break room. His weathered face lit up when he saw me. "Clint! How the hell are you?"

"Good, I guess. I'd be better if I could figure out who's killing off our residents with arrows."

His face tightened. "This has got the missus all worried. She won't sit on the porch anymore. Barely goes outside. She keeps threatening to make me quit my job. Says she'd rather I go back to wrangling 'gators."

"Tell her she can't have you back," I said. "We need you too much."

"Yeah..." Dexter's voice trailed off and he stared down into his coffee cup. After a while of silence, he said in a low voice, "This thing with Susan...I believe it's going to get bad."

I took a seat across from him and leaned forward, my heart pounding like a kick pedal against my chest. "What do you know?"

"I got a call from Bill this morning. He said it was a *courtesy call*, just letting me know he was looking to indict one of my officers." Dexter looked up. His jaw was set. "I told him Susan was your officer and you were my Chief. I also told him we weren't going down without a fight."

My chest swelled with emotion. I wanted to reach over and hug Dexter, but didn't. Instead, I pursed my lips and nodded. "Thanks, Dexter, I really appreciate the support."

"I'm not gonna lie, I don't know if it'll be enough. Bill's got a hard-on for that girl in a bad way, and he won't stop until he gets her."

"Why? What the hell did she ever do to him?"

"I'm not sure," Dexter said, "but it's got to be bad."

We both sat in silence for a while until Susan popped into the break room. She greeted Dexter with a smile and a slap on the back. "What're you up to, Dex? The missus keeping you out of trouble?"

"She's trying, but she can't put a bridle on the devil." Dexter stood and nodded in my direction. "I'll leave you two to get this bastard before he kills anymore of our people."

When he was gone, Susan told me Melvin didn't have any luck with the arrows. "The shop owner told him the suspect most likely ordered them online."

I nodded, and then told her about Bill Hedd's call to Dexter. "What on earth could you have done?" I asked.

A bewildered look had fallen over her face. "I swear to God, Clint, I have no clue. I don't know why that man hates me so much."

"Well, you did kill one of his assistant district attorneys."

"But he had it coming—he was reaching for a knife. Besides, he was just a piece of shit criminal in a suit, nothing more."

"I know, but maybe Hedd didn't think so. You know how some people refuse to believe the worst of those who are closest to them?"

"I guess you're right." Susan sat with her arms propped on the table, shaking her head. "I can't think of anything else that could've caused him to hate me so much."

I was about to ask about a possible feud between their families, but Lindsey pushed through the door and interrupted me. "Chief, Chloe's here. She wants to talk to you about the case."

CHAPTER 26

When I was seated in my office with Chloe, I asked if she'd gotten with her family.

"Yeah, I talked to my mom and dad, but they've never heard of Betty Ledet or Isaac Edwards." She lowered her eyes, staring at her feet. "Mom asked about you. She wanted to know how we were doing."

"What'd you tell her?"

"I told her we were doing okay."

Relief flooded over me, as I realized there might be a chance of reconciliation. "Chloe, you have to know how sorry I am. And I'm going to fix this. I'm going to see a doctor and get a script for sleeping pills, or something. Anything to help fix this."

When Chloe looked up, her eyes were misty. "I love you too much to let this come between us. And I do know you'd never do anything to jeopardize what we have."

I stood and walked around my desk. Chloe met me halfway and we embraced for a long moment. Her firm breasts were pushed up tight against my chest and I could feel the beating of her heart against mine. I wanted that moment to last forever, but a knock at the door drew us apart. She wiped her eyes quickly and smiled. "I'll see you tonight, okay?"

"I'd love that." I reached for the door, but stopped. "Can you do me a favor?"

"Sure, anything."

"We're looking to question the driver of a faded green Ford Thunderbird who was wearing hunting gear and an orange hat. I'd like you to put it out to all the networks."

Chloe reached into her purse. After pulling out a notepad and pen, she began writing furiously. "So, do you think the driver is the killer?"

"We're not sure, but the car was spotted at the front of Isaac Edwards' street on the day of his murder and was seen in the area of the cemetery last night. I don't think it's a coincidence."

Chloe nodded and leaned up to kiss me on the lips. "I'm on it."

I opened the door and found Susan standing there looking a little impatient. Chloe greeted her with a smile on the way out and then Susan came in and dropped into the same chair Chloe had just vacated. She kicked her boots up on my desk and crossed her arms. I sat at the corner of my desk and stared down at her. "Nothing," I said. "She talked to her parents and they've never heard of Betty Ledet or Isaac Edwards."

Susan was thoughtful. "These are three different people from three different walks of life. What event might bring all of them together in one place? And how many more of them are going to die? Or be exhumed?"

"Maybe they all worked together at the same job?" I offered. "People of all ages and backgrounds work together."

"That's unlikely. Betty was a waitress at a small—"

I jumped up. "But she worked at the hospital before that! Maybe they worked there, too."

"Now you're talking."

I rushed behind my desk and shook my mouse to stir my computer monitor awake. When the display appeared on the screen, I clicked on the database icon and typed in my username. I stopped and pursed my lips.

"Forgot your password again?" Susan asked.

I nodded, trying desperately to remember it.

"Just give up and use the cheat sheet already."

Sighing, I pulled open my bottom drawer and snatched up the index card that had my passwords scribbled on it. I found the right one, typed it in the appropriate box, and hit the log-in button. When the program was up, I typed in Frank Rushing's name and ran an employment search. Susan stood and walked around my desk, leaning on my chair to study the results as they appeared on the screen.

"Nothing in the medical field," she said.

"These records aren't always complete."

"Try Isaac Edwards."

I did, but he hadn't worked in the medical field either. "What else might connect them?"

"What if they were her patients?" Susan asked.

I frowned. "The hospital would never give us that information."

"Let's call their families. You call Chloe and I'll call Mrs. Edwards."

Without waiting for me to answer, Susan rushed off to her office. I called Chloe and she put me in a three-way call to her parents. "No," her dad said when I posed the question. "Pops always made his doctor visits, but he hadn't been to the hospital in about twenty years before he died."

Too long ago for Betty to be a working nurse. "If you don't mind me asking, how'd he pass?"

"Massive heart attack," Chloe said. "He was involved in a single car crash and the first responders found him dead in his truck. After an autopsy, it was determined his heart attack caused the crash."

"We're just glad no one else was hurt," Chloe's dad said in a low voice.

I thanked them and hung up, wondering what to do next. I was still staring at my computer screen when Susan rejoined me.

"Isaac was hospitalized when he was a boy after being bit by a copperhead snake," Susan said, "and he had shoulder surgery when he was in college, but that's it, according to his wife."

"What else can we check?"

"What about their addresses?" Susan asked. "Maybe they were all neighbors at one time."

"That's a good idea."

As I cross-referenced all of their previous addresses against each other, Susan began flipping through the crime scene photos on her laptop. When I was done, I shook my head. "Nothing. The closest Isaac and Betty got was a few miles from each other and Frank never even lived in Mechant—"

"Wait a minute!" Susan sat upright in her chair and moved her face close to her computer screen. "This is it! I've figured it out."

CHAPTER 27

"What is it?" I wanted to know.

Susan turned her laptop around and shoved it across my desk so I could see. "Look at this picture."

I leaned close, squinting to see. It was a picture of Melvin holding something in his hand. He was at the crime scene at Isaac's house. "It's a piece of paper. So?"

"It's the jury duty subpoena."

My expression must've been blank as I stared at Susan, because she pounded her fist on my desk. "They served on a jury together! That's how you get three people from completely different backgrounds to be connected to one killer."

I suddenly thought back to the diverse group that served on the grand jury and my mouth dropped open in awe. "Damn, you're right!"

"Maybe, and if we are, nine more people are going to die—unless we can figure out who they convicted."

I snatched up my phone, called Chloe. When she answered, I asked if her grandfather ever served on a jury.

"As a matter of fact, he did," she said. "But it was a long time ago. I was, like, in third or fourth grade at the time. I remember asking Mrs. Sadler what jury duty was and she explained all about the court system. She told me a story about her serving on a jury once and I found it fascinating."

"Do you remember anything at all about the case? The defendant's name? The offense?"

"Wait, do you think the killings and his grave desecration are related to that case?"

"Maybe. Do you remember anything at all?"

"Of course not...I was a kid. I just remember someone saying something about him having jury duty and I thought he was in trouble and I was afraid."

"Ask your parents if they remember anything." Before she could respond, I hung up. "Susan, can you get with Peter and see if he remembers anything?"

"I'm on it." She grabbed her stuff and walked out of my office, waving as she disappeared through the doorway.

Next, I called Isabel. She answered on the first ring. "Hey, Clint, what can I do for you?"

"This case we're working—all of these arrow killings—we think the victims might've served together on a jury at some point. Is there any way you can research their names and find out who the defendant was?"

There was a long pause on the other end of the phone.

"Isabel, you still there?"

"Yeah, I'm here. I'm thinking." She was quiet for another long moment. When she spoke, it didn't sound promising. "We'd still have juror questionnaires from all of the major cases we've tried over the years, but everything's filed in the defendant's name, so there's no way of looking them up by jurors."

"Can you go through all of them by hand and search for the names of our victims?"

"I'm sorry, Clint, but we've had hundreds of jury trials just since I've been here, and maybe thousands all total. There's no way we could go through all of them. We could maybe try by year, if you knew that, but it would be next to impossible to just start searching through random cases from random years. I'm not saying it's totally impossible, but we don't have the staff or the time to even begin such a massive undertaking." After a short pause, Isabel said, "You're certainly welcome to come dig through the files yourself, if you like. I'll make them available to you, beginning with this year and working back as far as you want to go."

I scowled. Like Isabel, I didn't have the time or personnel to go shooting blindly into the dark. "Can you at least ask around the office to see if the names Betty Ledet, Isaac Edwards, or Frank Rushing mean anything to anyone?"

"Sure...sure, I'll do that."

I told her bye, but she stopped me before I could hang up.

"Clint, should we be worried?"

"What do you mean?"

"If we did put some bad guy away and he's now out of prison and killing jurors, wouldn't he also come after the prosecutor who tried him?"

The thought hadn't occurred to me and I didn't want to alarm her, but she was right. "Look, there's no need to panic, because we don't know for sure that's the connection between them—it's purely speculation based on a hunch at this point—but if Susan is right, I'd say every prosecutor needs to be worried until we can figure out exactly who's doing this and who handled the case."

When we hung up, I decided to meet with Mrs. Edwards at the hospital and find out if she knew anything about her husband serving on a jury. But before I did that, I had one stop to make and a promise to keep. I backed out of the sally port and headed south on Main, turning right onto Orange Way. I slowed my Tahoe as I neared Orange Way and came to a stop in front of the mailbox. I radioed Lindsey to let her know where I was and then stepped out into the afternoon air. It was almost three o'clock and I realized I'd forgotten to eat again. Cursing myself for being so forgetful, I strode toward the front door to Ty Richardson's house. He must've heard me drive up, because the door flew open and he bounded across the wooden porch and leapt to the ground.

"Hey, Sheriff, what're you doing here?" His tone was cheerful and he was smiling big. He'd cleaned up quite a bit since I'd first seen him. His beard had been trimmed, his hair cut, and someone had apparently taken a fire hose and a gallon of bleach to him. His clothes were not new, but they appeared clean, and he'd lost that wild look in his eyes.

I didn't feel like explaining the difference between a sheriff and a chief, so I just shook Ty's hand, wondering if I should still give him the Hot Wheel. What if he was taking his medication and had forgotten all about the garbage truck? I wasn't sure how that worked, so I decided to play it safe. "Hey, Ty, it's good to see you again."

"Why are you here?" he asked. "Did you bring my car?"

I smiled and pulled it from the shirt pocket of my tan uniform shirt. "Here it is."

Ty's face scrunched up when he saw the Hot Wheel. "Um, that's a toy. I thought you said you were replacing my car that got crashed?"

I cursed myself again for even trying. Thinking quickly, I changed the subject. "So, Officer William Tucker says you saw a prowler on your property. Care to tell me about it?"

"It wasn't on my property and it wasn't a prowler," Ty corrected.

"It was a bush and it was over there." He pointed toward the back of the street.

I looked in the direction he pointed and nodded. "Was it at night or daytime?"

"It was in the morning and the sun was out."

"Okay, thanks for calling it in. I'll have my officers make extra patrols down the street." I shook his hand again and turned to walk toward my Tahoe. "Call if you need anything."

"But Sheriff," Ty hollered after me, "what about my car?"

CHAPTER 28

Chateau Parish General Hospital

Stella Edwards was eating dinner with the help of a lady about my age when I appeared at the door to her hospital room. She wasn't as gaunt as when I'd first seen her. I knocked on the door and both women looked in my direction. The younger woman stood, putting down the tray she'd been holding and hurrying to greet me. "Are you here about my dad?"

I nodded. She introduced herself as Tiffany Edwards Fischer and she began bombarding me with questions about her dad's murder. With the patience born of many such encounters with grieving and confused family members, I provided as much detail as I could without giving away too much. When she was satisfied she knew all there was to know about her dad's murder, she took a deep breath and exhaled, letting her shoulders droop. "This has been so hard on us," she said.

"I understand and I'm very sorry."

Tiffany looked up at me, raising her eyebrows. "You understand?"

"Yeah, I lost my wife and daughter a couple years ago." I shook my head. "The bad news is…the pain never goes away."

We talked for a few more minutes and then I asked her and Stella Edwards if Isaac had ever served on jury duty.

"Why, yes," Stella said. "He had to serve for over a week. He even worked the weekends. I remember him being really mad about that."

My pulse quickened. "Do you remember when? Or what the case

was about? Or who was involved?"

"I think it was a murder, or something," Stella said.

Tiffany shook her head. "I remember Dad talking about it—a rape case, I believe."

I pulled out my notebook and pen, looked up at Tiffany. "Would you remember any names?"

"Oh, no, that was like twenty years ago—at least."

Chloe would've been in third or fourth grade twenty years ago. *This was it! We might've found our connection.* I asked them to try and remember as much as they could about the case and then excused myself to call Susan. Once I'd found a lonely corner in the hallway, I got her on the phone.

She began talking before I could even say hello. "Clint, this is the connection! Peter remembers Betty being on a jury and her having a hard time with the case, because it involved a man who'd raped his wife."

"Did he remember the defendant's name?"

"No, but he did say the trial was during the winter—he remembers Betty complaining about having to go out and spend a bunch of money on warm dress clothes—and she was eighteen at the time."

"Winter…twenty-two years ago." I jotted the information in my notes. "Thanks, Sue—you did some great work!" I hung up and called Reginald Hoffman on his cell phone. When he answered, I apologized for calling him so late and, while I had him on the phone, asked if they'd heard anything more on the hearing. He told me the grand jury was still set to meet in two weeks.

"I was hoping your boss had changed his mind," I said.

"We've been working on him, but it's no use. His mind is set on this one."

"Do you have any idea why he's gunning for Susan?"

"None at all, I'm afraid."

Grunting, I changed the subject and filled him in on what we'd learned so far. I asked if he could get someone to go through their files from twenty-two years ago and dig up every rape case that was tried in the winter. I offered to go through the files myself looking for the names of the jurors, but he told me that would be the easy part.

"The hard part is getting my hands on the files in the first place," Reginald said. "We keep all of our old major cases stored in a secure location off campus, but I don't know if we'd have any rape cases—unless it was an aggravated rape."

"It could be," I said. "I'm not sure. I just know a husband raped his wife."

"Okay, I'll see what I can find out."

I reentered the hospital room and asked Stella and Tiffany if they were able to remember anything specific about the case that might've stuck out, but they said they'd already told me everything they could remember. I thanked them and drove to the office, where Susan's Charger was parked in the sally port alongside William's and Amy's.

Marsha, my night shift dispatcher, looked up from her log book when I walked through the door. She pushed a tuft of snow white hair out of her eyes and pointed to my office. "The kids are in there looking at the GoPro video."

"Did Melvin turn in yet?"

Marsha shook her head. "He's out on the water. Something about someone spotted the monster 'gator that nearly killed Dexter."

My heart fluttered at the mention of the giant beast and my knees got weak. When word had spread about the attack, people began calling the mysterious alligator *Godzator* and everyone seemed to have a theory about what had happened to it. Some thought it had died from the bullet wounds and transformed into a ghost, forever haunting the swamps of Mechant Loup, while others swore it was still out there, waiting for a chance to get revenge on any human that crossed its path. While no one knew for sure what had become of the monster, there was no denying the benefit to the tourist industry around town. There had been a sizable uptick in swamp tours since the *Legend of Godzator* had crossed the Mechant Loup Bridge, spreading far and wide by word of mouth. While most of the townspeople were sorry for Dexter's arm, they were happy to see the healthy influx of tourists.

"How sure are they that it was the same alligator?" I asked.

"Melvin said they were tourists and they sounded scared to death, so it probably looked bigger than it actually was." Marsha's brows furrowed when she noticed the look on my face. "Chief, I'm sure that alligator is somewhere at the bottom of Lake Berg. Probably nothing left of it but a few bones and some bullet holes."

"God, I hope you're right."

I stepped into my office and found Susan behind my desk with Amy and William huddled behind her looking at the computer monitor. They all looked up. "Your monitor's bigger than any of ours and we can see the video better," Susan explained with a smile. "I guess that's one of the perks of the job."

"You know my door's always open." I walked around to stand

beside Amy, who tossed her long blonde hair back and moved over to make room. They were viewing the video from Isaac Edwards' GoPro and they were at the spot where he'd just ended his run and was cooling down by walking short laps in front of his house. As he reached one end of the lap, he turned and the camera panned the area across the street from his house. Susan paused the recording at that point and we all leaned closer to study the scene, searching for anything that might indicate a person was there. I'd cross-trained as a sniper when I worked SWAT in the city and I was taught to see the little things; a round or square shape where there shouldn't be one, a spot of foliage that didn't quite match its surrounding, a color different from what you'd expect to find in the forest, movement that wasn't consistent with the wind—generally, anything out of the ordinary. As I studied the tree line and the surrounding area, I saw nothing that would indicate an attack was imminent. The grass in the field was short-cropped and evenly colored and the ditch was well maintained. Other than the lone tree situated near the center of the lot and a short, stout bush off to its left, there were no possible hiding spots or signs of human presence.

I studied the tree first and then the bush, but didn't see anything around either that resembled a human.

"I don't see anything," Amy said, straightening to shift her gun belt around on her hip. Marsha had once said Amy wore her pants too tight and her collar too loose, but all I cared about was her productivity. No one else seemed to care about how she dressed, except for some of the more conservative women in town whose husbands gawked every time Amy was around. I'd fielded at least a dozen complaints from these women. When I told them she wasn't violating the department's dress code and there was nothing I could do about it, they were less than impressed. At least three of them took their complaints to the mayor, who was less diplomatic than I had been.

I scowled. "I don't see anything either."

Susan hit the play button and the GoPro went back into motion when I suddenly caught my breath. "Stop the video—that's him!"

CHAPTER 29

"Where?" William asked. "What do you see? There's nothing but grass and trees."

I hurried around my desk and grabbed the stack of crime scene photographs Susan had printed earlier. I returned to my spot beside Amy and spread several of the photos on the desktop. I pointed to one of the photographs we'd taken of the field across the street from Isaac's house. "The bush in the video—it's not in the picture."

"No shit!" William whistled when Susan backed up the video and hit the *pause* button. "How'd you even catch that?"

"It just hit me—there was only one tree in the middle of the field when Susan and I worked the scene." I leaned closer to the monitor, strained to pick apart the details of the bush. The quality of the film was surprisingly crisp for such a small recording device and I thought I could make out some linear shapes that could've been parts of the bow or arrows. The face was concealed behind a mask of burlap and natural vegetation—the job of a real pro. "He's wearing a ghillie suit," I said.

"A what?" Amy asked.

"It's a big leafy suit that snipers wear to conceal themselves in wooded areas," I explained.

"Hunters sometimes use them, too," Susan offered, "but I've never seen one that blends so well and looks so durable. Most of the ones I've encountered looked like camouflage papier-mâché and they got ripped up after one trek in the woods."

"This one is handmade for sure," I said. "This guy either knows what he's doing or he knows where to find instructional videos on the internet."

"You think the internet taught him to shoot a bow?" Susan asked. "Because I think he's pretty good—too good to learn that shit on his own."

I couldn't argue with her. I drummed my fingers on the desk and remembered Ty Richardson. "William, I bet—"

"I know what you're going to say," he interrupted. "Ty Richardson saw the killer."

"What're you talking about?" Susan asked.

"I'll tell you in the car." I turned to Amy and William before we walked out. "I want y'all doubling up tonight. Keep your eyes peeled and be on the lookout for that green Thunderbird."

They nodded their heads in unison.

"Don't let your guard down," I warned, before turning to hurry off with Susan. It was getting dark as we jumped into my Tahoe, so I turned on the headlights and pulled onto Main Street. Several reporters started scurrying about, gathering up their gear and rushing to their vans, but I stopped to tell them there had been no new developments and they could relax. They misinterpreted my gesture as a willingness to talk, and they began firing off questions. I smiled and, closing my window, drove away.

My cruiser sliced through mosquitoes and other flying insects on the drive to Orange Way—just a street north of Lacy Court—and I had to spray my windshield and turn on the wipers to keep it clear of smudge. As I drove, I told Susan how Ty had reported seeing a bush walking through a neighbor's yard. "At first, I just figured his mind was playing tricks on him, but I think he really saw our killer."

I made a sharp right off of Main onto Orange Way and cruised to the back of the street. I pulled to a stop in front of Ty's house and we stepped out. I paused to stare toward the houses across the street. Lacy Court—Isaac Edwards' street—was just beyond the trees that bordered the back yards of those houses. It was very plausible Ty saw the killer lurking in the area. He'd provided the first real clue as to how the killer was getting close enough to the victims to kill them without being seen, and I had brushed him off. Shaking my head, I walked around the Tahoe and followed Susan to the front door.

I swatted at a mosquito while we waited for someone to answer the door. It didn't take long for us to hear heavy footsteps pounding to the door. When it opened, Ty's mom stood there in jeans and an oversized T-shirt. Her smile was pleasant. "Hey, Chief, Ty told me you bought him the car. That was very sweet of you."

"It's nothing," I said, shuffling my feet. I didn't like being called out for doing good deeds. "Is Ty around? We need to talk to him about something he might've seen a couple of days ago."

The lady turned her head and hollered, "Ty! You've got visitors."

I thanked her and she walked back into the house, leaving the main door ajar and letting the screen door slam shut. Susan and I stood there in silence until Ty finally appeared in the doorway, casting a cautious glance from me to Susan and then back to me.

"Sheriff…is that you?"

"It is, Ty. How are you?"

He relaxed and stepped through the screen door and into the full light of the porch. "Good to see you." He looked at Susan. "I remember you. I think you came here before. You were nice."

"I try to be," Susan said, flashing a smile that accentuated the dimple on her cheek.

"Yeah, you might be able to help us, Ty," I said.

"I'd like that."

I pointed toward the back of the street. "Remember that bush you saw back at the neighbor's house?"

His eyes lit up. "Yeah, it was something else. I've never seen a bush move before. At first I thought my eyes were playing tricks on me, you know? So, I closed my eyes and opened them again like you're supposed to do if you're not sure about what you're seeing, and it was still there."

"Can you show us exactly where he was standing?"

"Oh, no, Sheriff."

"What's that?" I asked.

"It wasn't a *he*—it was a bush."

"I'm sorry. I stand corrected." I started over. "Can you show us exactly where the bush was when you saw it?"

"Sure, it was over there." Ty pointed to an opening between the houses across the street. "It was walking in the trees behind the houses and it was heading toward the back of the street."

"Did it have anything in its hands?" I asked.

"Bushes don't have hands," Ty answered flatly.

But it has legs? I wanted to ask, but decided against it. "Gotcha…did you see anything hanging off of its limbs?"

"I did. There were a lot of leaves."

I thanked Ty for his time and grabbed a couple of flashlights from the back of my Tahoe, tossed one to Susan. We crossed the street and dipped between the houses. When we made it to the tree line, we began scanning the ground with the flashlights, searching for any hint that a person had been through there.

"I'm no tracker," Susan said, "but there seems to be a faint path through here." She shined her light along a break in the thick underbrush. She was right. There seemed to be some smashed leaves and grass, as well as some broken twigs, along a stretch of woods. We followed to either side of it, both of us concentrating our light to the center of the trail, hoping to find anything that might lead us to the killer. The going was slow, because we lost the trail a half dozen times, but twenty minutes later we finally ended up at the edge of a clearing. We shined our lights across an empty field that boasted one lone tree, and saw Isaac Edwards' house.

"Wow," I said. "Ty saw our killer."

"You think the guy in the ghillie suit is also the guy in the orange hat?"

I was thoughtful. "It has to be. The Thunderbird was seen at two of the scenes. It can't be a coincidence."

Susan and I squatted and surveyed the ground at our feet. The grass and leaves were smashed in a small circle, as though the killer had waited here for some time. I was about to step out into the field when Susan called out to me.

"Clint, look here!"

I looked where she pointed and whistled when I saw a cigarette butt on the ground. My first thought was DNA evidence and I said as much.

"I'll stay with the evidence," Susan offered. "Why don't you go back and get your crime scene box?"

CHAPTER 30

Tuesday, October 13
Mechant Loup Police Department

It was half past midnight when Susan and I finally finished securing the evidence in the lockers. I bid her goodnight and walked out into the sally port. There were at least seven news vans still parked along Main Street when I backed my Tahoe out of the sally port. Most of the vans were cloaked in darkness, but light glowed from the tinted windows of two of them, and a head popped up when they heard the automatic garage door.

I stopped backing up when I saw a marked Charger drive up and park on the street. Amy stepped out and ambled to my door. I shot a thumb toward the news vans. "I think they're working in shifts, taking turns watching us."

"They jump up every time I drive up or leave." Amy smiled mischievously. "I sped off earlier and they started chasing me. I pulled up at Cig's and got some gas, a cup of coffee, and two donuts. They weren't happy."

I laughed and told her goodnight, but she stopped me. "I'm actually glad you're still here." She took a deep breath, exhaled slowly. "Um, I just wanted to let you know I stopped your girlfriend for speeding and I gave her a warning. She was heading—"

"Shit!"

Amy raised her eyebrows. "Did I do something wrong? Should I have written her a ticket?"

I laughed, waved my hand dismissively. "No, I was supposed to meet her at my house this afternoon and I totally forgot." I cursed myself inwardly. "I just got so busy with the case and everything was moving so fast."

"I'm sure she'll understand," Amy said. "She's really nice—and pretty."

I nodded and thanked her. I'd never known Chloe to speed through town and I couldn't help but wonder why she was in a hurry. Had there been another attack somewhere else in the parish? Surely Sheriff Turner would've called me and the other vans wouldn't still be here. I waved to Amy and drove off, calling Chloe's cell.

"Clint! I was just about to call you. My dad spent all night digging through my grandpa's things because he remembered him having a newspaper clipping from the trial. Well, he found it and I'm heading there now to get it."

A surge of energy pushed the tired right out of me, but then a thought struck me. "Wait—are you going to share the information with me, or is it for your story?"

She laughed. "You'll get first dibs. Catching a killer is more important than my story."

Chloe agreed to meet me at home later and we hung up. I called Susan next to let her know we might have a break in the case, and she made me promise to call as soon as I knew something. I turned into my driveway and shut off the engine. I could hear Achilles barking from the back yard. He knew the sound of my truck and could hear it from halfway down the street.

I pulled off my uniform shirt and tossed it on the sofa as I made my way to the back door. Once outside, I sat on the bottom step and stared into Achilles' eyes as he sat beside me. His ears were perked up and his long tongue was hanging out the side of his mouth. "You missed me, big man?" He slurped his tongue in his mouth and clamped his jaws shut, cocking his head sideways. I laughed. "Yeah, I know you did."

I don't know how long I sat there with my elbows propped on my knees, but my eyes started to close and I must've nodded off because Abigail's terrifying screech caused me to bolt wide awake. My left elbow slipped off my knee and I nearly spilled onto my face. Achilles jerked to his feet and stared at me, waiting for me to tell him what to do. I rubbed my eyes and swatted at a mosquito that had drilled for red oil on my neck. "Let's go inside, boy."

Achilles followed me through the door and plopped down on the floor in the kitchen. He was asleep within seconds. I envied him. Although he twitched sometimes in his sleep and I wondered if he was dreaming about the day he got shot, he was still able to sleep on his own. He was stronger than me. I shook my head and thought about hitting the vodka. I had two bottles left and would need to get a new supply tomorrow, unless I could find a doctor who'd discreetly prescribe some sleeping pills. *What if they didn't even work?* I shook off the thought and turned on the television. The news from earlier was being rebroadcasted and I settled on the sofa to watch it, waiting to hear back from Chloe. It wasn't long before a banner flashed on the screen that read, "Possible serial killer operating in small Louisiana town." I sighed. Once again, our quiet little town was making a lot of noise in the national news.

"A deranged person is going around killing people and desecrating corpses with a bow in Mechant Loup, a small town in rural Louisiana," the anchorwoman was saying. *"Once again, it seems like Police Chief Clint Wolf has his hands full as he tries to determine who would want to target three people from three very different walks of life with no obvious connection or relationship. No secret to controversy, this case has thrust the newly appointed police chief and his department right back into the spotlight. If you'll remember, back in July of—"*

I turned off the television and tossed the remote on the coffee table. I didn't need to be reminded of last year. I was about to call Chloe when Achilles' head snapped up and he stared toward the front of the house. Just then, I heard a car door slam outside. Before I could get up, Chloe hurried through the door.

"Sorry I'm home so late," she said. "My dad wouldn't—"

I met her halfway and put a finger to her soft lips to stop her. "Wait, what did you say?"

She cocked her head sideways. "My dad wouldn't stop talking?"

"No, before that."

"I'm sorry I'm late?"

"You called this your home."

She looked around at the boxes that Achilles has scattered around. "Yeah, I thought we moved in together."

"I thought you changed your mind."

She smiled. "I overreacted a little. I am disappointed that you felt the need to hide it from me and I might have some trust issues going forward, but I want it to work out between us. I love you."

"I love you, too, Chloe." I leaned forward and kissed her for a long moment before settling down on the sofa to look at the newspaper clipping.

Chloe pulled a large, faded yellow envelope out of her purse and placed it in her lap. "This is it," she said.

The clasps were still in place and it looked like the envelope hadn't been disturbed in years. "Y'all didn't open it yet?"

"My dad thought it was evidence and didn't want to get his prints on it." Chloe chuckled. "And I didn't want to look at it without you."

"How'd your dad know it was the newspaper article if he didn't open it?"

Chloe turned the envelope over to show me a simple phrase scrawled in ink at the top, left corner, *Newspaper article from trial.* "Gramps was very organized," she explained. Taking a deep breath, she unfolded the small metal clasps that held the flap in place. She tried to flip it open, but the flap was sealed. Using one of her painted fingernails, she scraped at the edge of the flap and was finally able to force it apart, tearing part of it in the process. She placed the torn pieces on the sofa beside her and gently expanded the envelope until she was able to see inside. Her brow furrowed as she reached in and pulled out a thin, rectangular piece of paper. It was definitely a newspaper clipping. She looked at the front of the clipping, and then turned it over.

"What the hell?" we both said in unison.

CHAPTER 31

Seven hours later…

Susan and I arrived at the district attorney's office just as the secretary was unlocking the front door. I'd called Isabel first thing in the morning and caught her driving her kids to school. When I explained what we had, she told me to meet her at the office at around eight-thirty, warning me she might be a little late. The secretary didn't know anything about the meeting, so she had us wait in the lobby until she could reach Isabel. As we waited, there was little conversation between Susan and me. She was no doubt worrying about the upcoming hearing. I was thinking about the same thing, but my mind was also on last night. I had tried to sleep but couldn't, so I let Chloe know I was having a bottle of vodka. She'd begged me to try and do without it, but I assured her it wouldn't work. I finally agreed to experiment with half a bottle. Turned out it did the trick. I was able to sleep without having nightmares and I woke up feeling less hung over than usual. I even felt recharged, and we both woke up happy with each other. After a quick breakfast, we'd both set off to our respective jobs, not knowing what the day would hold for each of us.

Susan and I had to wait for about ten minutes, but Isabel finally opened a side door and let us into their duty office. She apologized for making us wait and took a seat at one side of the desk, while Susan and I sat across from her. I pulled the newspaper clipping from the envelope and placed it on the desk in front of Isabel.

To our disappointment, the picture had been cut from the article and all pertinent data had been removed. All that was left was a picture of four jurors walking out of the courtroom in the background, and Reginald Hoffman walking toward the camera in the foreground. There was a man in a gray suit that Chloe had easily identified as being her grandpa, and the only woman in the photograph was definitely Betty Ledet—a younger and cleaner looking version of her, but her nonetheless. The other two jurors were young men—much too young to be Isaac Edwards.

Isabel studied the photograph. "I don't recognize any of them." She turned the photo over to look at the backside. "No date or anything on here?"

"No," I said. "Apparently, all Chloe's grandpa cared about was his picture. Her dad said it was his five seconds of fame."

Isabel reached to her left and snatched up the phone receiver, punched in an extension. After a few seconds she said, "Reggie, come into the duty office, please."

We made small talk until the door behind Isabel shot open and Reginald walked in. He nodded in my direction and then turned to look at Susan. He held her gaze for a moment and then frowned. "I hope you know I'm in your corner." His voice was low, as though he thought the room was bugged. "I'm doing everything I can to swing this thing in the right direction."

"I appreciate it," Susan said, before letting her eyes drop back to the photograph.

Isabel turned the newspaper clipping so Reginald could see.

"Is this from the old rape case you called about, Chief?" he asked.

"We think it is," I said.

"I'm going to the storage facility first thing this morning to see if we have anything from twenty-two years ago. Our computer system was purged about fifteen years back, so there's no way of checking how many rape cases we tried. I'll have to go through each box manually, and that'll take a few days." He turned his attention to the newspaper clipping and grunted when he saw his mug on the front of the picture.

"Do you recognize any of these people?" Isabel asked.

"I know that ugly bastard walking toward the camera," Reginald said.

"I wasn't talking about the defendant," Isabel joked. "I meant the jurors."

Reginald shook his head. "I don't recognize any of these people. I mean, we have so many trials here that jurors start to look the same to me. They kind of all blend now. And the picture definitely looks old, because I don't have that tie anymore—or those pants—so it'd be really hard to remember anyone from twenty-two years ago, if that's when we believe this picture was taken."

"We're pretty sure." I looked at the picture and then at Reginald. "Like all of us, you've definitely put on a few pounds over the past twenty years, and you look like a kid in that picture."

"And I was working for the sheriff's office at the time," he said. "That's a sheriff's badge clipped to my belt."

"Could this have been a case you worked?" Isabel asked.

Reginald studied the picture more, holding it up to the light. "Are y'all sure they're jurors? They could be regular people leaving court for any number of reasons."

I pointed to Chloe's grandfather in the picture. "This is Frank Rushing, the guy who was ripped from the grave and shot through the chest with an arrow."

"I heard about that." Isabel shuddered. "That's about as creepy as they get. Whoever's doing this is really angry." She turned back to Reginald. "Come on, Reggie, don't you remember anything about this picture?"

"I mean, I must've been a part of it if I was dressed up and in the picture, but I've testified so many times in court."

"How many of your rape cases made it to trial?" Susan asked.

"I've testified in a dozen, or so, rape cases, but I've had bit parts in most of them—maybe handled a piece of evidence or participated in the interview." He pulled out his phone and scrolled to the camera feature on it. "I'll take a picture of this and circulate it among the sheriff's detectives. One of them might remember something."

"How long have you been working here at the DA's office?" I asked.

"A little over twenty years now, so the timing would be…" His expression changed as his voice trailed off. He reached a hand to his face and rubbed his chin, lost in thought. His complexion was a little paler than a second earlier.

"What is it?" Isabel wanted to know.

"Um…the last case I worked before coming here was a murder. This could be it."

Isabel frowned and nodded. "The Lance Duggart case. You think this is it? We wouldn't know anything about it then, because our office had to recuse itself. The DA's office over in Magnolia Parish took over the case."

It was common for district attorneys and judges to remove themselves from cases when there was a potential conflict of interest, and the interest didn't get more conflicted than having the DA's wife killed.

"Isn't he the guy who killed Bill Hedd's wife?" Susan asked. "I remember hearing about that when I was little."

"Lance Duggart vowed to get out of jail and kill all of us—the jury, the judge, the DA, me." Reginald looked up. "And my wife and kids."

"He was sentenced to life without parole," Isabel said. "It can't be him."

"But he's got family." Reginald snatched up his phone and began making a call. "I'm heading to the Magnolia Parish DA's Office now to look up the case. If it's connected to Duggart, no one involved in the case is safe."

"Which of their prosecutors handled the case?" I asked.

"His first assistant did," Isabel said. "They tried it here in Chateau. Took over one of the government buildings and worked out of there for about two months. I had just gotten out of law school and remember it well." She sighed. "It was a bad time for us. Bill was crazy with grief and couldn't run the office. He was always gone and his first assistant was a lazy piece of shit." She nodded. "Everyone's glad he's gone."

I asked Isabel if she could have some of her employees search through their in-house files. "Isaac's daughter was sure it was a rape case and I'd hate to lose a day searching through the wrong case."

"Absolutely," she said. "I'll get someone on it right away."

CHAPTER 32

Friday, October 16

I woke up to thunder grumbling outside and my cell phone's annoying alarm screaming at me to wake up. I reached blindly for my phone and turned off the alarm. Chloe stirred beside me and wormed her head between my arms and against my chest. I smiled. Things were going well between us. She had been more encouraging about my drinking issues than I'd first thought, and I regularly cursed myself for not having more faith in her. With her help, I was sleeping on half a bottle of vodka a night. I tried to kick it cold a few times, but as soon as I'd fall asleep I'd see Abigail's face and wake up in a terror. For some reason, the alcohol helped to quell the demons in my head and we were both starting to realize this would be a natural part of our lives now—something we'd just have to learn to live with. Chloe was okay with it as long as it remained manageable and wasn't progressive. She'd tried to talk me into seeing a psychologist, but backed off when I said I'd drop to half a bottle. Just yesterday I'd promised to work on weaning myself down to a quarter of a bottle, and that pleased her a great deal.

While I was thrilled that our relationship was going great, I was even more thrilled that no one had been murdered or any corpses desecrated in four days. The investigation had stalled and we were awaiting DNA results on the cigarette and arrows. Reginald had located the list of jurors for the Lance Duggart case, but none of them matched up to our victims. Isabel was calling daily to update me on their progress at the storage facility, but, so far, they were coming up dry. She feared they might've destroyed the file, since it most likely wasn't a capital offense.

In town, we had canvassed the neighborhoods of each attack at least three times, but no one could tell us anything. We'd searched high and low for the green Thunderbird and Chloe had plastered it across all media outlets in the area, but it seemed to have disappeared. The town had gone back to normal as the story faded to black and people went about their busy lives, but the police department hadn't gone back to normal—and we wouldn't as long as a killer was on the loose. While I knew there was more to do and the case needed my attention, I had other things on my mind at the moment.

I placed a hand over Chloe's curvy hip and ran it up her smooth skin until I reached her breasts. She groaned and leaned closer into me. "Want to be late this morning?" she asked.

I nodded and we both slipped out of bed and raced to the bathroom. We stood naked in front of the sink, loading our toothbrushes and eyeing each other with naughty intentions. After we were done brushing our teeth, Chloe pushed her perky breasts against my torso and pulled my mouth down to hers, kissing me aggressively. I grabbed her buttocks with both of my hands and lifted her off the ground, carrying her back to bed. We had just plopped onto it when my cell phone began ringing. I ignored it and we continued kissing and exploring each others' bodies with our hands. My phone finally stopped ringing, but a second later it beeped to indicate I'd received a text message. As I began to wonder if something was wrong, it beeped a second and third time, and then started ringing again. "Leave us alone!" I yelled, and we both began laughing.

"You'd better get it," Chloe said. "It might be another dead body."

My mood suddenly fell. "I sure hope not!" I rolled to a sitting position and snatched my phone from the nightstand. I saw that the missed calls had been from Melvin. I checked the text messages. The first two were from Melvin:

Chief, where r u. can u please call

Hey, Chief, I need you to call me asap please

The third was from Susan and I could read her excitement in the message:

Clint, wake the hell up! We know who the killer is!

"They know who it is!" I said, jumping to my feet and scrambling to find some clothes. I hadn't ironed a fresh pair of uniform pants, so I grabbed the pair I'd thrown in the hamper the night before.

Chloe leapt out of bed herself, pulling on her panties, and slipping into her bra. "Who is it? The killer—what's his name?"

"I don't know yet."

She stopped in mid-motion—one breast hanging over the cup of her bra—and eyed me with suspicion. "You don't know, or you don't want to say?"

That stung, but I knew I deserved it. I finished buttoning my uniform pants and walk over to her. I cupped her face in my hands and looked into her eyes. "I'm sorry for lying about my booze problem, but I meant it when I said I'd never lie to you again." I kissed her until her tense shoulders relaxed and then I pulled back to look into her eyes again. "I don't know who it is yet, and that's the truth. But when I do know, I won't be able to tell you."

She scowled. "Okay, I guess this is *Chief* Wolf speaking, which means you'd better get your hands off of me before my boyfriend, Clint, gets home."

CHAPTER 33

I had rushed out the door without tucking in my uniform shirt or tying my boots, but I didn't care, and Lindsey didn't seem to notice when I walked into the office. She knew what I was looking for and pointed to the interview room, which also served as a conference room. Susan and Melvin were bent over a stack of documents and they both looked up when I entered. Susan looked down at my boots and then at my shirt, and shook her head. "Who dressed you?"

"I don't even know if I remembered to put my socks on." I then checked my holster to make sure my pistol was there. "What do we have?"

Melvin explained that the crime lab had faxed over the results of the DNA tests and it showed they'd gotten a CODIS (Combined DNA Index System) hit, where the DNA from the three arrows and the cigarette butt we'd recovered from our crime scenes was matched to an offender who had already been entered into the system.

"Who's the suspect?" I asked, eager to find out who'd been hunting down the citizens of our small town. Once I had a name, I could track him down and put my hands on him.

Melvin handed me the crime lab report and I scanned it, searching for the culprit's name. I finally found it. "Gregg Daniels," I read out loud. I looked from Susan to Melvin, whose expressions were as blank as mine felt. "Who the hell is Gregg Daniels?"

Susan shrugged. "I have no idea. I've never heard of him before. Neither has Melvin."

"Did y'all run him in the system?" I asked.

"Yeah," Melvin said, handing me a criminal history report complete with his prison mug shot. "It seems he got out of prison a few months ago."

Melvin was right. Gregg Daniels had been released from the state penitentiary on July 27, after serving twenty-one years of a twenty-five-year sentence. He'd been arrested a dozen times before the long stint in prison, and it took me a few seconds to sift through all of his previous arrests before finding the charge that landed him in prison for most of his adult life—aggravated rape. A sick feeling formed in the pit of my stomach as a thought occurred to me. "If he's killing jurors for putting him behind bars," I said slowly, "it's only a matter of time before he gets to the victim." I turned to Susan. "Call Isabel and give her his name. Ask her to find his case file and send us the names of everyone involved in the case—from jurors to witnesses to victims to law enforcement."

Next, I asked Melvin to run a name inquiry and get every address ever listed to Gregg Daniels, as well as any vehicles registered in his name.

I went into my office and called Sheriff Buck Turner. When he answered, I told him we had identified the suspect through DNA evidence and, based on the newspaper clipping from Chloe's grandfather, we believed the incident occurred in his jurisdiction and Reginald Hoffman had assisted in some way. "Can you have one of your people try to locate the old file? I need to know as much as I can about the case and everyone involved."

"Sure," Turner said. "That won't be a problem."

"And Sheriff..."

"Please, Clint, call me Buck."

"Buck...everyone who worked this case is a target." I let that information sink in before continuing. "Gregg Daniels spent the last twenty-one years seething in prison, but he's out now—and he's pissed off."

"I'll put my people on high alert."

Once we'd said our goodbyes, I found the number for the state prison and dialed it. I needed to know all I could about Gregg Daniels. He was ruthless and unpredictable, and I needed to stop him as soon as possible—before someone else found themselves on the wrong end of a three-blade mechanical broad-head.

After pressing too many buttons and not getting a live person on the line, I finally started pressing "0" repeatedly until an automated message finally told me to hold on for an operator. When she came on, she transferred me to a Lieutenant who transferred me to a secretary who asked me to hold for the warden. Ten minutes later a heavy voice answered in a thick north Louisianan accent. "This is

Warden Grant. What can I do for you?"

I introduced myself to him and explained everything I knew about the case. "We're in the process of trying to track down Gregg Daniels' whereabouts, and I was wondering if you might be able to help us out."

"Hold on a minute." There was a long pause and I could hear fingers snapping against a keyboard. It was painfully obvious he had a hard time navigating the keys, but it wasn't long before he spoke again. "Go ahead and send me a written request on your department's letterhead and I'll see what I can find out."

I pulled the phone from my ear and stared at it, telling myself to count to ten before opening my mouth again. I put the phone back to my ear. "Warden, this is an emergency. For starters, I need to know who picked him up when he was released, I need a list of every person who visited him over the past twenty-one years, and I need to know who he called while he was there—and I need to know this in a hurry, before someone else dies. His current address would also be most helpful."

"Then I suspect you'll get that written request to me in a hurry."

I started to object, but the line went dead. I thought about calling back, but decided against it. It would only be a waste of time anyway. On a yellow sticky note, I jotted the list of things I needed from the prison and the fax number, and then brought it to Lindsey. I explained what I needed and stepped into Susan's office. She was on the phone, but waved for me to sit across from her.

"I'm on hold," she explained. "Isabel's got someone looking through their old computer system. She said Reginald thinks he might remember the case now, but he wasn't the lead detective. He said a female detective was primary—a Mary Cox—but she was killed in a crash a few years ago during a high speed chase. I actually remember when it—" She threw up a hand and turned her attention back to the call. "Yeah, I'm here. Right…okay…sure, thanks."

"Well?"

"She found an entry in the system, but it only has the disposition of the case. She's got someone going to their storage facility and she'll call as soon as they have the file in hand."

Susan and I sat in her office for fifteen minutes, talking about the case and bitching about the upcoming hearing. We finally stepped into the patrol section to see what Melvin was up to. We found him seated at his desk, which was next to Lindsey's work station, with Lindsey looking over his shoulder. "Is that him?" Lindsey asked, staring at the computer monitor. "He looks scary!"

Susan and I walked to stand behind Melvin. He had accessed Daniels' mugshot from the last time he was arrested and it was quite a picture. Daniels' eyes were so wide the brown of his irises were completely surrounded by a sea of white. His scruffy face and brown hair sticking straight up added to the insane look in his eyes. The zipper on his sweat jacket was low, revealing a series of scratches and claw marks on his neck and upper chest.

"His victim fought hard, it seems," Susan said in a low, stern voice. "I'd like to get my hands on him."

Melvin grunted. "Yeah, but you wouldn't scratch him—you'd punch him so hard his grandma would get a nosebleed."

"Who's his grandma?" Lindsey wanted to know.

"How should I know?" Melvin asked.

"You just said Susan would—"

"It was a joke, Lindsey," Melvin said with a smirk. "You know what those are, don't you?"

Lindsey socked him playfully in the shoulder and turned away. "See if I deliver anymore messages from your wife."

"Are any vehicles registered to him?" I asked.

Melvin shook his head. "None—not even back when he was a free man, but I did find his brothers." He handed me a printout that listed Daniels' relatives. He had two brothers—Farrell and Howard—but all of the addresses listed to them were at least five years old.

"Nothing current?" Susan asked.

"Nope. Not a thing." Melvin searched for more results and then whistled. "Farrell had a green Thunderbird registered to him, but the registration has been expired for two years."

"You mean he's driving around killing people in a car that has an expired tag?" Susan asked incredulously. "He'd better not let Amy catch him."

We all laughed and sat around while Melvin ran query after query, trying to locate anything that would tell us where Daniels had taken up residency. It was nearly an hour later when Susan's cell phone rang. She glanced at the screen and nodded, put it to her ear. She spoke back and forth with Isabel and then waved for Lindsey to bring her a notepad. With pen in hand, she told Isabel to read off the list of jurors from Gregg Daniels' case. I couldn't see what she was writing, but counted thirteen lines. Susan frowned, causing her dimple to dig deeper into her cheek. "Wait, is that it?" she asked, then said, "Okay, thank you." She hung up the phone and handed me the list. "They're not on here."

"What?" I read over the names of the twelve jurors and the one alternate, and then read over them again, but slower. None of them were our victims.

CHAPTER 34

"So, you think these will help me sleep?" I asked Doctor Leslie Garner, holding up the orange bottle of pink capsules she'd recommended.

"You could start to see improvement within five days, but it usually takes one to two weeks." She wrote some notes in my chart and flipped it shut. "Okay, that should do it for today. Come back and see me if you have any problems at all."

I thanked her and stopped to pay the deductible before heading home. It was four o'clock when I arrived home and stepped out of the Tahoe. Chloe was already there and I found her fussing over the living room. She dropped what she was doing and ran to greet me, beating Achilles by half a step. When she finally let go of my neck, she stared sideways at the pill bottle in my hand. "What are those?"

"I've decided to try something new. Susan suggested I go to a doctor and see about getting some—"

"So, when Susan tells you to go to a doctor, you go"—Chloe folded her arms across her chest—"but when I tell you to go, you make all kinds of excuses and refuse to get some help."

"No, that's not it. She told me the same thing you did and I told her I didn't need to see a damn shrink. That's when she said all I had to do was see a general practitioner and say I was having problems sleeping. So, I did." I looked up at Chloe. "I thought you'd be happy about it."

"I'm sorry." Her face softened and she hugged me again. "I am happy. This is a huge step and I know you're doing it for me."

"I am. I don't have a problem with vodka at all." I tossed the bottle of pills on the table and went in my room to change. "Want some grilled burgers?" I called over my shoulder.

"Sounds yummy."

As I changed into jeans and a T-shirt, I considered whether I should tell Chloe about the latest on the case. We'd run all of the names Isabel had given us, but we couldn't come up with a connection to Isaac Edwards, Betty Ledet, or Chloe's grandfather. Being that her grandfather was involved now, I would simply be updating a victim's family member, and not divulging information to the media.

I could tell Chloe recognized the conflicted look on my face as we began making the patties together, because she said, "Just say it. You know you will eventually, so just get it over with."

She was right, I knew. I made her promise to keep it to herself and then told her what we'd learned.

She stopped what she was doing and stood there lost in thought, her hands covered in ground beef. After a few moments, she finally said, "So, this Gregg Daniels is responsible for the killings and for desecrating my grandfather, but none of the victims served on the jury that convicted him?"

"Yep, you've been paying attention."

"Then why'd he pick them?"

I didn't have a good answer, so I didn't say anything. One thing was for certain—I needed to find Gregg Daniels before he killed again. Chloe started to ask another question, but my phone began ringing.

"Achilles, get the phone!" I ordered. "My hands are dirty."

Instead of picking up the phone, Achilles just cocked his head to the side and perked his ears straight up, as though trying to figure out what I'd said. I laughed and washed my hands off, getting to the phone just as it stopped ringing. It was the office. Groaning under my breath, I called back and Amy answered on the first ring. "Chief, I'm sorry to bother you, but we need you to come out."

"What is it?"

Amy explained how William had staked out Cig's Gas Station and finally caught the suspicious subject who had been asking about me. William had him bent over the hood of his cruiser handcuffed, and he wanted me to interrogate him. When I asked why he'd handcuffed the man, Amy said the stranger told William he had a message for me—and it was about my dead wife and kid.

My curiosity fully aroused, I said in a hurried voice, "Okay, I'll be there in a few minutes."

Chloe sensed something was amiss and gave an understanding

nod. "It's okay. I'll finish these up and keep them warm until you get home."

I kissed her and grabbed my pistol before heading out the door.

CHAPTER 35

Isabel Compton tossed back a lock of wet blonde hair and wiped sweat from her sticky forehead with a rag. "What if we destroyed the file?" she asked Reginald Hoffman, who only sighed and sank to a seat on a file box that was smashed and busted open on one end.

Reginald had come to her earlier in the day waving a newspaper article in the air like a madman and saying he knew how to solve the *Arrow Slayings* (as they had been dubbed by the media). While the picture Chief Clint Wolf showed them didn't ring any bells for Reginald, he figured his mom would recognize it, and he was right. He often complained about her saving every issue of every newspaper that ever had his picture or name in it, but he wasn't complaining that day. Isabel thought it was adorable how Mrs. Hoffman followed her son's career, and she loved the woman—well, not because she followed Reginald's career, but mostly because she brought fresh eggs and vegetables to the office on a regular basis. Come to think of it, Isabel couldn't remember the last time she'd eaten a store-bought egg, thanks to her.

As it turned out, the photographer from the newspaper hadn't been taking a picture of the jury in the background—he had been shooting Reginald. According to the article, Reginald was the defendant in a civil case where a suspect was claiming he used excessive force during an arrest. It had been a bench trial (meaning a judge heard the case, rather than a jury) and he had ruled in Reginald's favor. The article quoted Reginald as saying, quite simply, "The truth prevailed today."

After reading the article and scanning the entire newspaper, searching for any mention of the jurors in the background, Isabel had tossed the paper onto her desk and looked up at Reginald. "You won...good for you. Now, please explain how this helps us solve the arrow case?"

Reginald had stabbed the top of the paper with his index finger so hard Isabel thought he'd punch a hole through her desk. "We now know the date of the trial! All we have to do is find out what trial y'all were having on that date, and we'll find the jurors!"

Isabel had turned from Reginald and fired up her computer, accessing the ancient program that housed their files from twenty-one years earlier. It had taken her nearly an hour to peruse the records—with Reginald hovering over her, his foot tapping the floor in an annoying fashion—but she found an entry on January 23rd that made the blood in her veins slow to a trickle.

"Holy shit!" she'd said to herself, but loud enough for Reginald to hear it.

"What is it?" he'd asked.

She'd pointed to the file entry, which indicated Gregg Daniels had been found not guilty of simple rape after a six-day trial. The file entry was dated three days after the picture of Reginald had appeared in the paper.

Everything after that moment was a blur. Isabel vaguely remembered calling her husband to tell him she'd be late coming home, letting Bill Hedd know she was heading to the storage facility—that took twenty minutes because he had a hundred questions—and then holding on for dear life as Reginald raced to the facility.

Now, at least six hours later, she was starting to wonder if they'd ever find the file. She also wondered if she'd still be married when she got home, because she'd been too busy to answer her husband's earlier calls and it had to be nearing midnight. After wrestling with large boxes and digging a hole in the mountain of files, she and Reginald had finally located a dozen boxes from twenty-one years earlier. They had ripped them open and scoured every sheet of paper inside, but nothing they found had yet pertained to the first Gregg Daniels trial.

The storage facility was supposed to be climate-controlled, but it was smothering hot in their room. The only lights inside lined the hallways and it was hard to see in the deep shadows cast by the walls of boxes. This slowed their search considerably and she had resorted to using the flashlight feature on her cell phone—until an hour earlier, when the battery on her phone died. She didn't know if it was from using the light or from all of her husband's calls, but it was dead nonetheless. Reginald had begun using his phone, but the light was starting to grow dim.

"It's got to be here," Reginald said, rising slowly to his feet. Several slivers of paper slid from the box he'd been sitting on and he grunted, bending to pick them up.

Isabel started to turn back toward the mountain behind her when the flap of the box Reginald had been sitting on flipped to the side and she saw a name printed in black marker. "Reggie, that's it! The box you're sitting on! It's the Gregg Daniels file!"

She nearly knocked Reginald over as she rushed by him and dropped to her knees. She tore away the cover and coughed when a plume of dust rose up and engulfed her. The picking in her throat persisted and she sneezed several times, but that didn't deter her.

"Are you okay?" Reginald asked.

Isabel nodded and wiped away the tears, straining to read the small print on the file labels through the blur in her eyes. Reginald aimed his light in her direction and it helped. After a few minutes of searching, she finally found the file folder labeled *Prospective Jurors*. Her heart raced as she thumbed through the individual pages. There were lots of questionnaires—some filled out, some not—to go over, and a ton of notes by the prosecution team. Finally, her heart jumped to her throat when she found a diagram of the jury's seating arrangement and she saw Frank Rushing's name all the way to the left of the top row. She scanned the sheet and found Betty Ledet's name listed at the middle of the bottom row. Isaac Edwards was seated directly to her right on the chart. She made a note of the remaining eleven names, but didn't recognize anyone she knew. She held up the form with hands that shook. "This is the hit list," she said. "These people are going to die if we don't protect them."

Isabel and Reginald spent the next couple of hours comparing the juror questionnaires with the names on the seating diagram, digging out the questionnaires for each of the targeted jurors. The questionnaires contained addresses, telephone numbers, and other information that might prove helpful in locating the jurors. Isabel knew most of them had probably moved by then, but the addresses would at least help Chief Wolf verify that he was researching the right people.

When all of the questionnaires had been located, Isabel sat on a box and read the original police report. Early in the morning on March 8—twenty-two years earlier—Sandra Daniels called the sheriff's office and reported her estranged husband raped her. She told the deputies he was a cop, and she knew nothing would happen to him because it was her word against his. Since Daniels was a cop, Isabel knew he should've been easy to find, but it took the sheriff's detectives eight days to get him into custody. The trial started on January 17 of the following year and lasted into the weekend. It was on Sunday, January 23, that the jury finally found him not guilty. A newspaper clipping in the file quoted a juror as saying they found the former police officer more credible than the victim and the babysitter, who testified that she'd witnessed Gregg Daniels being verbally abusive to his wife on more than one occasion.

Isabel stared unseeing at the floor, lost in thought. She handed Reginald the case file. When he had finished reading it, he handed it back to her. "Why is he killing the jury that set him free?" he asked.

"That's exactly what I'm thinking," Isabel said. Suddenly, a thought occurred to her and she jumped to her feet, wincing when pain shot through her tired knees. She took a moment to rub them before saying, "What if he got it wrong? What if he's killing the wrong jury? He means to kill the second jury who convicted him, but he's mistakenly killing the first jury."

Reginald scratched his head. "How does he even know who they are? I've testified in dozens of cases and I can't remember any of the jurors—unless, of course, I knew them before the trial."

Isabel lifted the seating arrangement diagram and the questionnaires. "Defense attorneys get copies of these, too, you know, and the defendants are sitting right there with them, participating in their own defense. It would've been nothing for Daniels to swipe a copy and hold onto it for all these years."

Reginald was thoughtful. "Yeah, I see how he could've easily gotten them mixed up in that amount of time."

Isabel gathered up all of the paperwork. "You go home and get some rest. I'll bring these to the chief first thing in the morning."

Isabel and Reginald locked up the storage room and walked down the long hallway to the exterior door. When they opened it, Isabel gasped at the bright sunlight and involuntarily squeezed her eyes shut. "Damn it, Reggie, what time is it?"

Isabel could see Reginald look at his phone and shake his head. "I don't know. It's dead."

She sighed and made her way to his car. "Bring me to the office, so I can stop home and save my marriage before heading down to Mechant Loup."

"Do you want me to go with you?" Reginald asked.

Isabel shook her head. "We've spent enough time together for one night. Get home to your wife and salvage what's left of your marriage."

Reginald laughed. "My wife won't care that I've been out all night. She knows no one else wants me."

CHAPTER 36

William had the stranger on his knees with his back against the Charger when I arrived at Cig's Gas Station. I didn't run right over to where they were, but I sure wanted to. I held to a normal pace and when I reached them, glanced down at the rough-looking man. "What do we have here, William?"

"This piece of shit has been stalking the town looking for you," William said, holding the man's face up to the light so I could see it clearly.

I squatted next to the man and leaned close, not recognizing him. "Well, here I am. What do you want?"

"I've got a message for you, but you're going to have to work for it." The man sneered, thinking he was allowing the suspense to build. He was enjoying it a little too much and that irked me.

"I don't give a shit about your message," I said, refusing to give him the satisfaction. I stood and looked away as though I were bored, nodded to William. "Cut him loose and send him on his way. He hasn't broken any laws."

William stared blankly at me. "Just like that?"

I nodded. "Do it."

William paused, then jerked the man to his feet and spun him around. I could tell he didn't want to do it, but he finally removed the cuffs from the man and pointed toward his truck. "Get out of here before the chief changes his mind."

The man rubbed his wrists for a moment and then turned his beady eyes to me. It appeared he had come there to do a job, and he was going to do it. "I've got a message for you."

"I already told you I don't give a shit about your message," I said, but curiosity was killing me. It was all I could do to act casual.

The man nodded for a long moment, and then said, "Simon Parker sends his regards."

My blood ran cold at the sound of the name. Simon and his three brothers were responsible for killing Abigail and Michele. They were supposed to be locked up in La Mort awaiting trial for first degree murder. "That's impossible," I said coolly. "Simon's in jail."

The stranger laughed. It was a wicked laugh and his voice cracked, making it sound even eerier. "Yeah, well, I was in jail with him and he sends his regards." He shot a thumb toward the store. "I tried to deliver the message to you last year, but that bitch in there lied for you. Said some other joker was the chief of police."

"She didn't lie," I said. "She just didn't know."

"Well, Simon wants you to know he's getting out of jail soon and he'll be paying you a visit." The man spat a stream of tobacco juice in my direction. I followed it with my eyes and it landed near my boot. I looked back up at the man and there was a twinkle in his eye. "Simon said you're going to pay for killing his little brother," he continued. "And then he's—"

I moved quickly toward the man, and he stiffened up ever so slightly, as though expecting to get hit. "You tell Simon he'll never step foot outside of a prison again, but if he does, it'll be the worst day of his life and it'll be the best of mine."

Trying to regain his composure, the man slowly backed toward his truck, nodding his head as he did so. "I'll tell him," he said. "I'll tell him what you said."

"Tell him he's safe in jail, but out here"—I waved my left hand around—"his ass belongs to me, and I live for the day I can avenge my daughter and wife."

Without saying another word, the man turned and rushed to his truck and drove away. I stood staring after him for a long while, forgetting William was standing there until he cleared his throat and spoke. "Chief, are you okay?"

I shook my head to clear it and turned to him. "Yeah, I am—why?"

"You're holding your gun in your hand."

CHAPTER 37

Saturday, October 17

When I drove up to the police department in the morning, my eyes were bloodshot and I was tired. I didn't drink coffee much, but I felt like I needed at least a few cups. I'd made the mistake of trying the sleeping pills the doctor had given me, but they hadn't gotten rid of the nightmares—hadn't even made a dent in them. In fact, they were worse than ever and I couldn't help but wonder if it was because of the stranger's visit. At about midnight, I had made a mental note to call my friend in the city to find out the status of the case, and found myself chugging a half bottle of vodka—completely forgetting about the medication. The combination of alcohol and pills put me out like the dead, and I wasn't even close to waking up when the alarm went off in the morning. Chloe had nearly dragged me out of bed and forced food into my mouth, and I saw the look of concern on her face as I fumbled to get dressed and finally walked out the door. I kissed her to reassure her I was okay, but I felt off my game and woozy.

I barely noticed the car parked in front of the police department and I didn't give it much thought as I made my way into the station. Lindsey was at her desk and I started to ask why she was there on a weekend, but then remembered. Ethel used to be my weekend dispatcher, but she'd had a stroke at the desk one day and—although she'd recovered nicely—decided life was too short to spend it working. Lindsey agreed to work weekends until I could find a replacement, but after seeing the overtime pay on her check, she'd begged to keep the spot. I knew I needed to hire another dispatcher eventually, but it wasn't going to happen anytime soon.

Lindsey started to say something to me, but I just pushed by her and forged ahead, needing to sit before I fell asleep standing up and hurt myself. I nearly jumped out of my skin when something moved in the chair in front of my desk. It was Isabel Compton and she looked as bad as I felt. Her blonde hair was several shades darker than normal and it was stringy and plastered to her head. She wore a light-colored undershirt that had black smudges and streaks across it and her red skirt was rumpled and dirty. I wasn't sure, but it looked like there was blood oozing from a scratch on her left shoulder.

"Hey, Chief," she said. "Forgive my appearance, but I needed to see you first thing this morning."

"Is everything okay?" I asked, slowly taking my seat behind the desk. "I don't mean any offense, but you look like shit."

"Right back at 'cha." She smiled and her eyes twinkled, appreciating my candor. "It looks like we both had a rough night."

I suddenly remembered the grand jury hearing and leaned forward. "Is it about Susan? Is she in the clear?"

Isabel's face fell and she shook her head. "I'm sorry, but it's not about that." She handed me a yellow folder that had *Prospective Jurors* scribbled on the label.

As I opened it, she told me she and Reginald dug through their storage unit all night and had located the "kill list" that Gregg Daniels was operating off of, explaining he had been tried twice for raping his wife. He was found not guilty after the first trial, but he wasn't done with her. Unable to forgive her for reporting him, he attacked her the very next night and raped her again, this time beating her senseless and pressing a gun to her temple and threatening to kill her while he performed the heinous act. He was arrested a day later and ultimately convicted of aggravated rape.

"So, why is he out?" I wanted to know. "Why didn't he get life in prison?"

Isabel shrugged. "The judge set the sentence. There's a note in the file saying the DA's office pushed for life, but the judge thought twenty-five years was long enough."

"Tell that to the family of everyone he's killed since getting out," I mumbled, reading over the names of the jurors. Something didn't sit well with me and I brought it up to Isabel. "Why kill the people who set him free?"

"The best we can come up with is that he got the lists confused," Isabel explained. "He was privy to the same information we have and, if he kept a list of the jurors' names from both trials, it's reasonable to think he could've mixed them up after all these years."

I couldn't argue, as his DNA was on all the arrows. I thanked Isabel and walked her out to her car. She complained about the Louisiana heat when we got outside, and then begged me and my officers to be careful. I thanked her for the help and called Susan on her cell, asked her to return to the office. I stopped by Lindsey's desk and asked her to have Melvin, William, and Amy come to the office as soon as they could. She said she'd call them right away, and handed me a message from Sheriff Turner saying he couldn't find the files I'd asked about.

I then ran the names of the remaining jurors and printed out their current addresses. Four of them lived in Sheriff Buck Turner's jurisdiction, so I called him and asked if he could have some deputies go out to their houses and make sure they were safe. He agreed and took the information over the phone.

When I hung up with Turner, I spread the seven remaining questionnaires and address printouts on my desk, along with their driver's license pictures, and drummed my fingers. My eyelids felt heavy, but I forced myself to concentrate. Which one would he target next? I didn't have the manpower to station a guard at each of their homes, but if I knew who his next target would be, maybe we could be there to catch him and put an end to all of this.

As I pondered this, Susan and Melvin rushed through the door at the same time. Melvin was out of breath from exertion and Susan's face was flushed. "Lindsey said to get back here in a hurry," Susan began. "Something wrong?"

I went over the story I'd received from Isabel and pointed to the pictures. "We need to split up and reach out to these people as soon as possible."

"What do we tell them, Chief?" Melvin asked.

I explained that we needed to warn them they were potential targets of the *Arrow Slayer* and they needed to take every precaution to keep themselves safe. "If they own a gun, tell them to sleep, eat, and shit with it in their hand. If they have loved ones, tell them to do the same."

"What if they live alone and are unarmed?" Susan asked. "How do we keep them safe?"

I was thoughtful. "We don't have the resources to place an officer at each of their homes, but tell them they're welcome to stay here."

"Here? Where will they stay?" Melvin asked. "We can't fit seven people in this building."

"We'll get some cots," I answered, thinking on my feet. I began walking throughout the office—Susan and Melvin following silently behind me—inspecting every inch of the place. When I was satisfied, I returned to my office. "We can turn my office, the break room, and the interview room into sleeping quarters. We should be able to fit at least four cots in each room." I went on to explain how we would accommodate the potential victims and some members of their families, from feeding them to protecting them. "We'll take turns guarding this place. One of us has to be here twenty-four-seven and we can only leave one door accessible. Everything else has to be locked tight."

Melvin asked how we were supposed to guard the office while still handling complaints and trying to catch the killer.

"Maybe the sheriff can loan us some bodies." I studied the windows to my office. "We'll need to barricade all the windows in the office, and the jurors will have to stay inside until we catch Daniels. If they even peek outside he could get them."

"What if these people refuse to come with us?" Susan asked. "I mean, I wouldn't come live in a police station. I'd much rather stay home and take my chances—same as with hurricanes. I'd much rather take my chances at home than stay in a shelter with a bunch of strangers."

I shrugged. "We can't force these people to let us protect them, but we can certainly impress upon them how dangerous this Gregg Daniels is." I handed two of the packets to Susan, two to Melvin, kept two for myself, and dropped one on Lindsey's desk for William or Amy—in case one of them came out. Lindsey said they had left for home about an hour before I got to the station, so they were probably already sleeping. I told Lindsey not to let their phones ring too long. "If they answer right away and they both come out, tell them to reach me on the radio and I'll get them another packet."

Lindsey nodded her understanding, but her face was ashen. I knew she was scared. She loved reading crime novels, but she didn't like it when things got dangerous around the office. I put a hand on her shoulder. "It'll be okay, Lindsey. Trust me, we'll catch this guy, and everything will go back to normal."

She smiled, but I could tell she wasn't convinced.

Susan and Melvin had already bolted out the door and I followed suit, looking down at my paperwork to see which juror I'd selected for myself.

CHAPTER 38

Sergeant Susan Wilson sat in her police Charger studying the paperwork Chief Clint Wolf had given her. There were worry lines on her forehead, but it had nothing to do with the task at hand—or the possibility that she could be arrested for murder in a few days. No, the concern she felt was for Clint. His eyes were bloodshot that morning and he looked lethargic. She wondered if he'd had too much to drink the night before and if it would adversely affect his ability to concentrate on his job. Gregg Daniels was a brutal killer and definitely not someone to play with. She knew they all had to be at their very best if they were going to survive an encounter with him. Hell, even at their best there was still a good chance they wouldn't come out the other side in one piece. One-on-one, hand-to-hand, she wasn't worried about Daniels—or anyone, for that matter. *But how do I stop what I can't see?* The very thought made a shiver creep up her spine. She looked up and scanned her surroundings. She knew he could be out there right now, with an arrow aimed in her direction. Of course, she hadn't served on his jury and he shouldn't be mad at her. But—she glanced at the driver's license photo in her lap—Ava Harper had, and she needed Susan's protection.

Susan fired up the engine and left the police station, careful not to appear in a hurry. She smiled and waved at a reporter on the corner and yawned, trying to appear as casual as possible. Once she was out of sight, she picked up speed and raced toward Coconut Lane to check on Mrs. Harper. According to Harper's questionnaire from over twenty years ago, she had twin daughters who would be twenty-seven now, and she would be about fifty-two. Clint hadn't found a work history for her, so Susan hoped she'd be able to find the woman at home.

When Susan turned onto Coconut Lane, hers was the only car in sight. Most people were at work at that hour and the neighborhood looked like a ghost town. She slowed as she passed Mayor Dexter Boudreaux's house, wondering if he or his wife knew Mrs. Harper. Dexter's truck was gone and Susan didn't want to bother his wife when he wasn't home, so she continued toward the back of the street. She had almost reached the end when she found the address she was looking for printed on a large mailbox wrapped in brick. There was a car in the driveway, which was encouraging.

Mrs. Harper's house was modest and her yard immaculate. Susan caught a whiff of freshly-cut grass when she opened her car door and she noticed some grass clippings on the sidewalk extending from the driveway to the front porch. *Yep,* she thought, *my girl's home.*

When Susan reached the door she rang the doorbell and then—as was her habit—rapped on the frame in case the bell didn't work. It had been her experience that only a small fraction of all doorbells were actually operable, and she'd wasted lots of time early in her career waiting for people to respond to broken doorbells.

Susan waited for a minute, or two, and then repeated the ringing and knocking. As sweat formed on her forehead, she wondered when Autumn would arrive. She yearned for a change in the temperature and was ready to put this summer behind her. The thought brought back the memory of the impending grand jury decision. She started humming to block the thought from her mind and knocked on the door a little harder. No answer. She was about to turn away when she heard what sounded like a puppy screech at the back of the house.

"Mrs. Harper?" Susan called, making her way around the right side of the house. She listened closely, but didn't hear the sound again. She called out to the woman again as she rounded the front corner of the house and made her way along the side toward the back. That side of the house was wrapped in the shade of surrounding trees and was surprisingly cooler. As she made her way closer to the back of the house, where a cyclone fence separated the back yard from the rest of the property, she heard a strange gargling sound that propelled her forward. "Mrs. Harper?" she called again as she reached the fence. "Are you—?"

Her words were lost in her throat and it took a split second for her eyes to process what she was seeing. A lady—it had to be Ava Harper—was writhing on her back in the grass, her hands clutching a large arrow that protruded from her throat.

"Hang on, ma'am!" Susan sprang into action, jumping over the cyclone fence with the ease of a cat burglar while snatching the police radio from her belt. As she reported her location to Lindsey and requested an ambulance ASAP, she quickly covered the distance between herself and the woman and dropped to her knees. She placed the radio on the ground beside her and studied the injury, unsure of how she could help. The woman's eyes darted from side to side wildly, but the light was slowly fading from them. She tried to speak, but only air spilled from the bloody hole in her throat. "Don't talk, ma'am," Susan said. "Just hang on. Help is on the way."

A chill suddenly reverberated up and down Susan's spine as she realized the attack had just taken place. *The killer was still in the area!* Careful not to move her head, she turned only her eyes and scanned the area beyond the rear fence that enclosed the back yard. Her heart began beating against her sternum like a jackhammer when she saw the bush standing all alone about thirty feet from the cyclone fence. It looked oddly out of place. She sucked in her breath. *It's him!*

The killer moved ever so slightly. To the untrained eye, it could've simply been the wind rustling the leaves of a lone bush, but Susan knew the object was no bush and she knew he probably moved to draw back his bow. Sunlight glinting off of something shiny confirmed her fear—that was a three-blade mechanical broad-head...and it was most likely pointing directly at her, ready to rip through her flesh.

Susan thought quickly. Even if she was fast enough to get off a shot, she would have to do it while moving, because killing Gregg Daniels would release the arrow, and she had to get out of its path. Trying to move so slow that it would go undetected, Susan continued speaking to the victim while easing her right hand toward her pistol. When her hand was wrapped around the grip and her index finger poised near the release button, she stole another discreet glance in the killer's direction. He was still there, and so was the sparkle of light.

But then a sliver of doubt started to creep in. What if she took a shot and missed, hitting a nearby house and injuring or—worse—killing someone inside? That would surely give Bill Hedd all the ammunition he needed to lock her up. What if it wasn't the killer and she shot the wrong person?

Susan pushed the doubts from her head and readied herself. She took a few deep breaths, exhaling forcefully each time, and braced herself for what might come. This was it. Her whole life came down to this one moment. What she did next—and how well she did it—would determine if she lived or died. "God help me," she whispered, and exploded to her feet, simultaneously drawing her gun and whirling toward the threat. She was surprisingly calm. Everything around her seemed to slow down and her senses were heightened. The sound of her pistol dragging against the inside of the holster was loud in her ears. She felt the front of her chest move with each beat of her heart. She was very aware of the tickling of her skin as a single drop of sweat tumbled down her temple and all the way to her neck. The trigger felt hard against her index finger and she hoped she'd have enough strength to pull it. *Just a little higher,* she thought, as the front sight started to rise toward the bush. *I'm going to make it! I've got—*

There was a quick flash of sunlight against metal, but this time it was very close and approaching at an unnaturally rapid speed—much faster than her gun hand was moving. In a blinding instant, the object collided violently with the left side of her chest. Her breath was suddenly ripped from her lungs. The pain in her chest was excruciating and crushing. As a cage fighter, she'd been kicked in the chest by powerful fighters many times, but she'd never felt anything like this. Her head swam and her knees grew instantly weak as the impact of the arrow sent shockwaves throughout her torso. She clutched at her chest, gasping for air that wouldn't come. She couldn't hold herself up anymore and dropped to ground, her bottom hitting first with a violent thud, and then she rolled to her left shoulder. Her chest felt tight and the lack of oxygen was causing her vision to blur and her head to spin. *This is it,* she thought, *I'm done.*

Panic began to set in as she realized she was dying and she struggled to get some air into her lungs. It felt like an elephant was sitting on her chest, smothering her. She groaned and strained, but it was no use. She didn't have the strength to force the air to come. After a moment of feeble struggling, a deep peace slowly enveloped her entire being, and she stared unseeing at the bright sky. *To hell with your grand jury investigation, Bill Hedd,* she thought. *You'll never get me now.*

The pain was more than she could bear and her body shut down, her eyes rolling into the back of her head.

CHAPTER 39

I snatched my radio from my belt and called Lindsey. "Did I just hear Susan call for an ambulance?"

"Ten-four, Chief—there's been another attack."

I didn't need to ask where it had happened, because I knew exactly where she was—I had sent her. As I turned my Tahoe around and raced across town toward Coconut Lane, I began calling for her on my radio. When she didn't answer, I radioed Lindsey and asked if she'd heard back from Susan.

"Negative, Chief. Nothing."

Driving with one hand, I fished my phone out of my shirt pocket and called Susan's cell. It went straight to voicemail. Cursing, I picked up the radio again and called for Melvin Saltzman to see how close he was to Susan's location, but he was on the opposite side of town. I heard his sirens in the background when he keyed up his mic, so I knew he was barreling toward the scene. The radio came to life as Amy Cooke and William Tucker radioed that they were in service and heading to the scene.

I was flying blindly down the highway, my surroundings moving faster than my sleepy eyes could process, and I nearly collided with a car that pulled out in front of me. Luckily, there was no oncoming traffic and I was able to swerve around it and continue onward. I shook my head, gripped the steering wheel with both hands. I needed coffee and considered stopping for some before continuing to the scene. After all, Susan was there and she would control the scene until I arrived. M & P Grill was approaching to my right and I started to slow down. It would take but a second to run in and grab a cup of hot java. That's when I heard a message over the radio that chilled me to the core. I could tell it was William's voice, but I'd never heard him talk like that. His voice was a mixture or shock and pain, of panic and horror.

"Help! Help!" he screamed over the radio. "Susan's down! Oh, God, she's down! Get me a medic…I need an ambulance! Hurry up! She's dying!"

I was suddenly wide awake. My stomach churned and bile rose to my throat, burning like a swig of whiskey. Questions swirled through my mind. What had happened? How bad was she? My chest ached and I pulled at my collar with one hand as I tried to keep control of the Tahoe with the other. Coconut Lane loomed ahead and I smashed the brake pedal, swerved onto the street with no regard for my safety or my surroundings. I raced to the back of the street—hands trembling and head spinning—and jumped from the vehicle when I pulled to a stop behind William's Charger. My legs were weaker than I realized and I spilled forward, throwing my hands out to keep from biting the concrete. My palms burned and my right knee hurt, but I ignored the pain and sprinted around the house and toward the back yard, from where I could hear William screaming and wailing.

When the scene came into view, it was almost more than I could handle. William was on his knees cradling Susan's limp head against his chest. He was crying and rocking back and forth, blood on his face and arms. I started to yell at him to start CPR, but I crashed into a four-foot cyclone fence and flipped over it, landing on my head on the other side. I scrambled to my hands and knees, scurrying forward until I was beside William.

I grabbed at his arms and pulled him away, just as Amy ran up from the opposite side of the house. She helped me pull William away and then she yelled right in his face, telling him to get his shit together.

"She's not wearing her vest!" William yelled back at Amy. "We need an ambulance ASAP! She's going to die if we don't get help here now!"

Amy turned away from William and helped me position Susan flat on her back. Blood covered the front of her uniform shirt and a red arrow was resting across her torso. Her holster was empty and, as we were moving her body, I'd caught a glimpse of her pistol in the grass a few feet from her body.

Trying to keep my own shit together, I pushed my index and middle fingers to Susan's throat, searching for a pulse. There was none. Amy had dropped an ear to Susan's mouth and came up shaking her head. "She's not breathing!"

I figured we'd have to stop the bleeding while also giving her CPR, so I ripped open the front of her uniform shirt to expose the wound. I felt something hard and twisted as I did so, and realized her cell phone was in her shirt pocket and had taken the full force of the arrow's energy. While the phone hadn't stopped the arrow completely, it slowed it enough to keep it from penetrating her chest too deeply, but I knew it didn't take much to reach the heart.

William had settled down a bit and shoved a white T-shirt over my shoulder. I took it and pressed it against Susan's upper left chest, motioning for William to go around to the other side and hold the shirt in place while Amy and I performed CPR. I don't know how long we worked together, fighting to keep Susan alive, but it seemed like days. My arms ached, but I wouldn't let them stop. I felt like crying, but I bit back the tears and focused on the task at hand. I wanted to kill Gregg Daniels, but I didn't know where to find him.

Finally, sirens blew loud at the front of the house and several volunteer firemen rushed to our sides and took over. One of them yelled that Susan was in cardiac arrest and called for a defibrillator. I stood weakly to my feet and looked around. I was at a loss, not really knowing what to do next. I felt helpless. I glanced to my right and saw William standing there crying, staring down at Susan's lifeless body. He didn't even try to push away the rivulets of tears that flowed down his red face. Although Susan was young, she was mature beyond her years and was like a mother figure to William and Melvin. I walked up to William and took him in my arms and hugged him, telling him she would be okay, that she couldn't die. Although I was saying it to him, I was saying it more for me.

As I held William, I saw Melvin and two medics run around the house. Melvin's face was pale and he came straight to where William and I stood.

"Chief, is Susan going to be okay?" Melvin asked, his eyes flooding with tears.

I let William go and wiped a tear that had escaped from one of my own eyes. "Pray for her, Melvin. Pray like you've never prayed before."

We all stood in a semi-circle around the medics—William in street clothes and covered in Susan's blood, Amy also in street clothes and a shotgun cradled in her arms, Melvin with his hands on his head, and me just standing there lost—and watched as they administered a shock from the defibrillator. There was a moment of silent hope, as they waited and then checked her vitals again. One of the medics shook his head and they began preparing to shock her again. I was praying out loud, not caring who heard it. I begged God to spare her life and take mine. It was more than Melvin could take and he turned and sank to his knees, face buried in his hands, bawling hysterically. I stepped closer to him and put a hand on his shoulder, watching Susan's face intently. There was no movement whatsoever. Not a twitch of a muscle, not a flutter of an eyelid. She was graveyard still and deathly pale.

CHAPTER 40

When Susan didn't respond to the next shock, one of the medics hollered, "We've got to get her to the hospital *now*!" He emphasized the last word and they all sprang into action.

My officers and I backed away and gave them the space to do their job. None of us said a word until they were long gone and their sirens were a distant murmur in the air. Amy was the one who broke the silence. "We need to find this asshole and stop him. We need to avenge Susan."

I nodded and turned my attention to the dead woman. She had been shot in the throat and was lying on her back staring unseeing at the blazing sun. The scene had to be processed, the autopsy attended, next of kin notified; none of which I felt like doing at the moment. My only thought was going to the hospital to be with Susan. I wanted to be by her—

"Chief, is it okay to come back here?" boomed a familiar voice.

I looked up to see Sheriff Buck Turner standing at the back corner of the house. Detectives Doug Cagle and Mallory Tuttle were flanking him. I wiped my eyes in case any more tears had pushed through and strode across the yard to greet them. I extended my hand, but the large man wrapped me in a bear hug. He apologized for what we'd gone through and said he was there to offer his assistance. When he let me go, I looked over his shoulder and saw six SWAT officers piling out of a tactical van. They set up at strategic points around the house and stood guard while we talked.

"You've been through a lot, Chief," Sheriff Turner said. "And I know you'd rather be with your officer." He shot a thumb at Doug and Mallory. "They're my best detectives. If you want, they can process the scene for you and report their findings when you're ready. I've got a SWAT unit here to protect the scene and another on stand-by. Say the word and I'll send them to the homes of the remaining targets on that kill list, and they'll stay there until you tell them it's okay to leave."

Relief flooded over me. I accepted Sheriff Turner's offer and filled him in on what we knew. There was deep concern on Mallory's face as she listened. "Will she make it?" was all she asked.

I bit down hard and couldn't answer. I just frowned and shook my head, unsure myself of the outcome. I took a breath and thanked Sheriff Turner again before turning away and waving for Melvin, William, and Amy to follow me to our cars. With lights flashing and sirens blaring, we raced down Coconut Lane and turned north on Main Street, heading to the hospital as fast as our cars could travel.

I fumbled with my phone and called Chloe on the way to the hospital. She answered on the first ring and she was crying. "Oh, God, I'm so sorry about what happened!"

My eyes blurred and I blinked to clear them. "Look, I'll be texting you a picture of a guy named Gregg Daniels. I need you to report that he's the prime suspect in the Arrow Slayings and he's wanted for the attempted murder of a police officer. I need it going to every news outlet in the area."

Chloe was sniffling in the background, but I could tell she was focused. "Gregg Daniels...got it. Anything else?"

I thought for a moment and then nodded. "Yeah, put the word out that I'm offering twenty thousand dollars for anyone who provides information leading to the arrest of Gregg Daniels."

"Twenty *thousand* dollars?" Chloe asked incredulously.

"Should I offer more?" I asked.

"That's quite a bit of money. It should do the trick!"

"Can you do it?"

She said she would. I thanked her and hung up, because I was approaching the hospital. I parked along the sidewalk near the building and my officers filed in behind me. William had tried to wipe the blood off of his face and arms, but it only smeared across his skin. He looked like something out of a horror movie. "Get a nurse to help clean you off when you get inside," I said.

He nodded and we all made our way to the emergency room, not saying anything more and fearing the worst. I wanted to stay outside, because I knew once we entered the hospital and got the news, there would be no going back. It would be final.

We were still a few feet from the automatic doors when they slid open and a gust of cold air blew out to meet us. It was dimmer in the lobby and I had to squint to see better inside.

"Chief! I came as soon as I heard." It was Mayor Boudreaux, and his wife was with him, clinging to his good arm.

We all gathered around him. "Any word?" I asked.

He frowned and shook his head. "They're working on her. She was unresponsive when they brought her in. I'm so sorry for all of y'all. I know how close y'all are."

I thanked him and looked around. The hospital was quiet and the waiting room across the hall was empty. I pointed to it. "I guess we should wait in there."

A nurse left her station and approached William. "Are you injured?" she asked.

William just shook his head, and the nurse waved for him to follow her. "Let's get you cleaned up," she said.

When they walked away, Melvin and Amy followed me into the waiting room. Mayor Boudreaux and his wife were already sitting in a corner and it looked like they were praying. I sank to a chair and just stared across the room. Melvin paced back and forth at the far side of the room and Amy took the seat next to me. Time seemed to stand still. With each second that passed, any sliver of hope I had began to slip away.

We'd been sitting there for at least thirty minutes when the door to the waiting room opened. Amy and I jumped out of our seats and Melvin spun toward the door, but it was only William. I sank back into my seat and buried my face in my hands. I didn't know how much more I could take. My chest ached and I felt like vomiting. My breath was coming in short gasps and it felt like I couldn't take a deep breath, no matter what I tried to do. I was sitting straight up trying to catch that elusive deep breath when the door opened again and a doctor walked in. I studied his face, but he was a poker player. He'd obviously had to do this before and he waited until we were all gathered around him.

"So, when the arrow struck Sergeant Wilson in the chest," he began in a measured tone, "it disrupted the heart's rhythm and it caused cardiac arrest. It's what we call commotio cordis and it's more often than not lethal." He paused and took a deep breath, very aware we hung on his every word. "But in this case, we were able to revive her…"

I gasped and exhaled forcefully, only then realizing I'd been holding my breath. The relief was so powerful I couldn't stop the tears of joy from flowing down my face. Melvin screamed and jumped up and down, pumping his fist in the air in jubilation. William and Amy threw their arms around me and we all nearly fell as we rejoiced together. I caught sight of Mayor Boudreaux and his wife standing several feet away, and their eyes were also filled with tears.

CHAPTER 41

Monday, October 19

It was almost ten and I was standing near Lindsey's desk waiting for Susan to walk through the door. She had been released from the hospital early yesterday morning with orders to see a cardiologist first thing this morning. She had grumbled, but agreed to do what she had to do to ensure her healthy return to work—and the cage. Her first question to the doctor had been, "Will I still be able to get kicked and punched?"

With a straight face, the doctor had replied flatly, "No...not with that giant hole in your chest."

The hole hadn't been "giant" to start with, and the doctors had done a great job sewing it up. I knew firsthand they'd done a great job, because Susan had pulled open the top of her shirt to show me when I was finally able to visit her in the hospital. A little embarrassed, and nagged by guilt, I'd found myself staring at the exposed upper half of Susan's amble breasts, barely noticing the injury.

"How am I supposed to find a husband with this nasty scar on my boobs?" she'd asked, sounding as though the pain meds were having an effect on her.

I had forced myself to look away and commented how she was lucky she kept her cell phone in her shirt pocket.

"The doctor said it saved my life."

"I'm so happy it did," I said, "but can you promise to start wearing your ballistic vest all the time—not just some of the time?"

"Yes, mother," was all she'd said as she fumbled with the buttons on her shirt.

While Susan was recovering from the arrow attack, the rest of us were working around the clock trying to find the green Thunderbird and Gregg Daniels. Sheriff Turner had been extremely supportive, offering me whatever resources I needed. While my officers and I combed the town for the killer, he had his men combing the rest of the parish. So far, we hadn't found even a hint of his existence and the warden from the state pen hadn't responded to our faxed request yet.

Melvin walked out of the bathroom and shot his thumb toward the door. "She didn't get here yet?"

I shook my head. "I guess the doctor visit's taking longer than expected." I knew she had to undergo a battery of tests to ensure there had been no permanent damage to her heart, and I didn't care how long it took. I still hadn't shaken the feeling of almost losing her and I wanted to be sure she was healthy.

We had waited about another ten minutes when we heard footsteps on the wooden porch in front of the building. We were expecting her to come in through the sally port, but I figured her mom might not have felt comfortable doing so, and Melvin and I raced for the door. We fought to open it, but stopped dead when we saw Jerome Carter and Neal Barlow standing there with shit-eating grins on their faces. Their smiles faded and they backed off a bit, staring from me to Melvin, as though they weren't sure what was going to happen next.

"Oh, it's not Susan," I said, studying the two young men. "What are y'all doing here?"

J-Rock stuck his chin out and smiled. "We're here to collect the reward money."

"Reward money?" I asked.

Neal held up a newspaper article announcing the reward for Gregg Daniels' arrest. I smiled inwardly. One thing was certain—when Chloe wanted a story to go wide, it went wide. I was positive everyone in Louisiana and the three surrounding states knew the name Gregg Daniels. I touched the picture of Daniels. "Y'all know where I can find this guy?"

They both nodded.

I searched their eyes for even a hint of deceit or folly, but they were serious. "If y'all can tell me where to find him, y'all get to split twenty grand."

Both men's eyes widened and their faces broke into grins. "We know exactly where this Gregg fellow stays," J-Rock said. "We delivered some grass to him and his brothers the day he got out of jail. They said they were celebrating his release and even asked if we'd come back with some—"

Neal punched J-Rock's shoulder. "Man, shut up!"

J-Rock's eyes widened and he apologized. "I guess I shouldn't have said that."

I waved him off and told him I only cared about catching Daniels. I then ushered them to the interview room and Melvin and I sat across the desk from them. "Okay, this is show time," I began. "Tell us what y'all know and where we can find him."

Neal Barlow cleared his throat and nodded. "He's holed up in North Camp east of town in Bill's Settlement—and his two brothers are with him."

"North Camp in Bill's Settlement? Where the hell is that?" I asked.

"I know where it is," Melvin said. "I'll show you."

We talked to the young men a little longer and then I told them they could go.

"But what about the money?" J-Rock asked.

"When he's captured, you'll get your money," I assured him. They started to stand, but I stopped them. "And if I find out y'all spent that money on drugs, I'll track y'all down and kick both your asses!"

"Oh, no," J-Rock said. "This is our big break. We're going straight from now on."

Melvin walked them out and I sat there staring at the wall, thinking. When Melvin came back in the room, he sat on the corner of the desk. "What're you thinking?" he asked.

"There are three of them and two of us. We need better odds." If Susan were well enough to fight, we could've taken on six of them, but I knew we were at a disadvantage.

"I can call William and Amy out," Melvin offered.

I nodded and told him I had to head to my house for a minute. "Make sure you tell them to suit up and bring as much firepower as they have. We need to be ready for anything."

I hurried to my Tahoe and raced out of the sally port—tires screeching and the smell of burnt rubber filling the air—and headed home. Two of the news vans filed in behind me and tried to keep pace with me, but slowed down when I flicked my emergency lights on.

Once I got home, I hurried to the bedroom closet where my gun safe was hidden. Achilles tried to keep up with me, but his paws slipped on the floor and he slid headlong into the doorframe just outside my room. "Easy big man," I called out, my hand dialing the combination on my safe at lightning speed. When I swung the heavy steel door open, I reached past a half dozen rifles and grabbed the Colt AR-15 at the back of the safe. I shoved three fully-loaded, thirty-round magazines into my back pockets and slung the semi-automatic rifle over my shoulder. I then grabbed my Accuracy International sniper rifle and a box of bullets. I scanned the interior of the safe to make sure I didn't need anything else, shut the door, and spun the dial.

As fast as I'd gotten home, I was gone, breaking every traffic law on the books en route back to the office. My mind flashed back to my days on the city's SWAT team. It seemed like a lifetime ago. I couldn't count the number of times I'd been wrenched from a dead sleep to leave the warmth of my bed and rush out into God-knew-what type of situation. I had always taken the time to kiss Michele and Abigail and tell them goodbye before stepping out the door. On those types of callouts, I never knew if I'd return home alive and I didn't want them wishing they'd been able to tell me goodbye. I then remembered how I felt when Susan was lying there unresponsive, and I reflected on the ruthlessness of Gregg Daniels. *Clint, old boy, this could be your last day on Earth. You might finally get to meet up with Michele and Abigail.*

Surprisingly, I felt a tinge of regret—was nervous, even. I frowned as I suddenly realized I wasn't ready to die. There were things I wanted to do with my life now. I wanted to get to know Chloe much better and I was excited to see what would become of us. And I was fond of my job and cared about my employees. If I were gone, who would take care of them? I also felt that Michele and Abigail were looking down on me, and I wanted to make them proud.

As I steered through traffic with my left hand— lights flashing and siren blaring—I dialed Chloe's number with my right hand. I wanted her to hear my voice before I went after Gregg Daniels and I wanted to hear hers. Daniels had already displayed a willingness to kill a cop, so there was no telling how this would turn out.

Chloe answered on the fourth ring. "What's all the noise in the background? Is your siren on?"

"Yeah, I'm heading to a callout and I just wanted to talk for a second."

Chloe was silent for a moment. When she spoke, her voice was troubled. "Is...is it a dangerous callout? Does it have to do with what happened to Susan?"

"Dangerous for the person I'm chasing," I said, laughing to reassure her, but I didn't think she was buying it. "Yeah, we got a tip on Gregg Daniels, thanks to your work. It won't be dangerous, though. I've got plenty of backup and we're going to take him down so fast he won't know what hit him."

"It seems odd that you're calling before heading out like that. You sound different. This scares me." Chloe was quiet for a few seconds, then said, "It reminds me of the stories I've heard of people who call their loved ones when they know they're about to die."

"No, it's really nothing. I just wanted to touch base with you in case I get tied up for a while—like all night."

"Oh, okay." She was silent for another long moment and then said, "Please be careful."

I promised I would and hung up. The police department rolled into view and I massaged the brake pedal.

CHAPTER 42

I pulled into the crowded sally port and rushed inside, where Amy, Melvin, and William were suiting up. Amy was stretching the straps of her bulletproof vest into place, while Melvin and William shoved twelve-gauge shells into the tubes of their Benelli pump-action shotguns. Lindsey sat on her desk looking worried.

I grabbed a vest from the tactical closet in the hallway and pulled it over my shirt, adjusting the straps until the vest wrapped around my torso like a body cast. "Did Susan stop by?"

"Yeah, but she didn't stay long," Lindsey said. "She was feeling weak and tired, so her mom took her home."

It was hard for me to imagine Susan feeling weak and tired. Lindsey, on the other hand, looked like she was about to faint. She was hugging herself and shivering. "You okay?" I asked.

"I'm just a little freaked out, Chief." She shook her head. "I've never seen anything like this. I...I never thought something like this could happen here. And I'm worried that one of y'all will...will..." She lowered her head and I thought I detected a tear rolling down her cheek.

"It'll be okay," I promised. "I've done this a thousand times."

I felt the collective head-spinning of William, Amy, and Melvin in my direction.

"Are you talking about last year or before?" William asked. "When you worked in the city?"

"Something like that," was all I said.

"Like what?" he asked.

I walked over to him and readjusted the strap on his vest, closing up a gap under his armpit. "You don't want an arrow sneaking into that spot."

"What do we do?" Melvin rubbed his face with a hand that shook slightly. "I mean, once we get there...what do we do?"

"First off, just relax. It's okay to be scared. That's normal. Courage is not the lack of fear, but being able to function beyond your fear."

"I won't lie," Amy said. "I'm scared shitless—and I have been plenty of times on this job—but I don't run from it. I try to embrace it and use it to my advantage."

"Amy's right. Don't fight the nervousness or the fear. Accept it and feel it coursing through your body. Let it flow. If you try to stifle it, you'll only feel more anxious and distracted and you could make a mistake." I walked to my office and they followed. I removed the town map from where it was pinned on my wall and laid it on my desk. "Melvin, show me where this camp is located."

Melvin traced his finger along Bayou Tail showing how the waterway flowed along the northern end of town, and then cut back across the northeast corner of town and continued south. Seeing it on a map gave me a better perspective and I realized Bayou Tail rested on top of the town like a giant upside-down horseshoe.

"You see this northeast corner of town?" Melvin asked.

I nodded.

"Bayou Tail cuts it off from the rest of us except for this tiny pontoon bridge." He pointed to the bridge. "These people act like they're in their own world. When we have curfews for hurricanes or other natural disasters, they ignore the order and roam the streets. They think the law doesn't apply to them."

"Will we have to worry about them while we're trying to apprehend Daniels?" I asked.

"We shouldn't," Melvin said. "They usually just gather around and watch when we have to handle stuff back there."

Melvin pointed to the road that paralleled Bayou Tail to the East. "This road is called East Bayou Lane and it ends to the north right here." He stabbed at the map where the road ended, and then slid his finger to the right. "And that's where North Camp is located. It's an old hunting camp that's been abandoned for years. It doesn't have a legal address, so that's probably why nothing showed up on our computers."

William, who had walked around my desk and was seated in front of my computer, called us over. "Look, I pulled up the old camp on the satellite map. You can see it clear as day."

I stepped behind him and looked over his shoulder. The camp

was centered on a small patch of land that was surrounded on all sides by trees. A small dirt path cut through the trees at the very end of East Bayou Lane and served as the driveway. There was a narrow canal that flowed off of Bayou Tail to the south of the camp. I pointed to the part of East Bayou Lane that flowed over the canal. "Is this a bridge?"

Melvin nodded. "It's a stationary bridge. It doesn't open or anything."

"There's no way we get a car across that bridge without the Daniels brothers hearing us." I examined the area south of the canal. It was also covered in trees. "Do y'all think the canal is small enough to jump over or shallow enough to wade across?"

Melvin shook his head. "We'd need a boat of some type—a pirogue or canoe would do. I can get my truck and throw my pirogue in the back of it."

"William, follow Melvin. When y'all get his pirogue, meet Amy and me by this old barn." I tapped a barn-looking building one street over from the canal. There was a large shell parking lot in front of it and a row of houses north of it that would conceal our vehicles.

CHAPTER 43

I parked the Tahoe in front of the old barn and Amy and I dismounted quietly. Amy walked around and met me on the driver's side of the SUV, waiting while I grabbed my gear. I handed her my sniper rifle. "You ever shot a scoped rifle before?"

She nodded. "I killed my first deer when I was twelve."

"You murdered Bambi?"

"And ate him."

"Very well. It's got a hair trigger, so be soft with it." I slung my AR-15 over my shoulder and pushed my door until it clicked shut. I turned the volume on my police radio down and Amy did the same. I looked at her, nodded. We crossed the street and ducked between two trailers, eased to the far end, and crouched, scanning the tree line ahead of us.

"The canal is directly on the other side of those trees," Amy whispered. "Once we make it across that clearing we'll be home—"

"Hey, what the hell are y'all doing next to my house?" called a raspy voice.

I spun and saw a grotesque hairy belly coming toward us. Above the belly, there was a saturated shirt that was too short and probably three sizes too small for the figure it clothed. When the man who owned the belly saw my rifle, he stumbled back, stammered. "I...I...didn't...I didn't mean anything by it. Carry on. I didn't see anything."

"Sorry we startled you." I pointed to the badge on my chest. "We received word that a murder suspect is possibly holed up in that camp."

The man grunted, his belly jiggling with the movement. "That explains it, then."

"Explains what?" I asked.

"The wife swore she heard some gunshots the other night. Woke me up and tried to make me go see what was going on. I told her it was hunters, but she says it didn't sound like no normal hunting guns." He scratched a patch of stubble on his chin. "Glad I didn't get myself up and go look."

"What day was it?" I asked.

"Um…" The man's face contorted in thought. "I don't remember the day, but I'd say it was between two o'clock and two-thirty in the morning."

Just then, Melvin and William appeared behind the man and they were carrying a pirogue. The man moved aside to let them pass, asked, "Is it dangerous to be out here right now?"

"Deadly dangerous," Amy said, hoisting the sniper rifle in her hands.

The man gulped and stumbled backward, then turned and hurried up the shaky and cracked concrete steps that led to his back door.

"Amy, drop prone and cover us with the rifle," I said. "When we make it to the canal, we'll cover your approach."

Amy responded by dropping to her belly. She flipped the scope caps up and the bipod down as though she'd done it before, and pulled the rifle into the pocket of her shoulder. After staring through the scope for about a minute, she gave the *thumbs up*. "I've got an eye on the back of the house." Her voice was muffled from her cheek being smashed up against the stock weld. "No signs of life."

I turned to Melvin and William. "Stay directly behind me. If something happens, drop the pirogue and get back to Amy as quickly as y'all can."

"What about you?" Melvin wanted to know.

"I'll cover your backside." Without waiting for him to protest, I crouched low and shuffled across the ankle high grass of the open field. The sun was relentless. Sweat poured into my eyes, making it difficult to penetrate the dark depths of the trees that lay about fifty yards ahead of me. I blinked the moisture away, held my rifle at the ready as I cleared the distance in rapid fashion. When I reached the first tree, I squatted beside it and listened. The only sound I heard was Melvin and William's boots brushing the ground as they carried the wooden pirogue to where I waited. I studied every bush in the area, but they all looked real.

Melvin touched my shoulder, his breath labored. "We're here. What next?"

I turned and waved for Amy to join us. She scrambled to her feet and cleared the distance in seconds. When we were all together, we moved to the edge of the canal and spread out, leaving the pirogue on land.

"Let's watch for a while," I whispered to Amy, who was several feet to my right. She passed the message on to Melvin who passed it to William. The camp was situated with the front facing the driveway and the back facing us. There was no sign of movement from inside or the surrounding property; no noise whatsoever. Not a peep. I began to wonder if something was amiss. *What if this is a trap? Or a ploy to get us away from the station?* I suddenly felt a chill reverberate up and down my spine. We were here on the word of J-Rock and Neal Barlow—two criminals.

I silently cursed myself for not thinking this over better. If someone did want to attack the station, this would be the perfect time. Trap or not, I needed to get in that house and find out if they were really there. I studied the canal. It was wider than it had looked on the map and I wondered how much noise we would make getting the pirogue into the water.

I sidled over to where Melvin squatted. "Can we get the pirogue in the water without making much noise?"

He nodded, waved for William to help. They lifted the wooden boat from the ground and eased it into the water. Save for a tiny ripple and a rub here and there, they didn't make a sound. I handed Melvin my rifle. "Y'all cover me."

Melvin shook his head, handed the rifle to William. "I'm coming with you."

I didn't have time to argue, so I only nodded. Holding on to a low-lying tree branch, I put one foot in the pirogue and eased my weight onto it. The boat sank precariously low when I placed my other foot inside and let go of the branch, but it held me. Holding my arms out for balance, I took a series of tiny steps forward until I was at the front, and then slid to my knees.

The pirogue rocked violently when Melvin added his weight and water splashed over the sides. I sucked air, gripped the sides, but the rocking didn't last long. Once it had leveled out, William gave us a shove and the pirogue glided across the canal. When we neared the opposite bank, Melvin dipped a paddle into the water and slowed our approach. The front of the pirogue stabbed the soft mud and we lurched forward when it stopped abruptly.

Melvin shoved the paddle deep into the muddy bottom of the canal, whispered, "Chief, I'll hold it in place so you can get out."

I nodded and tight-roped it to the front tip of the pirogue and took a careful step onto the ground, and then another. I turned and held onto the pirogue so Melvin could make his exit. I glanced over my shoulder toward the house as we pulled the pirogue onto land, but all was deathly quiet.

Careful not to step on small twigs or dry leaves, we crept through the patch of trees until we reached the edge of the clearing. I took up a position behind a young oak tree and drew my pistol. I heard Melvin do the same.

I leaned to my right and studied the house. There were no windows at the back of the camp, just two entrances—both of them outfitted with screen doors. Five square posts supported an overhang that jutted from the structure. Beneath the overhang was a dried patch of dirt littered with tall weeds. The faded green paint was chipped something awful.

Melvin's arm appeared next to my face, pointing. "Look!" he hissed. "It's the green Thunderbird!"

My heart raced. This was really it. "Okay, we know he's here." I pointed. "We're going to sneak to the back of the house and have a look around. You keep your gun trained on the door to the left and I'll keep mine on the door to the right. If anything moves, shoot it."

"But, what if—"

"Don't hesitate and don't think about it. If something—anything—moves in that doorway, you light its ass up…you hear?"

Melvin nodded—eyes wide and beads of sweat pouring freely down his face. "Got it."

CHAPTER 44

Before we left the safety of the tree, I waved my hand back toward Amy and William. Although it was difficult to see them hidden behind the trees, I made out Amy's hand waving back to let me know she was covering us. Adrenalin coursed like acid through my veins. My thoughts went to Michele, Abigail, and Chloe. When this was over, I'd be seeing either Michele and Abigail or Chloe—of this much I was certain. I took a deep breath before entering the emptiness between the tree line and the house. We would be vulnerable out in the open, but it was the only way to get to the house. "Melvin, stay directly behind me."

I inched out of the shade and into the direct sunlight, paused. Both eyes were open wide to take in the entire area, but they were focused primarily on the door to the right and secondarily on the front sight of my pistol. If shooting broke out, that would change and my primary focus would be on the front sight.

There was no noise or movement in response to revealing myself, so I took another cautious step forward...and then another...and another. The sun's fiery rays beat down on my exposed skin. An occasional fly buzzed by my ear and I flinched each time, expecting to be impaled by a red arrow. Sweat ran down the center of my back, beneath the restricting body armor. But I pushed forward, moving steadily until I reached the shade of the overhang. I stopped, crouched near one of the square posts, listening. Nothing...not a sound.

Melvin had taken a position to my left near one of the other posts. He waved his hand to let me know he was ready. I dropped prone and low-crawled toward the door near Melvin. Patches of tall weeds rubbed against my face and arms, causing them to itch. I resisted the urge to scratch.

When I got close to the door, I rolled onto my back and sidled up against the house. I glanced at Melvin and made a motion to let him know I was about to open the door. He nodded, took up an aggressive kneeling position, and aimed his pistol at the doorway.

Holding my breath, I reached up with my left hand and slowly pulled on the screen door. My pistol was poised in my right hand, ready to destroy anything that moved. The hinges squeaked. I froze, listened. I could hear nothing over the sound of my heartbeat. I shifted my eyes to Melvin. He gave the *thumbs up*. I continued to pull the door open an inch at a time—pausing after each inch to listen—until it was wide enough for me to fit through.

I motioned with my head for Melvin to move forward. He scooted across the ground on his knees and left hand, keeping his pistol pointed at the door with his right hand. When he reached me, he shoved his left boot against the screen door to hold it in place.

I slowly released my grip on the screen door and rolled to my hands and knees. I pointed, whispered, "I'm going inside. Stay out here and don't come inside until I call you."

Melvin's gun hand trembled. He nodded, swallowing hard.

I rose to a crouch and crept up the shallow steps. The doorway was a dangerous place to be, so I didn't stay there long. I slammed my shoulder into the flimsy wooden door and it flung open. I darted into the room as quietly as I could, hugging the wall. I found myself in a kitchen that opened to a living room. I paused, listening to see if the noise had attracted any attention. Nothing.

I moved forward until I reached the wall to the left and then continued along a bank of cabinets, scanning the area as I walked. There was no sign of life, but at least two window units were buzzing steadily, pushing ice-cold air into the small structure.

When I reached the wall at the end of the cabinets, I moved to the right along it until I came to the living room opening. I squatted there, peeked around the wall. I could see a lounge chair and the back of a sofa. There was a door to the right in the living room, but it was closed. I planted my right foot out to maintain my balance, quickly peeked around the wall, and to the left, jerked my head back. There was nothing but a dark hallway. I stuck my head out slower the second time and peered down the hall. A closed door at the end looked to be a closet, two closed doors on the opposite side of the wall were probably bedrooms, and the only door on my side of the wall was open. I craned my neck to see better and realized it was a bathroom.

I heard a noise behind me and looked to see Melvin following the same path I had taken. When he reached me, he plopped down on his knees, panting. "I'm sorry, but I couldn't let you do this alone." He shuddered. "It's freezing in here."

I nodded, pointed down the hall on the left. "Cover that area while I check the room to the right."

Melvin gripped his revolver with both hands and aimed it down the hallway. I turned toward the closed door on the right side of the living room and took my time getting to it, rolling my feet from heel-to-toe, slowly transferring my weight so as not to cause the floor to creak. Once I reached the door, I glanced over my shoulder at Melvin. He was focused like a laser beam on the hallway.

Redirecting my attention to the room and making sure I wasn't standing directly in front of the door, I took the knob in my left hand and turned it softly. It moved without making a sound. I continued turning until I met with resistance and paused, my trigger finger tense. I counted to myself. When I reached *three*, I pushed the door open and dropped to my knee. I started to sweep the room with my pistol when a pungent odor stopped me in my tracks. I resisted the urge to gag, immediately recognized the smell.

I inched upward and the figure on top of the bed came into view a little at a time. It was hard to distinguish his facial features in the dim light. I surveyed the floor before I stepped closer, but didn't locate any evidence. I lowered my gun.

When I reached the side of the bed, I leaned over and examined him closer, checked for rigor. It was present. Dried blood was painted in streaks over his plump face and an arrow was buried deep in his head. I fished out my phone and activated the light on it. It was Farrell Daniels and he'd been shot at close range. *Poor bastard didn't know what hit him,* I said to myself. *He still thinks he's sleeping.*

I quickly examined the rest of the room, wondering why Gregg Daniels would kill his own brother. Maybe he was afraid Farrell would turn him in?

My pistol poised in my hand, I made my way back to Melvin, who looked up with a curious expression on his face. I eased past him and indicated with my head that I was about to enter the next room. He re-gripped his pistol and nodded his understanding. Moving to the first door down the hall, I turned the knob and gently pushed it open, ready for anything. A putrid odor floated on the cold air and greeted us like a bad mother-in-law.

Melvin scrunched his face, whispered, "Is that smell what I think it is?"

I nodded and entered the room, finding another man dead inside. Based on the picture I'd seen earlier, this man was Howard Daniels and he'd met with the same fate as Farrell—a red arrow through the head. But why would Gregg Daniels murder his own flesh and blood while they slept? Had they found out what he was doing and objected to it?

I waved for Melvin to enter and his eyes widened when he saw the dead man. "Oh, shit! Did Gregg Daniels do this?"

I pushed a finger to my lips. "Keep your eyes peeled. He has to be around here somewhere, and we're running out of places to look."

Gregg Daniels was keeping the house extremely cold, and my guess was he was trying to slow the rate of decomposition. But why?

My heart pounding in my ears, I made my way toward the last bedroom. Melvin was on my heels, his breath heavy. I positioned myself to the far side of the door and turned the knob. The door squeaked when I pushed on it and I froze. Despite the cold temperature, beads of sweat pooled on my forehead. I shuddered, imagining how it would feel to have an arrow penetrate my flesh. I had to force myself to open the door. I sighed when I realized the room was empty. A wallet and an ashtray full of cigarette butts were on the nightstand. I flipped open the wallet and searched through it, locating a prison identification card for Gregg Daniels. *He's definitely been here!*

I motioned for Melvin to follow me. There was only the bathroom left to check. Either Gregg Daniels was waiting for us in there—ready to ambush us—or he was long gone. What had we done to give away our approach? A chill reverberated up and down my back as I wondered if he had been out there watching us.

We moved stealthily down the hall. When we made it to the bathroom door, I reached for the knob, but hesitated when I saw the doorjamb. It was splintered. Someone had kicked open the door. I wiped the sweat from my forehead and gently pushed it open. I could hear the steady hum of another window unit in the bathroom and it drowned out the slight creaking of the hinges. I quickly peeked into the bathroom and pulled my head back, processing what I'd seen. The tub was to the right and it was empty. A pedestal sink was to the left. I couldn't see the toilet, because there was a makeshift privacy wall, but there was a mirror over the sink that might offer a view of the blind spot.

I let Melvin know I was going in and asked him to cover the back of the bathroom. Staying out of Melvin's line of fire and dropping to my knees, I crept along the floor, moving closer and closer to the back of the room. Slowly, the blind spot started to come into view in the mirror. When I could see the whole toilet area, I gasped out loud.

CHAPTER 45

"What is it?" Melvin asked from the hallway.

I stood to my feet and walked toward the privacy wall. "This isn't good, Melvin. Not good at all."

There, sitting naked on the toilet, was Gregg Daniels. Four red arrows protruded from his body. The first had been fired from the doorway and entered his left cheek, punched through his right cheek, and stuck into the bathroom wall, pinning his head in place. I couldn't determine the order of the remaining shots, but there was one in each shoulder and one through his groin.

A forty-five caliber semi-automatic pistol was on the floor near his right hand and it was cocked. There were two spent shell casings in the corner, so he'd gotten off some shots. I shined my phone light toward the doorway, looking for bullet holes on the wall and blood on the floor, but there were none. I then shined the light at the mirror across from Daniels and saw two bullet holes through it. Whoever killed Daniels was very handy with a bow and had taken him by surprise. I'd never heard of an archer winning a gunfight.

Confused, I sank back against the sink, waved for Melvin to join me.

He walked in and gasped when he looked down at the toilet. "Shit, that's Gregg Daniels, isn't it?"

I nodded.

Someone had wiped out the entire Daniels clan, but who? And why? This person had stealthily entered the house, taken out Farrell and Howard as they slept, and then caught Gregg with his pants down—literally. This type of operation took planning and real motivation. Like a true hunter, the killer had stalked Gregg Daniels and waited until the time was right to strike.

I couldn't say I felt bad for Daniels—he was a cold and ruthless rapist who got what he deserved—but I was confused.

There was a puzzled look on Melvin's face, too. "Chief, is it just a coincidence that Gregg Daniels was murdered the same way he murdered the jurors, or do you think someone did it this way to pay him back for the jury murders? You know; an eye for an eye?"

I thought about it. The frigid temperature in the camp would've slowed the rate of decomposition, which meant the men had been dead longer than they appeared. I quickly made the calculations in my head and guessed the approximate time of death for the three men was about a week. If my calculations were correct, Daniels could've shot Betty Ledet and Isaac Edwards, as well as Frank Rushing's corpse, but there was no way he shot Ava Harper or Susan. Was he working with someone else? Did that someone kill him and his brothers because they were getting careless? Or developing cold feet?

"Chief?" Melvin pressed. "What do you think?"

"I don't know what to think." We hadn't gotten any test results back on the arrows that were shot at Susan and Ava, so we didn't know for sure if Gregg Daniels' DNA was on them. If his DNA did appear on those arrows, someone very well could have killed him and then transferred his DNA to all of the arrows in an attempt to frame him for the murders. I looked at the a/c unit in the bathroom window. Whoever killed him had attempted to decelerate the decomposition process. I suddenly realized why…they didn't want us to know when Daniels was killed!

"Find the motive, find the killer," Melvin said, interrupting my thoughts. "That's what you always say. Who would want Gregg Daniels *and* the jurors dead? What do they all have in common?"

"Now you're thinking like a detective," I told Melvin, as an idea started to form in my mind. There was one person who might want all of them dead. I shot a thumb toward the front of the camp. "Tell Amy and William we're clear and that we have a crime scene to process."

Melvin nodded and hurried off. When he was gone, I squatted on my heels in front of Gregg Daniels and stared at the arrows protruding from his body. The shot to the groin was indicative of sexual vengeance and that was more than a little coincidental. Sighing, I called Isabel Compton. I figured she was probably sleeping—since she'd been up all night digging through their storage facility—but she answered on the second ring.

I told her where I was and explained what we'd found.

"Holy smoke!" she said. "He's dead?" I told her he was and she stammered for a bit before asking, "Then who in the hell killed the jurors?"

"It's still possible he killed some of them and another person shot Ava and Susan," I said, "but there's one other person who might have a motive to kill Gregg Daniels and the jurors."

"His lawyer?" she asked.

Shit! That was the only other person involved with the case that I hadn't considered. Of course, it didn't seem plausible to me that a lawyer would risk the death penalty or a life sentence simply for losing a case. And why would he kill his client? *No, that doesn't make sense.*

"I never thought of the lawyer," I admitted. "I was actually thinking of someone else—the person who lost the most."

There was a long pause on the other end of the line as Isabel tried to figure it out. Finally, she gasped. "Shut up! You don't think it was the victim, do you?"

"I do." I nodded for emphasis, even though she couldn't see me. "I need everything you have on the case, including the victim's home address. I need to find out who she is and try to figure out if she could be capable of murdering innocent people." I paused, and then asked, "Can you also send me the lawyer's information? Just in case."

Isabel said she would fax the entire file to my office right away. I thanked her and hung up.

CHAPTER 46

It was closing in on three o'clock when Amy and I began processing the crime scene. Melvin and William had set out to retrieve the pirogue and move our vehicles closer to the camp. After they were done, Melvin came into the camp and found us measuring the bathroom. "William's heading home to get some sleep," he said. "Can I help with the scene?"

I nodded, handed him the camera. "Shoot the other rooms if you don't mind. Make sure to get close-ups of the injuries."

Melvin slung the camera over his neck and walked out the bathroom. Amy and I continued measuring the scene and we were done within the hour. As I was walking out to pick up my measuring kit, something on the kitchen counter caught my eye. It was an envelope addressed to Gregg Daniels. The handwriting was messy, but I could make out the return address—it was the state prison. With gloved hands, I fished out the letter and began reading. It was from an inmate who had shared a cell with Daniels. The inmate was congratulating Daniels on his release and bragging about what he would do when he got out, too. After reading it twice, I shoved the useless letter back in the envelope and then stared at the address for a long moment. I'd accessed every database available to law enforcement, but couldn't find Daniels at this address, so how'd the killer find him? I pondered this as I set about picking up the rest of my gear.

When we were done inside, Amy and I went out to the driveway to inspect the green Thunderbird. After donning a fresh pair of latex gloves, I tried the doorknob, but it was locked. I asked Amy if she had noticed any sets of car keys in the house.

"None," she said.

I thought about this for a minute. "Someone else has been driving this car, and they still have the keys."

With her left hand, Amy slowly pushed some blonde locks behind her ear and scanned our surroundings, her right hand resting on the grip of her pistol. "You think he's out there right now watching us?"

I penetrated the shadows of the surrounding trees with my eyes, stopping on each bush to be certain it wasn't a human armed with a bow. "Let's wrap this up while there's enough light to watch our backs," I said.

Amy retrieved a slim jim from my Tahoe and we broke into the Thunderbird. An orange hunting cap was on the passenger's floorboard, along with a set of dark sunglasses. Other than that, the car looked clean. We tried to pop the trunk with the release button we found in the glove compartment, but it wouldn't work without the key. I called a tow truck to impound the car just as Melvin was walking out of the camp. "All done inside," he said.

Just then, I heard the sounds of tires popping on shells and car engines approaching. I turned and saw three hearses pulling up. Melvin, Amy, and I walked to greet the chief investigator for the coroner's office—at least that's what the badge clipped to the front of his belt said—when he stepped out of the lead hearse. He was an old guy with large-rimmed glasses and a skeletal frame. We led him into the bathroom first and I thought I heard his bones creak when he knelt on the floor beside the toilet. He lifted Daniels' shirt, felt around on his torso, and drew a circle over the liver with a permanent marker. Next, he removed a large thermometer from a leather bag he carried and stabbed it into Daniels' flesh.

After a few moments, he lifted the thermometer and jotted some notes in a worn notepad. Grumbling to himself, he repeated the process on each of the bodies, not saying an intelligible word throughout. When he was finished, he looked up at me, his eyes magnified by the glasses. "Well, um, you see, um, it looks like they've been deceased for, um, for a week or more, could be ten days. The low temperature, um, in this here house, um, helped to slow the, um, the rate of decomposition."

I nodded slowly. Gregg Daniels didn't kill anyone. He was only a patsy.

The investigator left the house and returned a few minutes later with his assistants and a gurney. After stretching the body bag on the floor next to the toilet, they tossed Gregg Daniels inside. Leaving the bag unzipped to allow room for the arrows, they loaded him onto a gurney and then wheeled him out to one of the wagons. They returned a few minutes later for Howard, and then Farrell. When all the bodies were locked in the wagons, the investigator handed me a piece of paper with some scribbling on it. "The autopsies will, um, be this evening, um, this evening at about six-thirty."

Melvin strolled beside me and we watched them leave.

"That guy doesn't look well," I said. "He belongs in one of those bags."

"Yeah, someone needs to tell him *he* died a week or two ago."

While I checked the crime scene to make sure we hadn't overlooked anything, Melvin wrapped the exterior in crime scene tape and posted a notice on the door prohibiting anyone from entering. We met back up in the driveway and I paused by the door to my Tahoe. "You want to attend the autopsies for me?"

He said he would, and I dragged my camera from the front passenger's seat and handed it to him. "We need those arrows sent to the crime lab and worked up as soon as possible. Of course, I wouldn't be surprised if they came back clean. Whoever's doing this is being careful not to leave even the slightest trace of evidence behind."

When Melvin was gone, I turned to Amy. "Are you coming with me?"

"Unless I have to walk back to the office," she said.

We didn't say much as we drove away from the scene, both of us lost in thought. I was hoping the report from Isabel had arrived and I wondered what it would reveal. I knew I had to proceed with caution, because I had absolutely no evidence to prove anyone's involvement. Well, except for Gregg Daniels. If evidence never lied, then a dead man killed at least two people and shot a corpse.

Amy broke the silence to apologize for her stomach grumbling and I remembered lunch. I offered to grab some burgers, fries, and milkshakes from M & P Grill. She groaned. "I love that place!"

Changing course, I called in the order and parked in front of the restaurant three minutes later. I handed Amy my card and asked if she could pay for the food while I made a phone call. She nodded and jumped out. While she was gone, I pulled out my phone and called Chloe. Without telling her too much about the case, I let her know I hadn't been killed by Cupid. She didn't like that I used the "k-word", but said she was relieved. I told her we were still on the hunt, and that prompted a dozen questions I couldn't answer. I promised to tell her more when I could and told her I had to go.

After I hung up with her, I called Mayor Dexter Boudreaux and gave him an update on the case. He had a dozen questions, too, but I answered all of his. When we were done, I navigated to my *Contacts* screen and searched my phone for a number from my distant past. When I found it, I sat there with my thumb poised over the green button, wondering if I should press it.

CHAPTER 47

My hand shook as the phone rang. I didn't know if it was due to the nature of the call or because of who I was calling. Finally, a clicking sound let me know the call had been connected, but there was a long moment of silence. I cleared my throat, said, "Hello? Are you there?"

"It's been years, Clint...*years!*"

I frowned. "I know and I hate to bother you, but I didn't know who else to call. Everyone I knew from the bureau either retired or—"

"Wait—so, after all these years of nothingness, you're calling for a favor?"

"I'm sorry, Jen."

Jennifer Duval and I had worked as partners for three years before hooking up after one of our division Christmas parties. We'd both been single at the time—she was still single as far as I knew—and neither of us had anyone worth spending Christmas with, so we'd spent it together. It was a great weekend filled with lots of sex, food, and relaxation, but she wanted more than a three-night stand. When I told her we couldn't carry on like that and still remain partners, she offered to transfer to another division or leave law enforcement altogether. I told her she shouldn't make life-changing decisions after a weekend fling, but she said she'd been having feelings for me for over a year, and our intimate time together only solidified them. Work was awkward after that weekend, but things got downright uncomfortable when I met Michele.

"Please give me one reason why I don't hang up on you right now," Jennifer was saying to me. "*One* good reason."

I couldn't think of any, so I simply kept my mouth shut, cursing myself for making such a monumental mistake.

"I called you every day after Michele died," Jennifer said, "but you ignored all of my calls. I must've left a hundred messages, but you never returned any of them."

"I was in a bad place," I said meekly, remembering the missed calls and the many messages of condolences. I felt guilty about not taking her calls, but I figured she was trying to get with me. When I'd first told her I met Michele, she had quit speaking to me and immediately transferred to a different partner in a different division. It was at least a year before she would tell me hello in passing, and another year before she would hold a conversation with me. Before long, she started getting too friendly—making sexual jokes or trying to bring the conversation back to that weekend—and I'd have to cut her off and remind her I was engaged to be married. It always seemed to piss her off and she'd say I was overreacting and for me to "lighten up".

There was a sigh of resignation on the other end of the phone. "I'm sorry, Clint. It just hurt my feelings the way you shut me out of your life. Some of the other guys mentioned hearing from you, and when you never called or even answered when I reached out to you…"

I thought I heard her voice crackle and guilt tugged at my very core. We had been such great friends before that Christmas together and it was my fault for ignoring the advice of an old wise man, who once told me, "Son, you can mix rum and coke or peanut butter and jelly, but you can never mix friends and sex." When I'd asked about friends with benefits, he had snorted. "Sex ain't no benefit, boy; it's a sacred privilege, never to be taken lightly."

"No, Jen," I said. "I'm the one who should apologize. I thought you wanted to pick up where we left off and I wasn't ready to move on—"

"Don't flatter yourself," she said. "Sure, I would've picked up right where we left off that Christmas, but I'd never tell you that. I wouldn't want it going to your head."

We both laughed and she asked why I was calling.

"Well, I'm working in Mechant Loup now and—"

"I understand y'all don't have televisions down there in swamp country, but the rest of us saw your face plastered on every news channel south of Canada last year." She laughed again. "We *all* know where you work now, Clint."

"Touché," I said, continuing. "So, this stranger rolls into town asking about me and he tells one of my officers he needs to deliver a message. I go out to their location and this guy tells me he did time with Simon Parker, and Simon says he'll see me again soon—claims he'll be getting out of jail."

I heard some shuffling in the background and she repeated what I'd said, apparently writing it down. "Okay," she said, "let me check on this for you. I'll get back to you by the end of the week."

I thanked her just as Amy was exiting M & P Grill with a large bag of food. I was about to hang up when Jennifer stopped me.

"Yeah?" I asked.

"It's good to hear from you. It really is."

CHAPTER 48

There weren't as many news vans staked out in front of the office when we arrived, and that made me happy. We were coming and going so much that they quit trying to follow us and, instead, just waited for me to funnel information to them.

Lindsey was waiting for me when Amy and I walked through the door. She stood from her desk and held out both hands. In one hand there was a thick stack of paper with a faxed cover sheet and in the other there was a single sheet of paper with a list of names and dates on it. Isabel's name was on the cover sheet attached to the thick stack, so I knew that was the Gregg Daniels file. I studied the names on the single sheet of paper, recognizing a few of them from minor cases I'd worked during the year. I also saw Isaac Edwards' name toward the bottom of the sheet and became curious. "What's this?" I asked.

"You're being audited," Lindsey said flatly.

"I paid my taxes." I handed it back to her. "Send it back."

She laughed and explained that the administrators of the law enforcement databases conducted spot checks each year to ensure officers were using the system properly and not abusing their privileges.

"So, what do I have to do with this?" I asked, not having time for such pettiness.

"You need to provide the case number and the reason for each search. I'll then send it back and we'll be all clear."

I grunted and hurried into my office, tossing the sheet to the side. I settled into my chair and dropped the case file on my desktop, eager to begin researching it. The file might hold the key to the murders and could provide us with everything we needed to put the killer away—if it was the victim who did it. I fished out the attorney's information and called Amy into my office, handed her a letter containing his information. "Can you look him up and see what he's been doing lately?"

"Sure." She took the sheet and walked out.

I turned my attention back to the file and read how Sandra Daniels had filed two complaints against her estranged husband, Gregg Daniels, and he had been tried twice for raping her. In the first trial, he had been found not guilty by a jury of his peers, who believed the former cop when he took the witness stand and said the sex with Sandra was consensual. I read a newspaper article and more paperwork before turning my attention to the second case file that detailed a brutal attack and vicious rape. The day after being freed on the first charge, Daniels tracked Sandra down at her house and attacked her. As I read the details of the cowardly act, I was happy he was dead and hoped he suffered greatly.

I was still sifting through the file when a shadow fell over my door and I looked up to see Susan standing there. I jumped to my feet and rushed around the desk to greet her with a hug. "Hey, how are you?"

When I released her, she cracked that crooked smile of hers and nodded. "The doctor says I'm good as new."

"Thank God!" I smiled big, unable to contain my relief and excitement. "I'm so glad to hear it."

Susan walked around me and stared at the mess on my desk. Four three-ring binders were open and spread out. "I heard you found Gregg Daniels dead," she said.

I nodded and told her the story. Picking up a large yellow envelope labeled *Crime Scene Photos*, I reclaimed the seat behind my desk, and she sat across from me. I shoved my hand deep into the envelope and pulled out a handful of photographs. I flipped through them one by one as we talked about the case and discussed the possible suspects. I was about to mention the lawyer when Amy came in and tossed the letter back on my desk. "It can't be the lawyer," Amy said, "unless he's a ghost."

I grunted. "How long has he been dead?"

"Six years."

I looked at Susan and raised my eyebrows. "That leaves only the victim, Sandra Daniels."

Amy handed me a computer printout and said she'd taken the liberty of running Sandra Daniels' name. "This is her last known address. It's off of Cypress Highway."

I thanked her and pointed to the chair next to Susan, who was reading over the files. I continued flipping through the photographs and cringed when I saw the pictures of Sandra Daniels' nude body. She had been banged up pretty good and there were bruises on her upper thighs and forearms. I flipped to the next picture that showed finger bruises around her throat and a red mark on her temple that was made from the muzzle of the pistol. When I came to focus on her face I nearly choked on my tongue.

"What is it?" Susan asked, looking up from the file in her lap.

"I...I know this woman!" I said, pointing to the picture of her face. "I know who she is!"

CHAPTER 49

Susan hurried around my desk and looked over my shoulder. Amy was right on her heels. I held up the picture so they could see.

"Who is she?" Amy asked.

I stabbed at her face with my index finger. "Their Sandra Daniels is our Sandra Voison."

"Who's Sandra Voison?" Amy wanted to know.

Susan's face scrunched up. "Why does that name sound familiar?"

"She's the postal worker who found Betty Ledet," I said. "That explains how she found Gregg Daniels when we couldn't. She delivered the letter from prison." I shook my head, disappointed with myself. "I should've figured it out sooner. When I interviewed her that day she bragged about knowing everyone's address. She even showed off her skills by calling out my address and telling me I needed to cut my grass."

"She's right about your grass," Susan said, picking up the picture and holding it close to her face. "So, this bitch shot me."

I twisted around until I could see her. "I'm going to make her pay for what she did."

"I want to be there when you arrest her," Susan said.

"I don't know if that's a good idea," I began slowly. "We don't have a shred of evidence against her, so we'll need a confession, and that means being nice to her."

"Oh, I'll be really nice to her. I'll sing her a lullaby as I put her to sleep."

By "sleep", I knew Susan meant choking her until she was unconscious, but I also knew she would restrain herself and do what she had to do to make a good case.

Amy was thoughtful. "I don't get it. Why wait so long to go after everyone? I mean, why not kill the jurors immediately after the trial?"

I shook my head. "She wanted all of them, starting with Gregg Daniels, so she had to wait for him to get out of prison. My guess is she's been preparing for this day for over twenty years."

"Hell, she might've applied for a job with the post office just to find everyone's addresses," Susan said.

After researching her address on the computer and finding a bird's eye view on the satellite, I gathered up the file and moved to the conference room with Susan and Amy. I drew a quick diagram of the house and surrounding area. She lived east of town on the opposite side of Bayou Tail. Her house was centered on an empty stretch of land along the bayou. It had the only red roof in the area. Sandra's closest neighbor was directly across Cypress Highway from her, but it was the only neighbor for at least a quarter mile.

I pointed to a patch of trees on the western bank of Bayou Tail. "I'll set up here and do surveillance—see what I can see." I slid my finger along Cypress Highway in front of Sandra's house. "Susan, do a drive-by and see if there are any cars in the driveway." I turned to Amy. "Meet with Melvin at the coroner's office and see if he needs any help. Afterward, get with William and call me on the radio. We can't arrest Sandra, but I want her house surrounded when we knock on the door. She's a potential cop killer—let's not forget that."

Susan rubbed the top of her left breast. "Can we make her buy me a new cell phone? That thing was six hundred dollars."

I smiled and headed for the door.

CHAPTER 50

I pulled to the shoulder of the road when I found the landmark I'd been looking for. It was an old gas station directly across the bayou from Sandra Voison's house. I'd planned to hang out behind it to conduct surveillance on her property, but I hadn't realized someone had turned the little building into an apartment. An old rusted out pickup and a faded blue boat were parked under the overhang and lights were on inside the house. I couldn't risk being discovered, so I drove farther south and grunted when I couldn't find an opening that offered an unobstructed view across Bayou Tail. The sun was going down behind me and the mosquitoes were already out in droves.

After parking down a cane field road, I grabbed the binoculars from my floorboard and jogged across Main Street and reluctantly squeezed through the thick underbrush. Most of the weeds were taller than me and some were as thick as my forearm. Pickers stabbed at my bare arms, leaving deep burning sensations I could've lived without. Sweat dripping from every pore, I finally pushed through to the water's edge and sank to the ground with my back to a cypress tree. I scanned the opposite bank. There was no mistaking the red roof on Sandra's house. I pulled the binoculars to my eyes and focused on her back yard. She kept a nice flower bed and her box garden was well tended. Her grass was neatly cropped and nothing seemed out of place...well, except for a large puffy object on the northern edge of her property. I couldn't make out what it was from my vantage point, so I started creeping toward my right. As I moved, I was very aware of the dangers that lay beneath the surface of the murky water, and I kept my right hand close to my pistol.

I had picked my way about twenty yards to the right when the face of the puffy object came into view—a bow hunter's target! I tightened the focus on my binoculars and saw a human silhouette target taped to it and there were red arrows buried in the chest, throat, and groin area. I snatched up my radio. "Susan, this is our killer. Where are you?"

"I'm on foot across from her house. Her mail Jeep's here and so is another car. I detected movement inside, but I can't make out how many occupants."

I told her to hold her position and I scrambled through the underbrush, fighting my way back to Main. Once I got there, I crossed the highway and jumped into my Tahoe, speeding toward the bridge that connected the west side of town with the east. I called Melvin as I drove, asking him where he was and how he was coming with the autopsy.

"We're done," he said. "I heard your transmission over the radio. Amy's with me and William's meeting us at the office. Tell me what you want us to do."

I gave him their assignments—two of them on foot behind the house and one in their car south of the place—and met Susan where she hid her Charger in the fields. I jumped in with her and sighed when the cold air hit my wet uniform. I wiped my forehead and stared out the window. The long, evening shadows had turned into thick waves of black. Knowing it would be easier for us to move under the cover of darkness, I'd told everyone to hold their positions until the last light had faded from the sky. That was now.

I keyed up my radio. "Let's move, gang."

Susan and I waited until everyone was in position. Once they were set, we cruised down the road and pulled into Sandra Voison's driveway. Instead of going to the front door, we went under the carport and tried to see as much as we could from the kitchen window on that side of the house. As Susan knocked, I waited and watched through a slit in the curtains. Before long, I saw Sandra making her way from the back of the house, dodging a sofa and the kitchen table before disappearing from my view to the right. I backed away from the window and stood to Susan's left, hand positioned on my pistol. I hadn't seen anything in Sandra's hands, but I didn't trust the woman one bit.

Light flooded the carport when she opened the door. She smiled at Susan. "Hello, officer. Can I help you?"

I wanted to tell her to cut the act and get her shit so we could go, but I took a breath and stepped forward. "Hey, Mrs. Voison. Remember me?"

Sandra squinted, trying to penetrate the shadows better, and stepped closer to the storm door. "Chief Wolf? Is that you?"

"Yes, ma'am."

Sandra pushed open the door and waved for us to enter. "I'm sorry. I didn't realize it was you out there. It's hard to see."

I followed Susan into the kitchen area and quickly surveyed the room, searching for any clue that might help us prove she was the killer. There were pictures in the living room, but it was cloaked in darkness and I couldn't see who was in any of them. Sandra pointed to the table at the center of the kitchen. "Please, have a seat."

Susan sat beside Sandra and I sat across from them. My gaze immediately fell upon a picture on the kitchen counter. It was in a rustic frame and the surface was faded, but that wasn't what had gotten my attention. I pointed to it. "Who's that?"

CHAPTER 51

Sandra turned her attention to where I pointed. The picture had been taken in the wilderness and the man was clad in a thick jacket, gloves, and knit hat. There was a long bow in his hands and the string was pulled back, aiming a wooden arrow at something. She frowned. "That's my late husband, Spencer. He was my only true love."

"This Spencer, was he a bow hunter?" I asked.

She nodded. "Exclusively. He didn't think it was fair to hunt animals with a gun, so he never did. He preferred the challenge of stalking close to his quarry and killing them, rather than doing so from the comfort of a deer stand three hundred yards away, where the animal would never have a fighting chance."

"Did he ever teach you to shoot a bow?" I asked.

"He showed me some things, tried to get me to go hunting with him, but"—Sandra shrugged—"it wasn't my thing." She stood suddenly and moved toward the sink, pushing her dirty blonde hair out of her eyes. "Care for something to drink?"

Susan and I both declined and I watched her move around the kitchen. I knew she was strong, because I'd seen her toss those mail boxes around like they were empty when I'd first met with her, and now I noticed how easy she moved on her feet.

"Do you still practice shooting your bow?" I asked.

She smirked as she poured a glass of water from the tap and returned to her chair. "I barely have time to eat, much less play around with some toy."

I made a mental note that she hadn't denied owning a bow. "So, does that mean you don't practice shooting your bow?"

"That's affirmative, Chief."

Susan gave me a nod, then looked at Sandra. "Ma'am, you haven't asked us why we're here."

"Because I already know why you're here. It's about the murder."

"What makes you say that?" I asked.

"I mean, why else would you be here?" Sandra took a sip from her glass and then set it down. "The only dealings I've had with the law was when I found Betty Ledet dead at her house."

I studied her face, knowing what I was about to do and waiting for any clue that might tell me she was ready to crack. I didn't need her to confess to killing any of the jurors; I only needed her to admit she'd killed her ex-husband. I could connect the rest of the dots myself. "Ma'am, do you know Gregg Daniels?"

The blood immediately drained from her face and she averted her eyes, not saying a word.

"What would you say if I told you he was dead?" Susan asked, leaning close to her.

Sandra's eyes widened. "Dead? What do you mean? Are you sure?"

I pulled out a picture of Gregg Daniels as we'd found him and tossed it on the table. "Dead as can be."

She recoiled in horror, but her eyes remained glued to the picture. When the initial shock wore off, she reached for the picture and pulled it close, studying it. I thought I saw the sides of her mouth curl up into a smile. Finally, she looked up and nodded. "That is him. He's really dead."

"How do you feel about him being dead?" I asked.

"I don't know how to answer that," she said.

"Just be honest," Susan offered.

"I'm happy he's dead. I wish I could've been there to see him take his last breath."

"You weren't?" I asked.

Sandra's face twisted into a scowl. "Excuse me?"

I pointed toward the back of her house. "If I search your place, will I find the compound bow that was used to kill him? Or red arrows with three-blade mechanical broad-heads like the ones used to kill him?"

Sandra's eyes narrowed and she fixed me with a cold stare. Finally, through gritted teeth, she asked, "Do you have a warrant?"

"No, but I can get one."

"Meanwhile," she said, "you can get the hell out of my house."

I stood and nodded at Susan. "We will, but you're coming with us."

Sandra turned from me to Susan and then back to me. "What on earth for?"

"For murder."

"Murder?" She stabbed the crime scene photo with her finger and laughed. "You think I did this? I wouldn't even know how to find him. I thought he was still in jail. He wasn't supposed to get out for another—"

"You thought he was in jail until you delivered that letter to him from prison." I watched more color drain from her face and wondered where all her blood was going. "Are you going to deny delivering his mail?"

"I deliver everybody's mail," she said.

"And you also know where everyone lives," I said. "Remember? You even proved it to me."

"Oh, I guess I killed Betty Ledet, too, since I delivered her mail, as well."

I nodded. "And Isaac Edwards, and—"

"Wait—you can't be serious." Sandra shoved her hair out of her face, glaring at me. "Do you really think I murdered all those people?"

I pointed toward the back of her house. "There's a human target back there with red arrows sticking out of the throat, chest, and groin areas—precisely where our victims were shot. You're the only one involved in the case who has access to everybody's address and you're the only one who knew Gregg was out of prison. Hell, *we* couldn't even find him, and we have access to all the latest databases available to law enforcement."

Tears began to form in Sandra's eyes. "I can't believe this is happening to me. I didn't kill Gregg, or any of those people."

"Really?" I leaned back and folded my arms across my chest. "Then who'd you share his address with?"

Sandra stared blankly at me. "I don't understand the question."

"Did you tell anyone where Gregg Daniels lived?"

"No."

"Are you sure? Because if you didn't, then no one else knew he was in town, and that means you're the only one who could've killed him."

Sandra's lips began to quiver and she lowered her head, not saying another word.

I pointed to the ashtray on her table. "You're a smoker and so is

Gregg. You knew enough to take cigarette butts from the ashtray in his bedroom and leave them at the scenes of the juror killings. And you rubbed your arrows on Gregg's body to get his DNA on them. You did a good job setting him up, and it might've worked had it not been for one thing." I paused a moment to let Sandra wonder what that one thing might be. "You didn't count on two drug dealers coming forward to claim the reward."

Sandra started to cry softly. "I'm not saying another word until I speak with my lawyer."

"Suit yourself." I stood and scanned the kitchen. "I bet we'll find the keys to that Thunderbird in here somewhere."

Sandra kicked back her chair and jumped up. "Not without a warrant you won't!"

Susan was on her feet before the first word left Sandra's lips. In an instant, she kicked Sandra's feet out from under her and dropped on top of her on the ground, jerking both arms behind her back. "Another thing you didn't count on," Susan said, "was me not dying. My only regret is not shooting you out there in that field."

CHAPTER 52

An hour later, Sandra Voison was locked in our holding cell and Susan and I were sitting around my desk filling out the arrest report and applying for a search warrant. William had returned to his shift and Amy and Melvin went home for the night. Once the arrest report was done and the warrant had been faxed to the judge's house, I called Mayor Boudreaux and updated him on the case. I was about to call Chloe and give her first dibs on the story when Susan picked up the database audit report.

"What's this?" she asked. I explained to her what it was and she scowled. "According to this, you ran a name inquiry on Isaac Edwards on October eighth."

I stared blankly at her. "Sue, I don't even know what today is."

"You didn't even know Isaac Edwards existed until he was killed on October tenth."

I reached for the report and she handed it to me. I reviewed it and nodded. "Yeah, you're right. I was in the grand jury hearing on the eight." I shrugged and handed it back. "It must be a mistake. I'll have Lindsey call the administrators tomorrow."

I reached for my desk phone to call Chloe but it rang under my hand, and I picked it up. It was my night shift dispatcher, Marsha, and her voice was laced with excitement. "Sheriff Turner's on line one and it's an emergency—there's been another arrow attack!"

My heart fell to my gut and stopped ticking. Susan saw the look on my face and turned her hands up. "What is it?" she mouthed.

Before pressing the button for line one, I told her what Marsha said. She stood with her jaw hanging as I answered the line and greeted Sheriff Turner.

"Clint, I know you got the killer, but there's been another attack. I think it's a copycat, because this one's different. It happened inside the house. Some kind of way, this slick bastard snuck by my deputy, broke into the house without making a sound, and executed Drake Alan while he slept."

I pushed the phone away from my mouth, turning to Susan. "Drake Alan—is he one of the jurors?"

Susan walked to the dry erase board on my wall (where we'd taped the hit list) and ran her finger up and down the printed names. I saw her finger stop on one and she turned to nod. "It sure is."

My mind raced as a few things began falling into place inside my head. "Sheriff, it's no copycat. It's the original killer."

"But this one's different, Clint. The victim wasn't—"

"It's different because the killer has to complete her mission before we catch her. She knows we're closing in on her." I snatched the Gregg Daniels file from my desk. Before hanging up, I told Sheriff Turner to activate his SWAT team and put officers inside the homes of every remaining juror. "We're dealing with a crafty individual and she might be one of us!"

CHAPTER 53

With Susan hot on my heels, I rushed into the holding area. Snatching the key out of the security drawer, I hurried to the cell door and shoved the key into the hole. Sandra stood and backed into a corner of the cell when I wrenched the door open, as though she thought I was going to attack her. I pulled the old newspaper article from the file and shoved it in her face. "The jury believed your ex-husband over you and your babysitter," I said, quoting from the article. "You had a daughter, didn't you? And Gregg Daniels raped her, too, when he was released from jail, didn't he?"

Sandra just stood there trembling, her eyes wide and her hands covering her mouth.

"Who is she?" I asked. "What's her name?"

Sandra shook her head. "I…I want a lawyer."

"Very well," I said. "I'm sure I'll find her picture at your house."

"You can't search my house without a warrant," Sandra called weakly, as I slammed the cell door shut and locked it back. "Stay out of my house."

"The warrant is probably already signed," I called over my shoulder as Susan and I rushed out of the holding area. "Marsha, did we get a fax from the judge yet?"

She shook her head. "Not yet."

"I'm calling him." Susan grabbed Marsha's phone and dialed the number. The judge answered and she spoke hurriedly with him, explaining the new developments. When she hung up, she gave me a thumbs-up. "He gave verbal consent to search Sandra Voison's house."

I rushed out of the office and jumped into my Tahoe, pressing the button to the automatic garage door as I did so. Susan slid into the passenger's seat beside me and told me to slow down on the way out of the sally port. "You don't want the media following us."

Knowing full well she was right, I forced myself to slowly back out of the sally port and onto the street. We smiled and waved at two reporters who stood on the sidewalk smoking cigarettes and talking. I cruised slowly down Main Street, traveling less than the speed limit, until the glow from their cigarettes couldn't be detected in my rearview mirror, and then smashed the accelerator, racing toward Sandra's house.

I jumped the bridge, headed south along Cypress Highway, and didn't slow down until we were a hundred yards away. I shut off the headlights and killed the engine, coasting into the driveway and smashing the emergency brakes. "Keep your eyes peeled," I warned Susan. "There's no telling where she is."

We rolled from the Tahoe and stalked toward the front door. Other than the sound of mosquitoes buzzing in our ears, all was quiet. Susan fished Sandra's keys from her front pocket and unlocked the door. We slipped inside and locked the door behind us. Using only our flashlights, we moved through the kitchen—pausing only to pull the curtains closed—and into the living room, where pictures lined three walls. One of the walls was dedicated to Spencer and it looked like a shrine.

"She really loved this man," Susan said. She turned toward me and her eyes were ghostly in the dim light. "I saw the same pain in her eyes that I see in yours."

I looked down, shuffled my feet.

Without waiting for me to respond, she continued. "You lost Michele while y'all were still very much in love. People say divorces are hard, but by the time a couple files for divorce, both parties already know things have eroded to the point of hatred. But to lose someone at the height of a relationship..." Susan shook her head. "No one should have to live through that."

I turned toward the opposite wall and aimed my light at the picture frames on that wall. Something familiar caught my eye and I walked closer, focusing the light on one of the faces in a picture with Sandra Voison. When the image came into full view, I nearly vomited. I know I cursed—a lot—because Susan rushed beside me asking what was going on and feeling me for injuries. I could only point at the picture...and curse some more.

Susan's mouth dropped open and she sank to her knees, rolled onto her butt, and leaned back against the wall. I sank to the floor beside her and my flashlight dropped from my hand. We both sat there staring into the blackness, neither of us saying a word. I could barely hear Susan breathing above the sound of my heart beating. I felt weak and tired…sick to my stomach.

CHAPTER 54

We must've sat there for twenty minutes before Susan asked, in a low and cracking voice, "What're we going to do?"

I'd spent the whole time wondering that exact thing. "I don't know."

Another moment of silence.

"We have to do something," Susan said.

I nodded, knowing she couldn't see me in the dark. It was another ten minutes before I spoke again. "I think I know what to do, but we'll have to play it cool...very cool."

"What do you have in mind?"

I told her my plan and she took a deep breath. "Are you sure about that?"

"It's the only way to do it without someone else getting hurt."

Susan sighed. "I sure hope it works."

"It's got to."

I helped Susan to her feet—not that she needed it—and snatched the picture frame from the wall before we walked outside into the warm night air. The drive back to the office took longer than the drive to Sandra's house, because I was dreading what we'd have to do. As I drove, I called Sheriff Turner and told him who our prime suspect was and asked that he tell only the most trusted members of his department. I shared my plan with him and he told me his people were available if I needed them.

Once we arrived back at the office, we stopped near the dispatcher's desk. "Call Melvin and Amy and ask them to meet us here at the station," I said to Marsha. "Tell them I'm sorry to bother them, but Sandra Voison is refusing to cooperate and another juror was killed right under Sheriff Turner's nose, so we need one of our people embedded with each of his SWAT members at the juror's houses until we can figure out who's committing the murders. Also, reach William on the radio and tell him the same thing."

I then went into my office to wait with Susan. Neither of us said a word, each lost in our own thoughts. I was hoping no one else would die that night, but I wasn't optimistic.

William arrived first. "Where's Susan and Clint?" he asked Marsha.

I couldn't hear what Marsha said, but William appeared in the doorway to my office. "So, what's this I hear about another murder?"

I frowned. "He's still out there, Will. Mrs. Voison won't cooperate and we've got no evidence to hold her, so we're going to have to let her go soon. Our best chance is to be at the next kill site when the killer arrives."

William nodded and took a seat next to Susan. "How's your wound healing?" he asked.

"As well as can be expected," she said. "I can't wait to get the stitches out. They itch."

We heard the side door open and Susan got up and walked to the door of my office. "It's Melvin," she said over her shoulder.

I stood to walk around my desk. "Let's meet in the conference room and lay out our plan."

William got up and walked toward the door. "What about Amy?"

Melvin heard him and called out, "She should be here any minute. I heard her go in service over the—what the *hell*?"

Susan turned abruptly in my doorway and kicked William square in the solar plexus, sending him reeling backward toward me. I rushed forward and put my left arm around his throat and grabbed his pistol with my right hand. "Get in here, Melvin!" I hollered. "William's the killer!"

Susan was moving forward and reaching for William's right arm when he punched her in the left breast, right over her wound. I saw her face twist in pain, but she kept coming forward. William clawed at my right hand, trying to pry my fingers loose from his pistol. Melvin was trying to get around Susan, but the space was cramped and he bumped into her, sending her flying into my desk. Melvin lost his balance and fell forward into William, knocking all of us off balance. I tripped on one of the chairs and fell backward with William crashing on top of me and Melvin on top of him.

I struggled to get out from under them while maintaining my grip on William's pistol, but William wasn't having any of it. He grabbed my right index finger and wrenched it sideways while biting into my left forearm. I didn't know what hurt worse—my finger or my forearm—but I tried to block out the pain and hold on while Melvin scrambled to get control of William's left arm. We struggled for what seemed like forever, knocking furniture down and stumbling all over each other.

Out of the corner of my eye I caught sight of Susan's foot stomping at William's torso. The first few strikes didn't seem to do much, but one finally connected and I heard him grunt. Melvin was able to grab William's left arm and peel it away from his body while Susan hooked his right arm in both of her arms and jerked on it, nearly taking my finger with it. She did some kind of twisting movement that placed her legs across William's chest—kicking Melvin in the face in the process—with his right arm between her legs. With a grunt, she gave her hips a thrust upward and I heard a sickening crunch as William's arm bent ninety degrees in the wrong direction. William screamed in pain and his body relaxed, no longer interested in fighting.

Susan and Melvin jerked William off of me and slammed him onto his face, cuffing his arms behind his back. William cried out in pain, begging them to release his broken arm.

"You're lucky we don't kill you!" Susan said, reading him his rights as she pulled him roughly to a standing position.

CHAPTER 55

I rolled to my feet in time to see Amy arrive in the doorway. "What in the hell is going on?" she asked, both hands planted on her hips. "Marsha's hiding under her desk and it looks like a tornado came through here."

"It *feels* like a tornado came through here." Melvin said, trying to catch his breath. "I'd like to know what's going on, too. That's one of our own standing there in handcuffs!"

I picked one of the chairs off the floor and sat William in it. "William is Gregg Daniels' stepson," I said.

There was a collective gasp from Amy and Melvin.

"Daniels didn't just rape his estranged wife when that jury let him go," I explained. "He also violated William."

We all stared down at William for a long moment, sitting there with his head down. Finally, Susan addressed him.

"I understand why you killed Daniels and you might've even gotten away with it," Susan said, "but why murder all those innocent jurors? They didn't ask to serve on the—"

"They weren't innocent!" William spat the words. "They promised my lawyer they wouldn't hold the word of a cop in higher regard than the word of the victim, but they all lied. My mom and I were raped twice—once by Gregg Daniels and again by the justice system!"

"That's bullshit." I grabbed the file from my desk and held it in front of William. "There's nothing in here about you being raped."

"You wouldn't understand unless you've been through it."

I tossed the file back on my desk and crossed my arms. "Help me understand. You owe everyone in this room at least that much for betraying us."

William sighed and his voice quivered. "I was just a kid. I liked girls before he had his way with me. Afterward, I...I...it made me confused. I didn't know who I was anymore—didn't know what I wanted. He stole my innocence, took away my boyhood. There's no forgiving that." William was crying. "You can't know how it feels growing up with that secret, with that pain. We only have one life and he robbed me of mine. There would never be any going back...no do-over, no reset. He ruined my life forever."

I scowled, realizing he was telling the truth. "Why didn't your mom tell the police?"

"She didn't even know. He beat her unconscious and then attacked me. I think he realized he could get the death penalty for what he did to me, because he cleaned me up and told me if I told anyone he'd come back and kill me and my mom." William wiped his leaking nose on the sleeve of his uniform, shaking his head. "He didn't have to worry about me saying anything. Do you know how embarrassing that is for a little boy?" William shook his head. "I was never telling anyone anything."

"How'd you find the jurors?" I asked, already knowing the answer.

William shot his head toward my desk. "You leave your password in the bottom drawer—we all know it. I didn't want anything traced back to me, so I got on your computer when you weren't around." He mumbled an apology and said something about feeling bad because I'd always been good to him. "I just figured if anyone checked they'd think you looked up the names as part of the investigation."

"Did your mom know about this?" Susan asked. "Is she involved?"

"She's not involved, but I think she suspected something was wrong when she heard the names of the victims and found out they were killed with red arrows. She remembered every one of those jurors. She hated them, too. When I was growing up, she'd point them out in public and tell me they were the ones who let Gregg out so he could hurt her again." William sighed. "I never forgot them and never forgot about what Gregg did to me. Hell, I couldn't forget— she wouldn't let me. Every time she'd point them out, I'd relive that night."

"So, that was your target in the back yard?" I asked.

He nodded. "My dad taught me how to shoot when I was small. We'd spend hours in that back yard, shooting until our forearms were bruised and our fingers bleeding. I still go there to practice, because it makes me feel close to him." William stared off. "Life was great when he was alive. If he would've never died…"

"She has to be involved," I pressed. "She's the one who told you where to find Gregg Daniels."

"But she didn't know I would kill him. She just told me she'd delivered a letter to him and she told me to stay away from that side of town. She didn't know what he did to me and she didn't think I'd go after him."

I was quiet and Susan asked him why he'd waited so long to start killing jurors. He said he never planned on going after the jurors, but when Daniels' death didn't provide the closure he thought it would, he figured it was because the job wasn't finished—the mission was incomplete. "I felt like the only way I could get my life back and become whole again was to kill everyone responsible."

"How'd you get Daniels' DNA on the arrows?" I wanted to know.

"That was easy." William grinned, almost proud of himself. "I just rubbed the nock end of the arrows against the inside of his cheeks, like we do with buccal swabs. I kept the bodies cold, knowing it would slow the rate of decomposition, making it difficult for y'all to determine the time of death—*if* y'all ever found him." William's grin faded and he shook his head. "It was the perfect plan, but y'all found him way too soon and ruined everything."

I looked up when I saw Melvin approaching at a slow walk with his fists clenched. "So, in your twisted little mind, you blame all those people for what happened to you and that's great. But why did you shoot Susan? Why would you do that? You're supposed to be our brother. We're family! We don't attack each other, no matter what!" I quickly moved between Melvin and William, afraid Melvin would start beating him.

Tears were flowing freely down William's face now and he was bawling. "That's the one thing I feel the most guilty about," he said through sobs. "I'm so sorry, Susan! I didn't know what to do. They all needed to pay for what they did to me and I couldn't let you stop me before the mission was completed. I thought you were wearing your vest, so I aimed for your trauma plate, thinking you'd be fine and it would only buy me some time to escape." He turned his red face toward her. "I swear, if I would've finished making everyone pay, I would've let you kill me before turning my bow on you."

Susan frowned. "I can't explain it, William, but I'm not even mad at you. I feel sorry for you."

When we were done talking to William, I moved him to the holding cell reserved for male prisoners, where he would stay until the prison van picked him up and transported him to the hospital. I then set about releasing his mom. She begged to speak with William and I let them talk for about ten minutes. When she was gone, Susan and I searched William's Charger and found his ghillie suit, a compound bow, and six arrows wrapped in plastic. We also found the keys to the Thunderbird hidden under the spare tire wrapped in a latex glove, right where he said they were. He said he didn't have time to hide the evidence after killing Drake Alan, because I had called him into the office.

Once Susan and I had packaged everything in the evidence lockers, we met with Melvin and Amy in the conference room. A pot of coffee was on the table and they'd each had a cup, so Susan and I poured one for ourselves. The liquid was hot and strong.

Melvin scratched his bare head. "Chief, how'd you know it was William?"

I explained how the old newspaper article mentioned Sandra's babysitter, which told me she had a child. "When we searched her house, we found a picture of William—well, a million pictures of William—in her living room. One of the pictures was of him shooting a bow with his real dad, Spencer Tucker."

"I still can't believe I've been working with a killer all these nights," Amy said, shivering. "Do you know how many times I've turned my back to him, trusting he would cover me? He could've taken me out at any time."

"Yeah, and we've been friends for years," Melvin said. "He doesn't look like a murderer."

"Do they ever?" I asked.

CHAPTER 56

One week later…

The sun was setting in my back yard on the first Monday after William's arrest and I still couldn't shake the feeling I'd gotten when I found out he was the killer. Susan and I had talked about it often in the past week, but we couldn't put it to rest. William was one of our own. If he could betray us, anyone could.

Chloe was trying to wrestle a toy away from Achilles, but he wasn't having any of it. He jerked it from her grasp and raced off, taking a victory lap around the yard. Chloe approached me at a stumbling jog and plopped down on the steps. "He's got a lot of energy!"

I flipped the chicken on the grill for the last time and joined Chloe on the steps, smiling as I watched Achilles finish his lap and drop the toy at her feet, begging her to pick it up again. She rubbed his face and told him she was too tired to play anymore, but he pretended not to understand. He dropped to the ground, his face in his paws, and made a motion like he was going for the toy, but stopped. When Chloe didn't respond to his teasing, he grabbed the toy and bolted off, stopping a few feet away to see if she'd given chase. When he saw that she hadn't, he dropped the toy and ambled toward a shady spot in the yard and lay on his side, panting.

"He's such a beautiful dog," Chloe said.

I agreed with her and put my arm around her shoulders. "And you're such a beautiful girl."

She snuggled against me and smiled. "I love it when you say things like that."

"I love it when—"

A sharp ringing sound interrupted my sentence. I'd been expecting a call from Jennifer Duval to update me on the status of the Parker case, and I hoped that it was her. I jumped to my feet and rushed into the house.

"Wait," Chloe called, trying to catch up with me. "Finish what you were saying."

I snatched up my phone and looked at the display screen. It was Jennifer. I swiped the screen and pushed the phone to my ear, asking her what was up.

"It's not good, Clint."

"What is it?"

"I spoke with the assistant handling the case and he said the Parker brothers are set to be released in two weeks if they can't come up with more evidence."

"What?" I leaned against the counter, feeling as though the wind had been knocked out of me. "Released? How can the DA's office just release them? They murdered Michele and Abigail!"

"I know," Jennifer said, "but they said the case is purely circumstantial and they don't feel they can win. He said he'd rather let them out now and wait for more evidence, rather than trying them on a weak case and losing. You know yourself if that happens they can never be tried again because of double jeopardy."

I knew she was right, but I didn't like hearing it. Numb, I told her goodbye and ended the call. Before I could put my phone down it rang again. I absently put it to my ear and said, "This is Clint."

"Chief, you need to get here quick!" It was Melvin and he was so excited he was stumbling over his words.

"What's going on?"

"It's Susan—she just got arrested."

My jaw dropped. "*What?*"

"Two sheriff's deputies just took her into custody. They got a call from Bill Hedd saying the grand jury had indicted her for murder and she was to be taken into custody immediately and..."

I didn't hear the rest, because I snatched up my keys and sprinted for the door, leaving Chloe and Achilles wondering what was going on..

BJ Bourg

BJ Bourg is an award-winning mystery writer and former professional boxer who hails from the swamps of Louisiana. Dubbed the "real deal" by other mystery writers, he has spent his entire adult life solving crimes as a patrol cop, detective sergeant, and chief investigator for a district attorney's office. Not only does he know his way around crime scenes, interrogations, and courtrooms, but he also served as a police sniper commander (earning the title of "Top Shooter" at an FBI sniper school) and a police academy instructor.

BJ is a four-time traditionally-published novelist (his debut novel, JAMES 516, won the 2016 EPIC eBook Award for Best Mystery) and dozens of his articles and stories have been published in national magazines such as Woman's World, Boys' Life, and Writer's Digest. He is a regular contributor to two of the nation's leading law enforcement magazines, Law and Order and Tactical Response, and he has taught at conferences for law enforcement officers, tactical police officers, and writers. Above all else, he is a father and husband, and the highlight of his life is spending time with his beautiful wife and wonderful children.

http://www.bjbourg.com

Made in United States
Orlando, FL
17 February 2024

43767594R00139